STALKER

DI Benny Mitchell is attending another course, leaving Sergeant Jennifer Taylor to investigate a mysterious phone caller who is targeting pregnant women. Early information leads Jennifer to suspect someone who cannot have children – is he wreaking revenge on those who can? It seems to make sense, but why then is Mitchell's wife, Ginny, also receiving threatening phone calls – she isn't planning any more children. As Ginny's harassment intensifies, Jennifer becomes convinced that her inspector's wife is at risk from someone much more sinister – and Mitchell is barred from taking any part in the search for his wife's stalker.

STALKER

STALKER

STALKER

by

Pauline Bell

Magna Large Print Books
Long Preston, North Yorkshire,
BD23 4ND, England.

British Library Cataloguing in Publication Data.

Bell, Pauline
   Stalker.

   A catalogue record of this book is
   available from the British Library

   ISBN   0-7505-1716-6

First published in Great Britain 2000 by
Constable & Company Ltd.

Published in Large Print 2001 by arrangement with
Constable & Robinson Ltd.

Magna Large Print is an imprint of Library Magna Books Ltd.

Printed and bound in Great Britain by
T.J. (International) Ltd., Cornwall, PL28 8RW

For Aileen

1

Virginia Mitchell heard the telephone ringing as she wheeled the twins' double buggy up the garden path. However, she still took time to watch Caitlin, who had lingered by the gate, as she jumped into the centre of a large puddle. Six-year-old Declan, puzzled that his sister's antics were going unreproved, carefully used his finger to join up the separate raindrops on the clear plastic canopy that protected the twins from the worst of the weather.

After a moment he nudged his mother. 'I can hear the phone.' Virginia turned back to the door and deliberately fumbled the key in the lock until she was sure there was no sound of a message being recorded on the answering machine. Then she shepherded her wet children into the entrance hall.

Declan was reproachful. 'It might have been Daddy.'

'If it was, he'll ring again. Take your wet things off. Then you can help Caitlin whilst I see to the twins.'

Declan sat on the bottom stair and tugged disconsolately at a wellington boot. 'It might have been Jamie to ask if I could play at his house.'

'You can go another day. It was probably just someone wanting to sell double-glazing.'

'What's that?' Declan asked, as Virginia had known he would. Satisfied to have distracted him, she embarked on a lengthy explanation whilst her hands removed padded jackets and thick trousers from the fat limbs of Sinead, the impatient twin. Michael, the placid one, sat on in the buggy, well entertained by watching his siblings disrobe.

Declan walked over to the window and inspected it. Having checked that, as he'd thought, there was only a single sheet of glass, he frowned. 'If you'd hurried to answer the double-glazing man on the phone we would have got it fixed.'

Virginia grinned. The child was as persistent as his father. 'We can't afford it for this year. We've only lived here a few weeks and there are other jobs to be done.' Having towelled her own short curly hair, she began to deal with Declan's identical mop. Caitlin's lank straight locks, inherited from her father, had been protected by a hood.

Declan nodded solemnly. 'Jamie has double-glazing. I just didn't know it was called that. At his house, when it's dark outside, you can see two of me in the glass.'

10

The flashing light on the answering machine caught his attention as he wriggled his head out of the towel. 'There are four messages. Can I press the button?'

'No!' The boy looked up in surprise at his mother's tone. 'Get your library book out of your bag. We'll do your homework reading now whilst Sinead and Michael are quiet in the playpen, then we'll play Treasure Trove when they're in bed.' Knowing his mother's intense dislike of board and card games, Declan realised that she felt her refusal to let him play the recorded messages had been unfair and that he was being humoured. He recognised an opportunity to exploit. 'Can we have ice cream and raspberries out of the freezer for pudding?'

Caitlin was sitting at the table, carefully fitting the piece with Jess's face and whiskers into her Postman Pat jigsaw puzzle. As usual, she pricked up her ears at the mention of food and seconded the plea. Virginia agreed to it, listened to Declan's reading, fed all four children, bathed the twins and settled them in their cots, then paused by the window to gather herself.

Wet slashes across it distorted her view even of the small portion of the garden lit through the uncurtained glass. Usually, Virginia liked rain, liked to feel drizzle on her face, to see webs pearled with moisture. Today, it irritated her. Even Declan had trailed through it dejectedly, declining to join in his sister's puddle jumping. She knew that fear of her own wrath had not stopped him and hoped it was because he now viewed such activities as childish rather than because he had picked up her own unease without knowing the cause.

It was not really cold for the first week in November but the damp caused a miserable chill compounded by the cheerless house. To be fair, it was a very comfortable house. Even though the decorations were more to the taste of the previous owners than to their own, it was not hideous and in any case it would soon be changed.

She settled with as good grace as she could muster to the game of Treasure Trove which lasted almost until Caitlin's bedtime and left Virginia with another worry. Wasn't it time that Declan had learned to lose? 'It's a stupid game anyway!' he had announced after a careful count of the 'gold bullion' showed Caitlin to be the winner.

This further anxiety provided a useful counter-irritation. Calmly, Virginia read stories, then shooed the two older children to their rooms. Declan, knowing why he was in disfavour, did not plead to stay up his rightful extra half-hour but he had a request ready when his mother went to tuck him into bed. 'If it's one of my friends on the answering machine, will you come and tell me what they said?'

Virginia smiled. 'If one of your friends has left a message, I'll let you come down for a minute and listen to it.' Satisfied, he turned his face from his mother before putting his thumb in his mouth.

Downstairs, she debated with herself whether or not to draw all the curtains. If she left them open, she could see if anyone came close to the house. If she closed them and he was there, at least he wouldn't be able to see in. The answering machine winked at her mockingly. She began another argument with herself. Should it wait until she'd had a fortifying G&T?

This was ridiculous. Virginia got up, drew the curtains briskly on the dank night – to keep the heat in, she told herself, until the man on the phone had sold them their double-glazing – and poured herself a drink. She would have had one anyway, even without the messages to face, though probably not quite so early.

The messages all proved to be welcome. Her mother said hello, her friend Jennifer wanted to see the new house, her part-time employer would like her to work Thursday and Friday this week and her husband, as usual, would be late home. His voice, even on the tinny machine, restored an atmosphere of normality. 'Sorry, Ginny, but I can't let the paperwork mount up when I'm going away tomorrow. We nicked the lad who's been lifting all the school computers this morning. He wouldn't believe we'd got on to him all by ourselves. Thought his mates had shopped him so he produced this long list of names and telephone numbers to get his own back. I've got to write a small book about it for Mr Clever. See you as soon as I can.'

One day Benny would refer to Eric Kleever, his new detective superintendent, in this manner in his hearing. Virginia did not think the great man would be amused. As the machine switched itself off Declan's head appeared round the door. 'I heard the machine. Was it Jamie?'

'No it was Gran and Daddy and Auntie Jennifer.'

'You mean Jennifer Taylor who works with Daddy?'

'We don't know another Jennifer, do we?'

'Well then, she isn't my auntie, not my real one. She's your friend and Daddy's ... colleague!' He finished the speech triumphantly, pleased at having remembered the unfamiliar word almost in time.

'Declan, you're pushing your luck. You've forty-five seconds to be back in bed.' He saw she was serious and disappeared. Cheerful again, Virginia made a dual purpose call to her parents, passing on most of the family gossip and arranging for the twins to be minded whilst she worked at the end of the week. As she replaced the receiver, she heard footsteps not far from the back window. She knew that her neighbour took her toy poodle out into the back garden at about this time and again just after eleven. Sternly she forbade herself to check and picked up her glass again.

Curled up in an armchair she began mentally to go through a list of all the people she had met since they moved house a month or so ago and her harassment had begun. She was a friendly, outgoing woman who took an interest in the people around her but she knew that these contacts were just oiling the wheels of society. She had thought of these new acquaintances only fleetingly whilst actually in their presence. Had a smile, a kind word, been interpreted as something deeper, triggering a response out of all proportion to her intentions?

Since the move she had met very few men apart from the ones she had known for ages. The children, of course, had brought her into contact with other families, new teachers. There were men on some of the checkouts at the supermarket half a mile away, mostly young Asian men, but she did not have the impression that her unwanted caller had any kind of a foreign background. Caitlin's nursery school had a male teacher and the caretaker was a man. Some of the neighbours, naturally, were men. She and Benny had been invited to a drinks party at the home of Lee Hillard and his partner Gill who lived opposite. Most of the residents of the street had been there.

She had spent more time than she could spare lately, listening to the war exploits of the aged ex-RAF officer four doors away, but she thought she would recognise his voice even if it were disguised. Virginia finished her drink feeling more puzzled than anxious. The chap was most probably harmless – just so long as neither Declan nor Caitlin became involved in any way. It was a pity Declan was so fond of the telephone.

Suddenly, it rang again. Just as suddenly, Virginia knew that she didn't think her caller was harmless at all.

On this same evening, Detective Sergeant Jennifer Taylor, rejected as an aunt by Declan Mitchell, had hoped to be sharing an evening meal with her two young daughters. Instead, she was knocking on a door in Bramall Street in pursuance of her duties.

Even in this dull, wet weather the house looked welcoming and well cared for. The living-room window, giving on to a small square garden that separated the house from the street, had its curtains still drawn back. The room so revealed was lit by lamps on low tables. Plain painted walls gave the prominence they deserved to an assortment of pictures.

Only one was big enough and sufficiently conveniently placed for Jennifer to examine it as she stood back on the path waiting for the door to be opened. The river scene was anonymous, the buildings vague and figures on the bank dressed in costumes of another age. Something of its style and atmosphere suggested France to Jennifer.

She had abandoned her study of the print in favour of rubbing her hands and stamping her feet by the time footsteps were heard inside. The door opened and a girlish voice apologised. 'You must be frozen. Come and get warm before we talk.'

Jennifer, who knew her fashion, labelled the girl Laura Ashley rather than Roland Klein. Her pale brown hair was fringed down to her well-shaped eyebrows, the rest of it shoulder length, flicked up at the ends. Her face was carefully made up in no-brighter-than-flesh tints, whilst slim ankles and T-bar shoes showed below the almost ankle-length skirt. The dress was nipped in to emphasise the girl's tiny waist. Both women paused so that Jennifer could give Miss Weston's appearance the attention it deserved.

'Faye Weston?' Jennifer was puzzled.

17

'That's right.' The girl led the way into the lamplit room and arranged herself on an easy chair. When she realised she had lost Jennifer's attention to the French print, she spoke again. 'Do sit down. Thank you for coming straight away.'

Jennifer sat neatly in the matching chair and revised her initial estimate of Faye Weston's age. Not a young girl. Possibly turned thirty. 'You say you've been getting abusive calls, Miss Weston.'

'Yes.'

'And the caller is suggesting that your partner is promiscuous and your baby may be born with AIDS?'

'Yes, that's right.'

'How long have these calls been going on?'

The woman shrugged slightly. 'A week or two. We aren't sure because neither of us took much notice at first.'

It seemed, to Jennifer, rather too serious an accusation to be ignored. 'Was this suggestion made from the beginning?'

'No, first we just got silence, funny breathing. Then the voice asked if we were pleased about the baby. We'd talked about the calls and agreed not to say anything to the caller, so we just hung up without answering. Then he said the things about AIDS.'

'Can you remember the exact words?' The woman shook her head. 'Did you hear any

18

sound that came over the line to give a clue to the caller's identity or to the place he was calling from?'

'I told you. Neither of us took much notice. We tried dialling 1471 but he'd withheld his number, of course.'

Jennifer said, wondering if it were wise, 'You don't seem much concerned that what the caller said might be true.'

Faye Weston seemed quite calm, as though nothing could concern her. She considered Jennifer's comment. 'I'm as sure as you can be about another person. The father's my brother so I think I'd know. We're quite close, and, after all, I've known him for a long time.'

Jennifer swallowed as Miss Weston eyed her solemnly. She appeared quite sane. Feeling her way carefully, Jennifer tried another tack. 'It seems likely, doesn't it, that your caller is someone who knows you very well, intimately, in fact?'

'Why?'

'Well, it isn't obvious to other people yet, is it? You certainly don't look pregnant to me. Who've you told about it?'

Miss Weston sighed, then gave Jennifer a humourless smile. 'You've only got half the story, haven't you? It's my partner who's pregnant – about five months. Quite a lot of people know and almost everyone disapproves.'

Jennifer relaxed as things clicked into place. 'You're a lesbian couple... And your partner is pregnant by your brother?'

'That's right. Colin and I are very alike so he's the next best thing to me. Megan didn't like the idea, didn't enjoy it much. It's lucky she fell on so quickly.'

Jennifer wondered if the old-fashioned terminology was intended to go with the dress. Her curiosity overcame her tact. 'How did you decide on who would carry the baby?'

Faye Weston was not in the least offended, just anxious to explain. 'We each had a full medical and there was nothing to choose between us physically, but Megan hadn't got a close male relation – well, not one who was willing anyway.' She stopped speaking and looked up at the ceiling as muffled footsteps were heard. 'That's Megan getting up.'

'Finding pregnancy tiring, is she?'

Faye looked surprised. 'Not particularly. She does shift work at the shirt factory. She's on ten till six then she gets up at teatime so we can spend a bit of time together.'

'And you?' Faye looked enquiring. 'What work do you do?'

'Oh, I'm writing a novel.' She waited for Jennifer to be impressed and to beg for details. Since the sergeant merely added to the notes in her book, Faye supplied them unasked. 'It's a romance set at the end of last century.'

Wondering about the nature of this fictional romance, Jennifer hurried on. 'Are you going to baby-mind as you write or is Megan going to give the shirts a miss and let the proceeds of the novel keep you all?' It occurred to her that the two girls and the baby too could live for a good while on the proceeds from selling the picture that was still demanding her attention.

Megan Scott had made an unobtrusive entrance and answered for herself. 'Neither the baby nor I will get in the way of Faye's writing. I shall carry on with the shirts and use the factory crèche.'

Jennifer regarded her with interest. Megan's complexion was probably naturally pale but it was overlaid with a mask of white foundation that seemed hastily applied. Her hair was roughly chopped, short pieces on the crown of the head standing on end. Jennifer thought it would be naturally dark but its texture suggested that the matt black was assisted. The eyes were magnificent, black-lashed, blue-grey with clear whites. In spite of her general presentation, the pregnancy made her look womanly.

The remarkable eyes were fixed sternly on Jennifer. 'Does that help to sort out the phone calls?'

Jennifer blushed and waited for Megan to make herself comfortable on the couch. 'Sorry, I was just being nosy. Have you had any harassment besides the phone calls?'

Megan qualified their shaken heads. 'Mind you, we don't keep looking behind us or listing the cars parked outside, but certainly we haven't been bothered in any other way.' The voice was quiet and deliberate, betraying neither region nor class.

'What made you change your minds?'

'About reporting it?' Megan clasped her hands over her swollen stomach. 'When I first went to the antenatal clinic I heard that one of the other girls had been having calls like ours. At the end of all the comic exercises and horror films of deliveries, we gather round for story time – when we have our worries sorted out, if we're silly enough to confide them. I could see that one of the girls was trying to work herself up to asking something but never managed it.

'I offered her a lift home. I'm quite good at getting people to talk and I'm a bit older than most of them, old enough to disbelieve old wives' tales, but it wasn't anything like that. She'd had some calls from our friend and she was scared that what he said to her was true...'

Faye sat forward, folding her skirt primly, to give her second-hand version of the rest of the story. 'She didn't know whether to ask for a test, have a termination or what.'

Jennifer turned back to Megan. 'Who is she?' Megan considered, then evidently deciding that further co-operation was in the other girl's best interests she fished in the pocket of her black dungarees for a diary with a tiny pencil in its spine. She wrote on a page, tore it out and handed it over with a warning. 'She won't want to talk to you. She's scared of her bloke.'

Jennifer nodded her agreement to tread carefully. 'Have you logged calls – kept records of times and what was said?'

They shook their heads. Megan said, 'As Faye probably told you, we were going to ignore it. After all, we're used to abuse...'

'Once I saw Megan wasn't upset, only annoyed, we thought... Well, he doesn't have much of a life and–'

Jennifer sat up. 'You think you know who it is? You recognise the voice?'

'Not exactly.' Megan wriggled on her cushions with a discomfort that was not entirely physical.

'So, who is it?'

'Look, can I explain it my own way?' She waited for Jennifer's nod. 'I was in the local surgery and came out of one consulting room as Clare Chase came out of another. She's a neighbour. It was over a month ago and I didn't have the bump on me that I have now. My parents had just been told about the baby and they were giving us hell. Still are. Clare's always miserable, with good reason, so I suggested we should drown our sorrows in a cup of coffee. It was a couple of days after that we had the first call.

'Our immediate families were the only other people who knew that I was pregnant and they were getting all their enjoyment out of criticising us to our faces. It wasn't any of them—'

Inevitably, Faye finished the story. 'So we asked Clare if she'd told anybody. She said no a bit too quickly. We were sure she'd told Justin.'

'Her boyfriend?'

'Her husband. He's a cripple. He got MS soon after they were married—'

This time Megan cut in, anxious to defend their friends. 'We thought it was the sort of thing you might well do to get your own back on the world if you had to watch it from a wheelchair at only thirty-three. We were more sorry for him than angry and we didn't want to make trouble for Clare. Unfortunately we already have done. She wanted to know why we'd questioned her and we told her. She wanted to assure us that Justin would do no such thing but it was obvious she was uneasy and now I think she suspects him as well.'

Jennifer listened to the two women until they had no more to tell, issued the standard instructions and warnings and departed exhausted. She would see Gemma Platt, the other persecuted girl, tomorrow. Now, since her own girls would have been in bed for more than an hour and there was no chance of tucking them in and saying goodnight, she'd trespass further on her mother-in-law's good nature and ask her to sit with them whilst she spent a couple of recuperative hours with calm, sane, cheerful Ginny.

Benedict Mitchell, acting Detective Inspector as from the beginning of October, could hardly believe he was voluntarily working overtime to catch up on paperwork. He had spent most of his police career thinking up devious schemes to avoid it.

He was pleased with the way his career was presently shaping up after certain events in his impetuous personal life had kept him a lowly DC for more years than was wise or usual for an ambitious detective. These included the seduction of his DCI's daughter, his consequent lively and satisfactory marriage and the fathering of three further children.

Mitchell had little patience with theories about ephemeral qualities that constituted good policing. He was sure his own progress so far was due to his asking blunt questions about what he wanted to know, having first sorted out the people who could give him the right answers. After his marriage he had continued to work happily on his father-in-law's shift, first as his constable and later as his sergeant.

Superintendent Cyril Petty, recently retired, had countenanced this slightly irregular arrangement because it worked well. Petty had endeared himself to DCI Browne, and his son-in-law Mitchell, in that respect at least. In most others, because of a combination of indecisive leadership and belligerent address, he had been unpopular. The large amount collected for the presentation at his leaving ceremony had represented a thank offering more for his departure than for his services to the Cloughton station.

His successor, Detective Superintendent Eric Kleever, however, seemed a man who played things by the book. Unhappy at having men so related on the same shift, he had been quick to offer DS Mitchell another step up the ladder in exchange for a transfer to the sub-station up the valley at Hubberton.

Mitchell, silently thanking Virginia for nagging and coaxing him through his inspector's exams at a time when actual advancement seemed only a theoretical possibility, had been willing enough to accept the promotion. The size of his family was making a house move increasingly

26

necessary, so to move to the other side of town had not been inconvenient. The remainder of the superintendent's conditions, however, had been less to his liking.

Kleever was a great believer in 'In Service Training', the phrase being endowed with capitals whenever he spoke it. Mitchell believed in it too, but his definition was more literal. He considered he was learning most about the job whilst he was 'in service' to the people of Cloughton and district. He expected to be little wiser about how to cope with their problems after the four days of his course in Wakefield on which he would embark the next day.

Like the rest of the force, Mitchell was ready to co-operate with Kleever merely because he was not Cyril Petty, but he gave his friendship and loyalty cautiously and he was reserving judgement. Doubtless people had welcomed even Petty as a relief from his predecessor.

Virginia greeted her visitor more effusively than was her wont. 'I can't believe we've been here four and a half weeks and you haven't visited us.'

Jennifer shrugged. 'I try to spend my spare time with the kids. Do you know, it's four days now since I got home early enough to have a proper conversation with them before bedtime. I never hear Lucy's school gossip and Judith has just accepted Granny Jane as a substitute mother. Jane's a saint but I'm jealous of her.' She dropped on to a stool to watch Virginia make her stomach-searing coffee. 'It's strange not to be as familiar with your kitchen as my own.'

Virginia smiled, having followed her friend's train of thought. 'You'll soon know where everything's kept. Then you can make the coffee and it'll be drinkable. I'll show you round when I'm sure everyone's sound asleep. It's a nice house. The neighbours seem friendly. There's an old RAF chap a few doors along who thinks he won the war single-handed and a chap over the road asked us to his party so we could start getting to know everyone. They're all a bit keen on the social round. They'll probably drop us when they realise we like our guests in ones and twos–'

'Ginny – is everything OK?'

Virginia tried to look surprised. 'Why shouldn't it be?'

'One, you sounded fraught when I rang to say I was on my way.' Jennifer fetched the coffee tray to the table as Virginia made no move to deal with it. 'Two, your nails are bitten, both of which are unusual. Three, you're gabbling a load of boring small talk which is unheard of.'

Virginia fixed her eyes on her hands as she arranged cups and poured. 'I thought you were someone else ringing.' Suddenly, Virginia knew she was going to confide in Jennifer and, the decision made, she snapped back into her usual phlegmatic self. Succinctly, she described her harassment. '...I was in here with the girl next door the first time. The call was fairly explicit. Sounded a bit like a soundtrack from a blue film. I put the phone down not knowing whether to laugh or scream. I wondered if it was someone I'd met. Then I wondered if it had really happened.'

Jennifer remained silent, knowing that they had arrived at a crucial moment and she would not find Virginia similarly confiding again.

'A few minutes later he rang a second time. That call was worse. Then there was a gap for a few days. When it started again I was angry. I thought of having the number changed but I decided not to. Why pay for being a victim? Why miss getting calls from friends and have the inconvenience of letting everyone know the new one?'

'It's better than being frightened.'

'I'm not frightened exactly, just unsettled.' Jennifer gave her a hard look. 'All right then, I'm frightened. He must be watching me. He seems to know all about me. Nights are worst. I don't know where he is but my imagination tells me he's close. If he rings me every ten minutes I think I'll go mad. If he doesn't ring I imagine him outside, watching.'

'Ginny! Stop being silly. I suppose you dialled 1471 and the caller had withheld his number.' Virginia nodded. 'Then change *your* number – or get a trace put on the line, then we'll not only sort you out but we'll stop him doing it to anyone else. I'm surprised that Benny–'

'I can't do anything like that without Benny finding out.'

For a moment Jennifer was silent, coming to terms with her surprise. Then she asked tentatively, 'There isn't something wrong between you two?'

Virginia shook her head vigorously. 'Definitely not, but going on this course was one of the terms of Benny's promotion. It's in three sections, beginning this week. I can't see him going off to Wakefield tomorrow if he knows this is going on. Don't hassle me, Jen. It's the first thing I haven't shared with him since ... well, it's the first thing ever I've deliberately hidden. It wouldn't be so important if it weren't for the kids. Some calls come during the day and Declan thinks the telephone and answering machine are his toys that he reluctantly allows us to borrow.'

'All the more reason–'

Virginia shook her head stubbornly. 'No. Benny would refuse to go and the new super might demote him. He's only acting DI for the moment.'

'Not if it was for a reason like that. He'll just arrange for him to go again later when everything is cleared up.'

Virginia suddenly stood up and began pacing the kitchen. 'Do you really think he might be doing it to someone else?'

Jennifer answered with another question. 'Ginny, you're not pregnant again, are you?'

Virginia managed a grin and sat down again. 'I think I'd almost rather have this than that. Why do you ask?'

'Tell me first if you've ever heard of someone called Justin Chase.'

Virginia pondered, frowning. 'I seem to have heard the name but I can't place it. Who is he?'

'He's thirty-three years old and crippled with MS. That's all I know myself at the moment—'

Screams from upstairs interrupted her and Virginia disappeared to investigate. She remained upstairs for some time and when she came down she was carrying a flushed, still confused and clinging Declan. Between them, they restored him first to calm and then, by means of a chocolate biscuit and five minutes of his favourite video, to positive glee.

When he was safely asleep again, Jennifer set off home, determined to renew her arguments next day. Virginia might be more amenable once her husband had safely departed on his precious course.

Alone again, Virginia battled with an urge to ring her husband and ask him to come home. Keeping this problem from him was proving more stressful than the harassment itself. Born into a police family, she knew it was her duty to make an official complaint against her persecutor. Police families also knew, though, that it did an officer's prospects no good to have too many family responsibilities. She knew too that being in the bad books of one's immediate superior officer could block a junior officer's promotion for years. If Superintendent Kleever had an obsession with courses then Benny had to attend them and she was not going to be his excuse for refusing.

When her unintended pregnancy had begun in her first year at Oxford, Benny had put his own career on hold. He had done more than his share of child minding whilst she obtained not only a first degree but also a master's. Now it was her turn to cope whilst his career prospered. He was thirty-four and it was time to be moving forward.

Nine years younger, her turn would come again when the children were all at school. Jennifer might well be proved right about the reasonableness of Mr Clever, but for the present she was not taking the risk. She jumped as the phone rang again.

Benny's voice, peevish with frustration, told her that the computer thefts were not all history as he had hoped. Two more schools had been broken into that evening. Virginia commiserated with him, described the more entertaining aspects of Jennifer's visit and rang off.

Virginia's anonymous caller watched Jennifer leave the house, saw the living-room light go off and the bedroom light go on. He resisted the temptation to telephone now. He would call in the morning and describe Virginia's evening to her. Then he would describe how it would have been if she had spent it with him.

Virginia heard the engine of a large and probably expensive car start up, then the purring died away as the vehicle approached the end of the road. Determinedly she kept away from the window. Resolutely, she switched off her bedside light.

2

Out of her husband's sight, Clare Chase leaned against her kitchen wall to catch her breath after helping him downstairs. It was not often that Justin agreed to accept such assistance so it promised to be a bad day.

The stairs these days were always a struggle but, usually, he merely asked a favour of her that took her away to the cellar or garden where she could not watch his awkward and painful efforts to descend. There was equipment he could have applied for that would have been useful to the pair of them but Justin's pride in both his physical manhood and their beautiful home had so far kept ugly mechanical aids to a minimum.

'I can manage at the moment with a bit of help,' he was wont to say, with a not unappreciative glance at Clare. 'Maybe, but can I?' Clare would ask, but silently. He would never complain on the days he was more unwell than usual. Instead he would express disapproval of everything and everybody that came his way. Marginally, Clare preferred this attitude. She admired his courage, his refusal to give in and be an invalid.

She made the washing up and tidying the kitchen last as long as possible. When it was finished, she would make his coffee and chat with him for a few minutes before going to work. He despised her job as a school dinner lady, blaming himself because she was not free to apply her talents to a more prestigious occupation.

Prestige Clare could leave alone, but she would have welcomed release from serving out sloppy, greasy food, watching the little animals scoff and fight and, worst of all, carrying away bowls full of nauseating leftovers. She was glad, on the other hand, of any pretext for getting away from close confinement with her husband for a couple of hours each day.

She remembered incredulously how, less than five years ago, she had engineered ridiculous manipulations of her own routine so that she could 'accidentally' bump into him and snatch a few minutes of his conversation. It was less than four years since they'd spent an ill-afforded, blissful honeymoon in Aviemore. She had preferred watching Justin skim over the slopes to learning to ski herself, but she had become quite proficient in a small way by the time they had to leave. Together, they'd planned to explore the world before raising an equally intrepid family.

After their 3rd anniversary, though, he'd

become ill. The symptoms were strange and had scared her. The day he had broken the news of his diagnosis to her had brought a kind of relief. It had been better than a brain tumour or other cancer, or some kind of mental disease. Then they had expected too much from his five-day course of Methyl-prednisolone, though the physiotherapy, the cornerstone of his treatment, had helped Justin take the best advantage of what strength he had.

The associated infections had followed inevitably, chronic ear and sinus problems, bronchitis and, what made his care more difficult than anything, the weight gain that resulted from a combination of drugs and his forced inactivity.

Clare raised a sudsy hand to brush away the self-pitying tears that she rarely allowed herself, then blinked away the fierce pain until further tears washed the detergent out of her eye. At least the small shock had restored her habitual resignation. She loved Justin, would have married him even if she had anticipated what was to be the nature of their life together.

She had left the morning paper within his reach. Dr Simpson had told her that, as he became increasingly housebound, she should talk to him about the everyday happenings in the district so that he continued to feel part of the local community. She did her best but he dismissed her offerings as trivial women's gossip and affected not to listen. She knew that he was actually paying close attention since, on a bad day like today, he would review the small events she had recounted in a condemnation on the fecklessness and passivity of his able-bodied neighbours. She switched on the coffee machine and returned to the living-room.

'Did you fetch the paper from the shop this morning?' he asked, without turning to her. Impatiently she pushed it closer to him. He knew she had. To get an 'all-round view of things' he insisted on a different paper each day, ranging from the *Sun* to *The Times*, but excluding for some unfathomable reason the *Telegraph*. This made delivery beyond Mr Platt's willingness to oblige. 'Let's hear all the latest then.'

He was right to consider the shop a better source of all the local news than the combined efforts of its staff could make the *Cloughton Clarion*. She gave him a list of the trivial events she had heard about, including a neighbour's modest lottery win, the loss of another's job and the second pregnancy of the newsagent's daughter. It occurred to her that these happenings were not in the least trivial to the people concerned that she could haven bitten out her tongue after delivering the last item.

Justine merely enquired, 'Without benefit

of clergy again, I suppose? Good job I pay my taxes to keep them all. Had he glanced towards the phone on his right, Clare wondered, or was it just one of his involuntary, uncontrolled movements? She knew how much Justin wanted a child for themselves, had watched him turning to the 'Hatches and Matches' on the inside front cover of the *Clarion* to see which of his acquaintances was newly enjoying fatherhood.

She sighed impatiently. Did he think there was nothing she couldn't cope with? If she were carrying a baby she would lose it with lugging him about. She could understand his bitterness but she could never condone the way he was taking his revenge. If the girls were right, that was, and it was Justin who was making the calls. She would never be able to bring herself to challenge him about it, never mind give him away to the authorities. If by some wonderful chance she was wrong she would have forfeited his trust for always.

She had thought of taking his mobile phone and leaving it on a bus. When she had asked to borrow it Justin said that it had disappeared, that he thought it had been stolen from the car. That story would make a good cover if the malicious calls were traced back to his number. She had searched the house but not discovered it.

Justin was still elaborating on Gemma Platt's unfitness to be a mother and Clare cheered up slightly as she remembered Megan saying that Gemma had already been pestered by the mystery caller. If it turned out to be Justin, he'd known about this pregnancy before this morning and Clare had not added to his temptation. The news, he declared, did not surprise him. Clare fled to the kitchen to escape the rest of the diatribe.

Her husband's voice came through to her as she poured the coffee. 'Dr Simpson has assured me over and over again that there's no reason why I shouldn't father a child...' She ran water to drown the words. She knew the script. It began with the doctor, progressed through the moral unfitness of the new parents who proudly announced the arrival of their offspring under separate surnames in the *Clarion* and ended with a suggestion, just short of an accusation, that she might be on the pill. Of course she was!

Why could he not see what a silly idea it was for them to have a child? There was no pleasure for him any longer in the sexual act. In fact on the rare occasions they attempted it, it had become indescribably difficult for him to maintain any position and the only sensation he felt was pain. Maybe he had given up hope and this railing at her was just another way of venting his frustration.

Clare stirred sugar into both cups of coffee and tried desperately to think of something, anything that she could look forward to. The highspot of the week seemed to be Justin's routine hospital visit on Friday when the best prognosis they could hope for was that his deterioration might slow down.

They did, of course, have blessings to count. Justin still had an interesting and well-paid job and an understanding employer. Clare chided herself for giving up her job in the library too soon. Maybe she needn't have left at all, but Justin's bad patch seemed to be the beginning of the end at the time. She knew she was becoming depressed. Their understanding GP was another blessing. Perhaps she'd go and talk to him as he often urged her to. Before the resolve could fade she got up and carried Justin's cup in to him. 'Won't be a second.' She left her own cup beside his and went up to the bedside phone to arrange an appointment.

That same Tuesday morning found the Mitchells at breakfast rather later than usual. It was not Virginia's turn for the school run. Michael and Sinead were fed and watered and not yet fighting in the playpen and their parents were enjoying the last of each other's company before the weekend.

Virginia was finding the companionable meal a mixed blessing. Having Benny there in any mood was better than his absence and this last brew of his excellent coffee stood in front of her. Fleetingly she wondered how, with the same equipment and raw materials, the end product could be so different for her. On the other hand, the phone might ring before he left and, meanwhile, his conversation consisted of a long complaint about the uselessness of everything he'd be doing the next four days.

'What happened about the school computers?' Virginia asked in an attempt to deflect him.

'Got passed down to Clement.'

'The new DC? What's he like?'

Mitchell shrugged. 'Pleasant lad – and efficient enough to take any action I might have taken myself, I suppose.'

'I thought he seemed a bit...' Virginia paused to pin down her impression of the young officer she'd met at the formal and rather stilted drinks party the new superintendent had held in order to meet his team. 'A bit withdrawn,' she finished doubtfully.

'Subdued, you mean. Not surprised. His wife died last year giving birth to their first child. The baby died too.'

Virginia was appalled. 'It's not the sort of thing you even begin to prepare yourself for

41

these days. What was the problem?'

Mitchell did not know. 'He applied for a move from North Yorkshire to begin again and it seems to be working out. He's a good copper.' Sinead walked to the side of the pen nearest to her father, closely followed by her brother who still preferred travelling on his knees. Mitchell offered each of them a finger of toast and some fatherly advice. 'When you two start work, make sure you don't have to waste time listening to so-called experts frantically trying to bolster up their egos by lecturing on courses.'

'I've taken their bibs off,' Virginia remarked with longsuffering as Sinead applied the buttered side of her toast to the front of her clean dungarees. In spite of all her resolutions, she added, 'If you feel so strongly, do you have to go? What happens if you refuse?'

Mitchell shook his head. 'Don't know enough about Mr Clever to get stroppy yet.'

'What's he like?'

'Well, you've met him. Beefy. Quietly spoken...'

'It'll make a change from Petty's roaring then!'

'Oh, but he can roar softly when things don't suit him. Wouldn't have got to super without.'

Virginia laughed. '"As gently as any sucking dove"?'

Mitchell smirked. '"I will roar as it will do any man's heart good to hear me." Thought you'd catch me out, didn't you? That's from the poncey play they were doing at Holmbrook School when that youngster killed her teacher.'

'I wouldn't call it poncey.'

'No, you'd call it *A Midsummer Night's Dream*. I recognised it when you thought I'd forgotten. How could I when it's the daftest bit of drama I've come across in a long time? But, if being able to quote Shakespeare means you're well educated, then I can so I must be.' Having talked himself into high good humour, Mitchell departed.

Virginia had been alone with the twins for just an hour when the doorbell rang. Ignoring the twins' roars, which were definitely not gentle, she dropped them back into the playpen and went to see who her visitor was. She opened the door until the chain stopped it but saw no one. On the step was a florist's box with a cellophane lid. It contained four orchids and a note, which read, 'One for each week since I met you.'

After some seconds, Virginia knelt down and picked up the box. She closed the door, locked it and slipped the chain back on. Going through to the back door, she drew both bolts across, her hand freezing on the top one as the telephone rang. After six peals, which, as always, silenced the babies, the answering machine clicked on and she heard Jennifer's voice.

She was not ready for another argument with Jennifer. She took the box of flowers into the kitchen. Her first impulse had been to put it and its contents into the bin, but the box was evidence and the flowers were beautiful and had probably only been touched by the florist. She could not, however, bring herself to put them into the Stuart Crystal specimen vase that Benny had given her and picked instead a small white china container left in the back of a cupboard when the previous owners moved out of the house.

Virginia made no attempt to arrange the blooms but took care with the positioning of the vase so that it was out of sight of the window. She lifted the box with the message still attached, holding it, as before, by the corners and taking it up to the spare room. More than an hour later, with the twins in their cots and asleep, she listened to Jennifer's message. The expected follow-up to last night's hearing was to be at two when Jennifer came off duty. Virginia had no intention of changing her plea.

Gemma Platt looked up as the bell over the shop door rang, hurriedly pushing the magazine she was reading under the counter. Then she leaned against the back wall, hip jutting. Without the swelling around the waistline and belly, her stance would have been provocative. With it she merely looked awkward and uncomfortable.

A stretch towelling shift dress accommodated the bulge and stopped short to reveal legs well worth baring even on this sharp morning. The girl had piled her hair on top of her head in an untidy bun. Nevertheless she had a generally attractive appearance. Her face was pert and pretty, her full pouting lips filled in with pearlised pink and outlined in another shade. Her eyebrows were pencilled in but followed the natural line. Her skin was flawless except for the fading bruising round one eye.

Jennifer, taking time over her appraisal, noticed Gemma wince as she levered herself away from the wall and came to the counter. Since the shop was empty she began her questions with no preliminaries. 'Who's the man who's been knocking you around?'

Gemma recognised authority in the woman's voice and stance and saw no point in denying the assault. ''E 'asn't touched 'er and I can look after meself. You from the Social?' Jennifer had failed to remark the small silent girl who sat on the floor behind the door sucking a lollipop. 'Say 'ello to the lady.' The child transferred her gaze from Jennifer to her mother and back again but did not speak. When Jennifer produced her warrant card, Gemma looked disappointed. 'Never thought Megan would shop me.'

'I'm sure she wouldn't. Since you haven't done anything wrong, she couldn't even if she wanted to.' Jennifer put the card back in her pocket. 'I wasn't trying to threaten you with this. I just wanted to be up front with you. If you're talking to a police officer, you should know you are.' Gemma seemed mollified but still uneasy. 'Look, I've no intention of causing trouble between you and your bloke. If he, or anyone else, comes in, I'm just a customer come to complain because you haven't delivered my magazine. On that condition, will you tell me as much as you can about the calls you've been having? You and Megan might be tough nuts but the next girl he picks on might go and have a backstreet abortion. Does your boy-friend know about it?'

She nodded. 'I asked him if we could both go for a test, just to be sure. 'E went ballistic.'

'Would you like me to put you in touch with someone who could fix it for you?'

She looked wistful but shook her head. 'It wouldn't do no good if Steve didn't go as well. If I've got it, it's only from 'im.'

'You don't have to sleep with him.'

The girl looked at Jennifer with disappointment. 'That's all you know – not even the half of it.'

Jennifer knew this was so. She had no understanding of the undoubted thralldom of an abused girl to a dominant man. She asked, 'Is Steve not angry about it? Maybe he'd–'

'Maybe 'e'd kill me if 'e knew I were talking to you. I wish I'd never told 'im about it, nor Megan neither. Steve says 'e's going to find the bastard and deal with 'im.'

'If he assaults someone he'll certainly have us to reckon with.' Observing Gemma's face, Jennifer went on quickly, 'There wouldn't be any need for him to know we'd been talking to you. That's a firm promise. Will you tell me exactly what the man said and contact me if anything else happens?'

The girl's story followed the one Jennifer had heard from Faye and Megan. In reply to the second request, Gemma agreed grudgingly. 'I'll tell Megan, get her to tell you.'

Jennifer offered advice which was refused on the subject of line traces but the girl did agree to log calls whenever possible and listen for any sort of identifying sound. When the door latch rattled, she changed her topic as she had promised. '...It's the third time that it's happened. If there's any more trouble I shall have to take my custom elsewhere...' When she met Gemma's indignant stare it occurred to her that she was overdoing things to the detriment of the family business.

Gemma pulled from under the counter the magazine she had been reading when Jennifer had first come in and handed it over. 'It only came in today. You'd 'ave 'ad it in the evening round.'

Jennifer glanced at the magazine, felt the scrutiny of her fellow customer and blushed. Gemma had exacted a full revenge.

Harriet Bradley had not been sick this morning, which was useful because the music examination to which her parents had been attributing her 'nerves' had taken place yesterday. Far from being overwhelmed by it, she had welcomed it, letting it fill her mind for a while to the exclusion of her greater fear.

Because she no longer cared about passing or failing, she knew she had played well, even brilliantly. Mr Lennox had said as much to Mummy. Mummy had beamed and Harriet knew she was making plans to drop the news of a distinction casually into the conversation at the PTA meeting or a dinner party. Mummy would have news soon that she wouldn't want to drop anywhere.

Harriet pulled off her knitted cotton nightdress with its printed Boyzone logo, shook back her straight blonde hair till it fell to her waist behind her and regarded her naked form in the wardrobe mirror. It was

slim, skinny to be accurate, with only a suggestion of raised soft flesh round her
nipples. She had a very immature body for a
fifteen-year-old.

Yesterday, in the showers at school, that
nasty coarse girl, Melanie Patchett, had told
her, in a voice that everybody could hear,
that she had tits like a couple of fried eggs.
Maybe it was a good sign. Surely a body like
hers wasn't capable of producing a baby.
Mother Nature wouldn't let a body grow a
child inside it when the breasts hadn't
grown enough to make any milk.

A year ago she hadn't even had a period,
had wondered if she ever would. Maybe
she'd just missed a couple because they
hadn't settled down yet. Her eyes were
drawn again to the small box on the
dressing-table. What a lot of money it had
cost – most of what was left of her birthday
money. Eight pounds and ninety-nine pence
just to get bad news! She'd have to do the
test this morning. Anything was better than
not knowing, she told herself desperately,
not believing it.

Not knowing was far better than being
certain and having to tell her parents. She
shut her eyes, which cut out her image in
the mirror and the pretty, cheerful wallpaper her mother had chosen for her, but
left everything else still frightening, taunt-
ing, threatening her. She'd count up to a

hundred, then she'd hide the box under her dressing-gown, go to the bathroom and follow the instructions.

The result would be negative. Her whole life could start again. Suddenly, she knew she was not pregnant. God would not give her such a terrible punishment just for disobeying strict orders and having a couple of drinks at Gary's party. It had seemed so important that night to show Gary that skinny people too knew how to get a life. That was Melanie's phrase. Harriet was not quite sure what it meant but she knew by her class-mates' standards, she hadn't got one. Ninety-eight, ninety-nine, a hundred. She grabbed the box and set off before she was tempted to begin at the beginning again.

Her father was coming out of the bathroom. He'd become awkward and falsely hearty now that she was growing up and he couldn't reach so easily to pat her on the head. 'Well, I'm glad we can have smiles over the breakfast table, at least until the next exam. You've no slippers on, Harriet. You'll catch cold!'

Harriet wondered how when she was walking on thick carpets in a centrally heated house. She locked the door and her fingers shook as she struggled with the seal on the box. She had chosen this brand because it gave its result in just two minutes instead of four. She had learned the instructions by heart and had no need to refer to them. Pulling out the white plastic stick she plunged it into her stream of urine and prayed, fervently but faithlessly. Her bladder empty, she raised the stick and saw the dreaded double blue line.

At eleven o'clock, Virginia picked up Michael who had fallen asleep on the floor and carried him to his cot. Sinead, similarly dispatched, received dire threats to be carried out if her wails should wake her brother. The child lay down obediently when her mother drew the curtains across to dim the bright if not warm November sun.

Thankfully, Virginia went downstairs, surveyed her cluttered living-room, let her eyes stray to the book of *Times* crosswords that Benny had given her to fill the long evenings of baby-sitting whilst he was away and succumbed to it. She had solved three clues when the telephone rang.

In a sub-station in Millton, near Ulverston over in Cumbria, the desk sergeant had deserted his post momentarily to go in search of a cup of tea. He had dropped only one of his usual three spoonfuls of sugar into it when the bell on his desk pinged. He was still stirring when it pinged again.

He hurried back to the foyer, spilling hot liquid into his saucer till his cup looked like an oversized boat on a small pond. He licked his scalded thumb as he regarded the small, slight, middle-aged man and the small stout woman who required his assistance. When he offered it politely both of them began to speak at once.

The woman deferred to the man who announced, half-defiantly, 'We think our son is missing.'

The sergeant raised his eyebrows over his half lenses. 'You only think so?'

'Well, we know he's missing. We think something has happened to him.'

'Something nasty,' the woman added, in case the sergeant should have misunderstood. He reached gravely for the pen behind his ear.

Seeing that his report was being taken seriously, the man's aggression disappeared and he gave a straightforward account of his grown-up son's plan to spend some time at the primitive cottage in Grasmere which was jointly owned by several members of his family. He went on to describe their subsequent discovery, after several weeks of silence from the young man, that he had not been seen there.

The man's recital was punctuated by sporadic and incoherent mutterings from his wife. '...got behind with his thesis ...

about time our side of the family had a turn at staying there … silly habit, walking by himself in the hills … not eating properly…'

At this last irrelevancy the man lost patience. 'He hasn't vanished through wasting away, Mavis! For goodness' sake keep to the point.'

The sergeant drew a form from the pigeonhole behind him and a further supply of patience from long service in his position. 'Let's get a few facts in writing, shall we? Can you give me your son's full name?'

The man cheered up at the sight of the form. This was how things were done. Now they were getting somewhere. 'Certainly, Officer. It's Richard Lee Hillard.'

3

Clare Chase was not finding her appointment with Dr Simpson as soothing as she had hoped. He had certainly welcomed her and not rushed her as she'd tried to express her anxiety and he had at least explained one seeming contradiction that had been puzzling her.

'No. I never encouraged Justin to try to have a child, but I did assure him, when he asked me, that the disease won't affect his fertility. That's important to a man, especially one who's had so many of his powers taken from him.'

'Yes, I can see that.'

Not sure which of her many questions to produce next, Clare fiddled with a button until the doctor asked, 'How do you feel yourself about having a child?' How did she? She wanted several, at least three, but she wanted them already born by now so that she would still be in her physical prime when they were adolescent. She wanted them to have an able-bodied father who would share responsibility for them and teach them to be happy by being happy himself. She wanted them to be free from the danger of any inherited, incapacitating illness.

She was far too confused and weary, however, to express any of her fears about potential parenthood in their actual circumstances. She merely muttered, 'I couldn't cope.'

The doctor was patient. 'I know that, but how does it make you feel? How much do you blame Justin for your lack of children, as well as for his possibly rash wish to produce one?'

'It's not his fault!'

He saw that, on this occasion, he was not going to coax his patient into a cathartic expression of her resentment. He was aware, equally, of the danger of her growing despair and the needs of the fourteen other patients booked in to see him at this particular surgery, quite a number of whom would already be waiting outside.

He sighed and pulled his prescription pad towards him. 'I know you aren't keen on the idea, but I think just now that you really need–'

'Does MS affect the brain?' Clare asked suddenly. 'The personality? Make the person act out of character?'

He knew she needed a straight answer rather than further probing. He could find out later what Justin had been doing to prompt the question. 'There are no mental effects. That's something to be thankful for but it brings problems. Patients understand exactly what's wrong, have to face the frightening "incurable" label. There's an emotional response to that, first shock and anger, which Justin has got over now. Then comes grief and depression, loss of sleep and appetite maybe. Certainly loss of self-esteem. It can certainly seem like a change of personality. Believe me, in the end there's acceptance and relaxation, but whilst he's working through to that you need some help.' He began writing. 'You mustn't feel a failure. I can't begin to express my admiration for the way you've taken all of this on.'

'You do what you have to do.'

'Yes, but when you had the option, to take it on knowingly. That's something else.' She looked taken aback and he wondered how long it was since the last time she had been verbally appreciated.

Dr Simson's receptionist, Debbie, looked round the waiting-room impatiently. Wasn't anyone going home this morning? First Mrs Chase had come out of surgery and gone straight back to the chair she'd been sitting on before going in. She'd been there for ten minutes now, staring at the floor.

Now the Bradley child had come out weeping buckets and she was sitting down again as well. Dr Fowler had gone out on an emergency call so none of her patients were moving, and that Asian woman who'd only registered last week had brought half her relations and all her children with her. At least, it was to be hoped that the present gathering represented all her children!

It was a change for smug little Harriet Bradley not to be accompanied by Mummy and not to be wearing a simpering smile. Debbie wouldn't be surprised if she'd got herself in the family way. It often happened to those little blonde, butter-wouldn't-melt types. If it had, Debbie would give a lot to be a fly on the wall when Mummy heard about it.

There were too many people in the world as it was. She had more sense herself than to be adding to them and having the best part of her life wasted on disgusting nappies and running noses. It was a nasty process that produced them anyway. One of the patients had once had the cheek to tell her theirs was a selfish attitude. Debbie didn't see how that could be. She did a useful, caring job and, in her spare time – well, once a year anyway – she sold flags for the hospice.

Damian was the practice nurse in this very practice. You couldn't, surely, get more caring than lancing boils for people, giving them injections, showing them how to take proper care of their children. This silent defence of her husband was interrupted by one of his grateful patients. "Ow the 'ell much longer will we 'ave to wait for Dr Fowler?'

'You needn't wait. The nurse can look at your ulcer for–'

'Nay, lass, you're not fobbin' me off wi' someone unqualified.'

'Then she'll be as long as it takes,' she told the beery old man, noting over his shoulder that Mrs Chase and Harriet were leaving together. The place certainly looked better for the removal of their miserable faces.

'Yes, I would like a tour of the house but it's not exactly top priority right now.' In the middle of a working day, Jennifer was determined to keep her meeting with Ginny to the point 'Even if you say you can cope, Declan's obviously picking up signals.'

'Rubbish! His nightmare was all about some unsuitable film he's seen at Jamie's house. I'll be following that up with his mother.'

'In the usual easy atmosphere in this house I don't think a film would have upset him.'

Suddenly, Virginia gave in. 'All right. Say all you've come to say. For the kid's sake, I'll go along with all of it except telling Benny before his course is finished.'

'On Friday?'

'No. All three parts of it.'

Jennifer knew she had to make the best of the concession Virginia had made. 'You need to log the calls, if possible tape them.'

'I have made a list of dates and times.'

'Well, let's be thankful for small mercies. The best thing is to hang up quickly. Don't give a reaction or he'll feed on it.'

'Common sense told me that, but hanging up without listening would be irresponsible. As soon as I put the receiver down I make notes of the phrases and expressions he's used. I'm trying to make sure I'll recognise his voice if I meet him face to face. Of course, he knows that. He always uses a half-whisper that's very difficult to pin down. He seems well spoken, though.'

'Any letters?'

There was a slight hesitation before Virginia replied. 'Not yet. He sometimes says he'll write.'

Jennifer drummed her fingers on the chair arm, reviewing the routine advice it seemed so strange to be giving to a close friend. 'I'm sure your house is secure but, if there's any little job that Benny thought it safe to leave till he came back, can you get it done today?'

Virginia considered. 'I don't think there is. At the best of times a copper's family is always at risk. With four small children to consider you fit chains and bolts before you

59

move in.'

'Right. Don't drive around without a car phone.'

'I never do. I can't leave the kids to their own devices if I run out of petrol or break down and have to find an emergency motor-way phone.'

'OK. Stick around with the rest of your family as much as possible, even if you don't tell them why. Couldn't you just tell your father?'

'Possibly. It would worry him. I'll think about it.' She went towards the window as a car drew up over the road, then shook her head impatiently and sat down again. 'I keep wondering if I'm partly to blame. You know I tend to poke my nose into other people's business. I may have given someone the impression I was especially interested in them...'

'Do you have a particular someone in mind?'

Virginia thought again then shook her head. 'We've met so many new people in the last few weeks but they all seem perfectly normal ... at least ... you know what I mean. Some of them are a bit eccentric but none of them would go in for this sort of obsession.'

'But the obsessive side of a stalker's character will only be apparent to the victim. Don't rely on the world-in-general's assessment if it opposes your own instincts. Tell me about this Lee.'

'I don't know much. He called one day to say he hadn't been in the street long himself. No one had invited him to anything so he decided to take the initiative, said that was his way. The party was for a couple of nights later, a fortnight ago last Saturday. It can't be him. The calls began a week or so before he came round.'

'He might have become attracted to you and had the party for that reason. Or he might have invited you because someone less extrovert encouraged him to. Who talked to you at this do? Did anyone try to get you away from Benny?'

'No one had to. We couldn't get a sitter at such short notice so I went first and came back at about ten so Benny could show his face. He wasn't all that keen.'

'So, who did you talk to? By the way, can we have some coffee? I skipped it after lunch, counting on getting some here.'

Virginia was indignant. 'You'd have been offered refreshments after your tour of the house if you hadn't begun this inter-rogation!' She got up and went into the kitchen, adding over her shoulder, 'You can make it yourself if you like.'

Jennifer hastily took advantage of the offer whilst Virginia continued her description of Lee Hillard's party. 'I got pinned into a corner by the Wing Commander. I'm not sure if that's his proper rank or his nickname. Then Gill, Lee's partner, rescued me. She said she'd only met Lee a few weeks ago. Getting into bed with people seems to be her way of getting to know them. Then she went off to do things in the kitchen. I didn't offer to help. I have to know people fairly well before I feel comfortable spoiling their food.' Both women grinned.

'I talked to Lee himself for a while, then I introduced myself all around. After that it was my baby-sitting stint.'

'So Lee was the only man you had an extended conversation with?'

'I suppose so.'

'But you didn't recognise his voice over the phone.'

Virginia shrugged. 'I just don't know, except that he's certainly well spoken. Perhaps I should find some trivial reason to ring Lee and try to make a comparison.'

'Perhaps you shouldn't!' Suddenly Jennifer caught sight of the flowers. She laughed. 'I'm beginning to think I don't know Benny at all. First you tell me he stayed late last night to clear up his paperwork–'

'Exactly. Ever since I got pregnant seven years ago, I've been the reason that Benny's career's been on hold and he's had a cavalier attitude to some aspects of the job because it didn't matter. His family commitments were stopping him getting on anyway. Now he's really being given a chance and he's so keen he's even keeping files up to date and, if it's really necessary, going back to theoretical learning, under protest of course. I'm going to do my damnedest to make sure I don't hold him back this time.'

'But that doesn't explain the orchids – or did you buy them?' Virginia shook her head. 'One for each child you gave him? That seems even more out of character. It's not even anywhere near St Valentine's day. We'd better drop this stalker business and start investigating Benny's other women.'

This at least was not on Virginia's list of concerns. Jennifer offered her a brimming mug. 'How does he like being up the valley?'

'He's quite taken with it. It's pretty country, a better view from his window and handier for dealing with the weirdoes who live up there. He thinks he'll miss out on some interesting town cases. It's mostly drug-related crime up there but he goes out on raids and, as you know, he's always enjoyed kicking the odd door in. It's the flip side of this neat finickiness.' Both women looked round the untidy kitchen, which had been Virginia's sole responsibility for only half a day. 'I don't bother with things so much when I know he isn't coming in to see the mess and get up steam about it. How're you getting on with your own funny calls?'

Jennifer described her encounter with Gemma Platt and picked over the previous day's interview with the lesbian couple.

'You obviously took to Megan.'

Jennifer considered. 'Yes, I did. She interested me. It struck me as strange at first that the apparently unwomanly one of the pair had undertaken the pregnancy but the more I talked to them, the more she struck me as the fitter mother. I think her appearance is probably a rebellion against someone, possibly parents whose ambitions for her were different from her own. She's gone into it with her eyes open – knows not to expect any help from the decorative Faye. She said she'd carry on with the shirts and use the factory créche. She knows she's going to be landed with both childcare and making the money.'

'I wonder how much writing will get done when the infant arrives.'

Jennifer tutted impatiently. 'About as much as gets done now, probably. I imagine it's a pseudo-occupation that leaves sufficient time for tittivating her face and dress.'

'You said they took very little notice of their call?' Jennifer nodded. 'It seems odd when the message was so sensitive and spiteful. Still, as one of them said, lesbians are used to abuse. They'd have no life at all if they were upset by it.'

'Have you heard from your caller today?'

Virginia's face was covered by her mug as she drank the last dregs from it but Jennifer was still watching her when she put it down on the table. They discussed the call until it was time for Jennifer to pick up her small daughters. She was unlocking her car when Virginia came running down the path to delay her departure.

'Jen! I've remembered who Justin Chase is. I've never actually met him but I have spoken to him by telephone.'

Jennifer was grateful to Superintendent Kleever for taking her fears seriously. She was convinced that Ginny was in danger and could not let her down. The two women had consulted together on many occasions and many subjects before. Mostly it had been Ginny who had dispensed common sense and sound advice, as though she, and not Jennifer, were the elder by several years.

Now Jennifer was betraying her confidence but she knew that she had no choice. The alternative was to risk rape or worse for her friend with the possibility of the Mitchell children being used to manipulate her. She had considered taking her worries to her DCI but that would be putting him in a worse dilemma than her own. Ginny was his daughter and Benny his son-in-law and ex-sergeant.

Maybe Mr Clever had been right to separate them after all. Possibly he was the best person to approach. If it was the super himself who recalled Benny from Wakefield, Ginny would surely have no objections. At any rate he was proving a good listener and Jennifer began to feel her task becoming easier. 'The DI didn't want to go on this course even without knowing this was happening–'

The superintendent shook his head. 'I think you're wrong there. Mitchell's a keen lad – likes his macho image of course but he wants to get on. All this anti-course chat is to keep in with the lads.'

'I think you'll find both the Mitchells more straightforward than that. If either of them says anything, it's meant.'

The superintendent shrugged. 'We'll see. Why hasn't she told him?'

Jennifer floundered through an explanation of her friend's determination not to be a further hindrance to her husband's advancement. Now that it was too late she realised that she had already told him rather more than Ginny might want her husband's boss to know.

He listened without comment, then asked, 'Why are you telling me now? It's been going on for four weeks and Mitchell will be back in forty-eight hours.'

'I've only known about it since yesterday.

What worries me today is that Virginia thinks there was a change in tone in this morning's call. Up to now, the calls have been obscene but the caller has seemed laid back, tempting her to be interested in him, as if he were having his kind of joke. Today, though, she says he sounded annoyed. He seemed to think she shouldn't be coming and going as she pleases with no reference to him.

'And, if I'm right about the flowers, he's been right up to the doorstep. She led me to think Benny gave them to her but it's not likely. If he did send flowers I can't see them being orchids – and why four of them? I think I've interfered too much, put her off telling me any more.'

'The chap needn't have delivered the flowers himself. He'd only need to order them.'

Jennifer felt relieved. 'True, and I know he's not been in the house. He said he could imagine her there with everything in place and no man to make a mess.' She explained the true nature of the Mitchells' domestic affairs.

The superintendent was silent for a few moments, scribbling notes. He looked up to ask, 'How many people knew Mitchell was going to be away?' Jennifer shrugged. 'Anyway, aren't you on this chap's track already? I thought Tom Browne had landed that nasty calls business on you.'

'He's the one I'd have consulted about Ginny if it hadn't been for all the tangled relationships.' Jennifer related her dealings with the pregnant girls, thankful to be no longer breaking confidences. She finished, defiantly, 'I don't think this one is the same man who's bothered Virginia.'

Kleever blinked. 'You think in a place the size of Cloughton we've got two separate malicious telephone callers at work simultaneously?'

'Yes, I do.'

Kleever gave Jennifer a long, silent appraisal. 'All right. Whether or not, we'd better do something about Mrs Mitchell. You couldn't move in with her till Friday, could you?'

This plan had been in the back of Jennifer's mind since she had first heard of Ginny's predicament but she turned it down again now. 'If I had no responsibilities I'd have done it already. I have two small daughters and no one else to look after them out of working hours. If I feel the Mitchell children are at risk I can't bring myself to move in and put my girls in danger too.'

'Tell me about this man Chase you've got down for the AIDS scare calls. Have you seen him yet?'

Jennifer shook her head. 'I've left him till

tomorrow as I know he'll be at home. I'm seeing Gemma Platt's boyfriend Steve Thacker tonight. I want some more information from Virginia before I see Mr Chase. She's met him – well, spoken to him through her work.'

'What does she do?'

'She's working for a small publisher on the industrial estate at Darleigh. They put out what Virginia calls "those rather dreadful books" full of pictures covering the last hundred years of trivial social history of various small towns, exploiting their isolationist tendencies. The chap in charge does most of the text himself, looking at pictures and inventing commentary as he feels led. That's according to Ginny. Actually, I rather like them. I've got one of Chesterfield where I was born and I shall get the Cloughton one with Ginny's pieces in as soon as it's available.

'She writes up company histories of the significant firms in each area. Sometimes she's working from old documents, sometimes making extracts from a longer, official history, sometimes interviewing retired workers for their reminiscences. And yes, you're right, the man who's harassing her could easily be someone she's met in the course of her work. Justin Chase is a case in point. He's the man she had to liaise with at Cantrells. As I implied, the current book is on Cloughton.'

'Well, there's the connection. You'd better keep your two separate callers theory under review. In the meantime, I'd give this Steve character a miss. Chase sounds more like our man – not that there's a great deal we can do about him until we get more co-operation from all the women concerned.

'Mrs Mitchell at least ought to have more sense. With traces, we've got a ninety per cent chance of nailing him. If she's kept all the rest of it from her husband, why can't she let them put one on their line and not tell him?

Jennifer sighed. 'All right. I'll ask her that.'

'And I'll give you Clement to keep half an eye on the Mitchell's house now the computer business is finally cleared up until I need him for something else.'

'But that means he'll have to know–'

'Of course it does! What did you expect me to do for you, wave a magic wand? Next you'll be wanting me to fetch Mitchell back from Wakefield to hold his wife's hand.'

An after-school hour spent in the reference library had given Harriet new hope. Sitting there she had faced the fact that she was going to have to help herself. No more counting. No more bargaining with God to live an impossibly holy life if He would take the baby away. He obviously wasn't going to help her and neither was Dr Simpson.

She had to learn what must be done and, if the library failed her, she had almost decided to swallow her pride and consult Melanie Patchett. It wouldn't matter too much about trusting her to keep the secret because she often spread scandals about girls she didn't like and, although the others all gathered round to listen and laugh, they didn't really believe her.

A boy came to share her table. Harriet was glad she didn't know him. He'd think she was doing Biology homework, but, even so, she arranged her arm casually round the big book to shield his eyes from the rather rude pictures. At first the medical dictionary had disappointed her. She had heard vaguely about children's rights and charters and had been hoping for information on clinics that would perform discreet – and painless! – abortions for schoolgirls.

Actually she had rather more faith in Melanie, though she hoped the tales about gin and knitting needles were just her usual vulgar jokes. The fat book contained no mention of clinics but, to Harriet's inexpressible relief, it suggested that an early pregnancy could be lost if the expectant mother failed to take care.

Suddenly she remembered an aunt who had some years ago lost a much-wanted baby when she had carried a trunk full of baby equipment down from the attic. Eagerly Harriet studied the kinds of movement that were considered ill advised. Hope sparked and then flared as she planned. She'd join the team of girls who helped put out and put away the gym apparatus and she'd make an effort in the lessons for a week or two instead of lounging around in a sulk because she'd been made to tie her hair back.

Perhaps it would be a good idea to change the furniture round in her bedroom. If Mummy was annoyed that would be all the better because then she could put it all back again. She could make a start now by lifting the fat book in a manner quite contrary to the advice it contained.

By the time she reached home she felt almost lighthearted. As she fitted her key in the lock she heard the phone ringing. It was probably one of her friends. Everyone knew her parents never got home until a quarter past six. She picked up the receiver but heard only small gasps, as though the caller had run for a bus and was catching his breath. She repeated their number, and, when there was still no message, asked politely, 'Have you got the wrong number?'

The voice answered only, 'Oh no, it's the right number, Harriet,' before the receiver at the other end was replaced.

4

DC Clement was well pleased with his latest commission from Superintendent Kleever. The young DC had suggested a list of ingenious pretexts that would have justified his presence outside his DI's house and had been disappointed to be told that it would not matter if he were seen. His only purpose in being there was to safeguard Mrs Mitchell, and if her tormentor knew he was being watched then so much the better.

Clement remembered Virginia as one of the few bright spots in the superintendent's ghastly party and was of the opinion that she was well worth watching. Her dress had covered what a good many other female guests had unwisely revealed and the mystery had been more intriguing than the displays. Besides, she had been kind to him when most other guests had taken his reserve for rudeness.

Clement contemplated the Mitchells' house in the gathering darkness, noting trivial details to keep his mind occupied and alert. None of the sets of curtains at the front windows matched any other, but the different colours agreed well enough with one another. The small frosted window would be the bathroom. The light in there kept going on and off and he imagined Virginia bathing the children and putting them to bed in turn.

He had watched her bringing them all home at end-of-school time, pushing a double pram with the two older children walking one each side, a handsome boy, very like his mother, and a rather solid, plain little girl. He and Virginia had ignored one another although he was sure she knew who he was and why he was there. Since she had gone inside she had not pulled a curtain to one side to check that he was still on duty.

She must have been a child bride. She only looked about twenty now and she had no bulges from producing all those children. The babies were about the age his own child would have been if... He shook away the memories and concentrated again on the task in hand. Virginia's hair must be naturally curly. She'd had it uncovered even though it had been raining and it looked none the worse. Anyway, the little boy's was exactly the same. It was a pity the other child had the DI's hair and walk and build. It was easy to see what the DI saw in his wife but Clement wondered what she saw in him.

After another hour, he slid out of the car and walked the fifteen yards up to number five and along the road beyond it. All the houses were medium-sized, respectable-looking and well kept up. There seemed to be a car in every drive but one, and others, probably belonging to the street's visitors, made his own inconspicuous. Clement rubbed his hands together and quickened his step, deciding not to take another walk without his jacket.

Passing number five for the second time, he glanced up the side of the house and saw, with some surprise, that Virginia's washing was still out on the line. He wouldn't have expected such sloppy housekeeping from such a trim-looking woman. Still, she had four small children to set her schedule awry. If the weather forecast were to be believed, she would be taking the clothes in tomorrow wetter than when they went out.

He grinned to himself as he climbed back into his car and switched on the engine until he was warm again.

The stalker entered the Mitchells' back garden with no particular intention beyond his desire to be physically close to Virginia. He felt he would learn to know her better, get inside her skin, by seeing the things that she had daily around her. He could do that well tonight. The rain had stopped before midnight and now, in the small hours, the sky was clear and the almost full moon gave sharp blue edges to gate, hedge and shrubs. It was cold and the wet surfaces were beginning to be filmed with ice. He trod carefully.

The garden was a credit to Virginia. With a neglectful husband and four small children she still found time to keep it immaculate. There was not a weed or a blade of grass in sight in the geometrical flower beds. The hedge was precision trimmed with corners, just as he liked his own. How could Virginia fail to realise how well matched they were? Sometimes he couldn't help feeling a bit impatient with her. He understood there were difficulties, of course. Although it could not be that she loved her husband, she would not want to hurt him or her children more than was necessary. He could have helped her with all that himself if only she hadn't hung up instead of speaking to him. And now she'd made it impossible for him to use the telephone.

In fact it seemed as if she was doing all she could to expose and disgrace him. At the very least she could have put his flowers in the window so that he could see them there and know she was enjoying them, but she seemed determined to ignore all his overtures.

Surveying the house itself from the shelter of a clump of old-established rhododendron bushes below the small terrace, the stalker suddenly realised how wrong he had been. The washing on the line had irked him when he first saw it there, gathering wetness and flapping untidily. How stupid he had been. Here was Virginia's signal. Of course she had to go through the motions of complying with police advice from her interfering sergeant friend, but here, cloaked by her having left household linen to drip beside it, was her answering gesture to him.

In a warm glow he gathered flimsy garments, crisp now with frost. The satin ones still felt smooth though as he stroked them, imagining the cups of the brassiere filled with the flesh of her breasts and the gathering of silk round the top of the brief pants covering firm buttocks. He dropped the filmy scraps into the inside pocket of his overcoat and crept out by the back gate, shutting it in slow motion and therefore soundlessly. He would examine the garments' colours and designs, imagine Virginia choosing them, climbing in and out of them, in the light and warmth of his own house.

Jennifer Taylor was not looking forward to her encounter with the Chases, chiefly because she was unsure how to approach them. If either of them was responsible in any way for the harassment of the pregnant women then her duty was clear. If neither of them was involved, then she would have made the miserable life they shared quite insupportable.

She had to make an arbitrary decision and did so, climbing out of her car briskly now that her mind was made up. Mrs Chase had not made the calls herself so it seemed fairest to be as open with her as possible, to offer to set her mind at rest. If Justin were innocent, then the sooner he was exonerated the better, in Clare's judgement as well as her own. If he proved to be the culprit then he probably needed help as much as blame.

Jennifer rapped on a clean and sparkling door painted in a cheerful red. The whole house had a more positive and well-kept appearance than she had expected. Its occupants too were a surprise. She had expected to find a consumptive-looking man, wasting in a wheelchair and tended by a bedraggled drudge. They proved to be a handsome couple. The girl was fair with hair expertly cut. Her face, admittedly bare, was relatively unlined. The man certainly sat in a wheelchair but he was broad-shouldered and powerfully built. No one had mentioned that he was black. A woolly cap of frizzy hair covered his skull and magnificent teeth made a startling white crescent as he smiled at her.

Their beauty magnified the tragedy. Forcing herself not to stare at them, Jennifer looked round the room into which she was ushered, her gaze settling on two framed photographs on a shelf of a pine dresser. One showed Justin Chase dribbling a football along a white beach. In the other, the couple sat on a rock, arms round each other's shoulders. Clare Chase wore a bikini that revealed no blemishes and her husband a bright sweatshirt over swimming trunks. Honeymoon photographs?

She turned back to the couple in the flesh. The man looked politely enquiring, the woman on her guard, so that Jennifer knew that her visit was half expected.

Clare threw her an appealing glance. 'I'm glad you managed to find time to drop in. Justin's got urgent work so shall we have coffee in the kitchen?'

This suited Jennifer's purpose well enough. She launched into her half-prepared speech, addressing the woman by her first name and urging her to be frank in her husband's best interests. Clare co-operated, thankful, Jennifer thought, that her duty to answer police questions now made it right to hand her problem over to someone else. She had no concrete evidence against her husband, had sympathised with Megan without feeling the least bit involved until Faye had voiced her suspicions. Faye had sounded so plausible that now Clare was reading something sinister into Justin's every remark. At the same time, however, she couldn't believe him to be guilty. 'Certainly, the old Justin wouldn't have dreamed of it.'

Jennifer noted the small but significant differences between Clare's account and Faye Weston's and she tried to persuade Clare to talk more generally about her circumstances and difficulties.

'I haven't really got any. In practical terms our problems are more than adequately catered for. We're both reasonably intelligent and we've found out about all the facilities that are available to help MS sufferers. We've incorporated as many of them as Justin can bear to accept into our set-up here.' She crumbled a biscuit between her fingers, letting the crumbs drop to her plate. 'His family is as supportive as Justin will allow, our GP is friendly and patient and Mr Cantrell, Justin's boss, has made things as easy for us as he possibly can.'

Clare put her plate full of crumbs on the table and gazed at it in silence. Jennifer waited, then prompted quietly, 'Are you afraid of not being able to cope financially, if and when he can't work any more?'

Clare answered without looking up. 'It might not come to that for ages, and, anyway, there's family money. It's been agreed it's all coming to Justin. Warren can fend for himself...'

'Warren?'

'His older brother. I shouldn't be telling you this because Justin doesn't know. It would infuriate him.' She reached over to the coffee pot and refilled their empty cups with lukewarm liquid that neither of them drank before she spoke again. It seemed as if she had been struggling to restrain the words from bursting out. 'It's just the mind-numbing boredom of living my life on hold. I can have no other role at present but waiting around in case he needs me. In some ways I shall feel less frustrated when he can do very little for himself and I'm busy all day doing everything for him.'

Jennifer tried to put aside her profound pity for this woman whose talents and beauty were slowly wasting. She took out a notebook to signal her change of attitude and made her questions specific. Motive was indisputable. Her job was to check on Justin Chase's actions and opportunities.

In Millton, near Ulverston, the desk sergeant at the little police sub-station was expecting a peaceful and pleasant evening. The dog that had worried, and in several cases injured, sheep on the surrounding hills had been identified and destroyed. His work would be cut by at least half now that no furious farmers were shouting the odds in the foyer.

The canteen seemed to have changed its coffee supplier so that the cups brought to him by the new young WPC could be drunk even when he was not actually dying of thirst. He was not supposed to specify woman police constable any more, as she constantly reminded him, and he gave her the old-style manner of address merely to prolong her presence as she berated him about it. As far as he could see, in fact, all was right with the world.

His heart sank, therefore, when, through the glass doors of the main entrance, he saw Mrs Hillard puffing her way up the steps. It took a further plunge when he realised she was not being followed by the dapper little man who had the knack of switching off her stream of incoherent utterances without giving her offence. Hearing a voice through the open door of the office behind the reception desk, he knew he was saved. PC Butcher could spend part of his first week in the force learning how to deflect time wasters. The sergeant exerted himself to the extent of raising his voice to call the very new constable through to the station foyer.

Mrs Hillard seemed to have begun her string of complaints whilst still outside and began her address to the two officers in the middle of a sentence. '...only you don't seem to be making much effort, even though you have put him on Missing Persons–'

The sergeant cut in on her gasp for breath, explaining that, in a way, she was right, that Lee was not what the force described as 'vulnerable', that they had no reason to suspect that he was a victim of foul play and that her son had the right to disappear if he wanted to.

Her glance was accusing. 'Lee wouldn't... Well, I suppose that's what all mothers say ... wouldn't be troubling you ... only it's my hubby who's really worried ... brings on his asthma ... so bad today he couldn't get here... Won't settle down again till we've got this sorted out.'

The frantic gasps that punctuated these attempts at coherent sentences made by the woman who had managed the journey made the sergeant fear for the respiratory system of the partner who had been considered unfit to come. 'I'm going to hand you over to Constable Butcher. He'll write down all you can tell us and we'll take it from there.' With a smirk he handed over both the woman and her file to his colleague.

Mrs Hillard followed the young constable as he ambled down the corridor. His sergeant's wink and nod had indicated that he was to use the draughtier of the two interview rooms. Nevertheless, when he had seated his interviewee on a hard upright chair he watched her begin shedding her outer layers of clothing. Still not comfortable she fanned away from her flushed jowls and chins the heat worked up by the rapid transfer of her bulk from the foyer, along fifteen yards of corridor to this cheerless little box with its chipped walls and its table decorated with cigarette burns and coffee stains.

Butcher knew that he had been fobbed off with a nuisance but he bore his superior no ill will. He was resigned to completing his stint at this back-of-beyond station and knew he would leave it with nothing on his record to impress the people who could offer him 'real opportunities'. Mrs Hillard enlarged on the subject of Lee's university career, thesis, promises of future employment and her disapproval of his friends.

One of them in particular, Charlie by name, had managed to annoy her most. '...ear-rings on a man! ... must be one of those ... kept Lee from his work ... brought up in a children's home ... what else can you expect...'

Her murmurings went largely unheard, though Butcher's pen busily kept pace. When his interviewee departed, his notebook read, 'Almost certainly escaped to grab his life back while he had the chance.'

This sentence was followed by as much as Butcher could remember of the shopping list his new wife had delivered verbally over the breakfast table and a magnificent doodle.

He put the book in his pocket and escaped the long way round to the station's little kitchen. He deserved a coffee before the sergeant played the next joke on him. Coffee was his generic term for the sandwich and large sticky cake that that beverage washed down. He took them to the table where he was soon joined by the other of the station's constables. He was a local man and an officer of rather longer standing. Butcher proceeded to describe his frustrations, flattered to find his older colleague paying rather more attention to his story than he had expected. His recital at an end, Butcher felt moved to a word of thanks for his listener's patience and interest.

The other officer brushed it off. 'It's just that I was at school with Lee and Nathan Hillard. Lee was a bit of a mummy's boy. I really couldn't see him giving her the slip like that. Though, if the worm's turned, I'm very glad to hear it.'

A telephone investigator arrived on Thursday whilst the Mitchells were still at breakfast, closely followed by the man who had been commissioned some time ago to cut out a stretch of rotten wood from the hall window. Declan and Caitlin were intrigued by such early visitors. When the first arrival explained to them that he had come to show Mummy how he had mended the telephone, Declan regarded him suspiciously. 'It's not been broken as far as I know.'

The man chuckled and glanced at Virginia. 'How old is he, ninety-nine and a bit?'

'I'm six years, one month and...' Declan began to count the extra few days, hiding his hands behind his back so that the man would not see him using his fingers.

Virginia hustled both children into coats and delivered them into the car that had drawn up outside with Declan's friend Jamie in the back. She found the telephone engineer efficient and reassuring. 'The trace is on now,' he told her, manfully swallowing her coffee in large gulps so as to be rid of it quickly. 'We can have up to seven thousand lines on trace at once, monitoring incoming calls. Now we'll know in seconds which number a call was made from, so long as you log the time and date of all malicious ones.' He shook his head as Virginia offered to refill his mug. 'No, sorry. I've got to keep to my time sheet. Of course there might be problems if a company number's used or if your caller has access to a phone that's not his own.'

Virginia had known there would be a catch. Reluctant to be left in the house with just the remaining workman, she went back to the kitchen, banging utensils unnecessarily to punish them for Jennifer's betrayal of her to Superintendent Kleever. Looking up, she noticed with a twinge of guilt the line of washing, heavy with rainwater, reproaching her through the glass. Benny's nagging about her housekeeping wasn't the pleasantest aspect of their relationship. She was pleased on the whole, though, that his obsession with order kept them up to the mark and compensated for her own casual attitude. She'd have to take it in before she delivered the twins to their doting grandmother and went to work. Now she would have to wash the school uniform clothes again. Since the weather was clearing, though, the towels could stay where they were till they'd blown dry again. Looking back at the line, she frowned. It had been full. Now the clothes reached only as far as the second flower bed. What was missing?

Virginia felt suddenly cold as she remembered. The far end of the line had held several pairs of lacy briefs with matching bras, several pairs of tights and Benny's favourite of her nightdresses, a filmy, scarlet scrap of silk. She closed her eyes as she worked out the implications. The stalker had been in the garden during the night in spite of the young constable's watchful eye. There was nothing to stop him hiding there during the day. She couldn't let the children play there any longer. If he was just outside the door she couldn't even leave them to play in a room of the house unless the outside doors were locked and bolted.

Could she, she wondered, trust the joiner, busy sawing in the hall? He had waved his credentials at her but Benny had engaged him and she didn't know the firm's logo or its workforce. She went out to the hall to watch him. He was still on his knees in front of the window and he continued his fiddling work without acknowledging her presence. Was that significant?

She walked past him, through to the sitting-room and looked out of the window, up and down the road. There was no sign of Clement but he had other work to do. She could hardly expect him to be there all day. She was lucky he could sometimes be spared when it was dark. She remembered how thankful she had been to see him as she had brought the children home the previous afternoon and regretted some of the furious vituperation she had heaped on Jennifer. She promised herself she would apologise for at least some of it at the first opportunity.

When she returned to the hall, the joiner

had packed his toolbag and was about to leave.

Harriet was finding the new arrangement of her bedroom furniture inconvenient but she would have to wait for a few days before putting it back. Mummy had merely remarked, 'It makes a change, I suppose.' She would want a reason if Harriet immediately moved everything back.

The baby still seemed to be clinging firmly inside her. She wondered who could be asked whether she should expect an immediate result from all this unaccustomed exercise or whether there was still hope that it would have the desired effect in time. She was not fond of physical exercise and only wanted to do what was necessary.

Unfortunately, her furniture had moved easily on some kind of rollers sunk into the bases. 'It's for easy cleaning, of course,' Mummy had explained. 'You don't think I clean around the edges! It's about time you were responsible for cleaning this room yourself.'

Harriet heard her parents' car doors slam as she was knotting her school tie. Going to the window, she watched them leave the drive, Mummy's signalling right for the local FE college and Daddy's left towards his office in town. She glanced at her watch and hurried downstairs. There would be trouble if her before-school jobs were not finished.

She took a tray to the table, stacked the breakfast pots and stowed them in the dishwasher. She poured herself more coffee, drank it and left her mug on the draining-board. Then she fetched her school books from Daddy's office where she had taken her homework for him to check. She was all ready to go out for the bus when the telephone rang.

Clare was relieved that Justin seemed to be having a better morning. He had washed and dressed himself, even though it was in sweatshirt and tracksuit trousers with no awkward fastenings, and got himself downstairs without her assistance. Immediately after breakfast, he had announced that he had a lot to do and she had heard him being noisily busy in his study. The phone in the living-room had murmured as it always did when his extension was being used, and, curiously, she could hear quite clearly through the door the soft clicking of his computer keys.

After a while there was an incoming call. Clare let it ring so that Justin could take it. After a moment his impatient voice called, 'It's for you. It's that hysterical girl you brought here the other day. I told you you'd have her on your back for ever once you got involved!'

Clare sighed, fearing that he was right. She lifted the receiver in the living-room, aware from the hollow echoing of her own voice that Justin had not replaced his own. 'What is it, Harriet?' She listened in horror to the distressed girl's incoherent message, able to fill in the gaps in her account from the more studied one Faye and Megan had given her.

She swallowed her fury and spoke as calmly as she could manage. 'I'm coming over, Harriet. When I arrive, I shall want some coffee before we decide what to do. Can you manage to make it?' There was a sobbing affirmative. 'I'll be about ten minutes.'

She replaced the receiver quietly before flinging open Justin's door and giving full rein to her anger. 'I'm going out. Since you were listening in you'll know where and why. And since the whole situation is the result of your jealousy and spite, you won't be surprised if I don't rush back to dance attendance on you!' She slammed the door on his protestations and drove the car noisily out of the garage and away up the street.

She had no experience of teenage girls, either hysterical or calm. She hoped Harriet was too busy making coffee, which Clare was sure she wouldn't be able to swallow, to have time to think of doing anything stupid.

The only strategy that occurred to her for when she arrived was to repeat to the girl her assurances that she was not alone as the victim of this evil man, so that it was unlikely that what he said was true. She would also point out that a test could be taken, easily, quickly and in confidence, to prove that both infant and mother were perfectly healthy. At least, after this scare, Harriet would see the problem of merely being pregnant in proportion.

Arriving at the large and gracious house, Clare realised that, before she said any of these things, she would need to do some serious listening. The girl needed to give expression to her fear and panic before she could take anything in. At least she had prepared the coffee and it did them both good. Clare sipped and forced her fury to subside whilst Harriet sobbed and hiccupped and searched her meagre vocabulary for ways to express her terror.

After some time the girl was ready to hear Clare's encouragements and to speak more than a couple of words without dissolving into tears again. Gary wasn't what Mummy called a nice boy, she volunteered, but he wasn't nasty either, at least Harriet didn't think so. No, she hadn't told him about the baby. He just might possibly want her to have it and then Mummy would have to know. It seemed that Mummy was the parent who must not be crossed or otherwise annoyed. The girl's father was obviously strict but to upset him was apparently not so unthinkable.

Clare looked at the thin, hunched shoulders and ravaged face and knew what the girl would look like when she was an old woman. It was easy to imagine the white-blonde hair as grey this morning as it fell, tousled and lank, round her shoulders. Clare spoke briskly. 'Let's see if we can establish a few facts. We need to see Dr Simpson, put him in the picture and ask his advice. We really ought to explain things to your parents too.'

The incipient hysteria threatened to return in full force. She hastily abandoned that line of reasoning, promising her own silence, at least for the time being, and stating her expectation that Dr Simpson too would keep her confidence if that was what Harriet really wanted.

As the Roman Candle sputtered yellow and white exclamation marks beside him, Detective Inspector Benedict Mitchell realised that he was completely happy. His stay in Wakefield was over for the moment, his digestive system had survived the shock of a meal cooked by Ginny after four days of excellent catering and Caitlin danced with excitement at his side.

Declan, conscious of his two and a half extra years, made 'grown-up conversation' with him. 'If you're a Roman Catholic, Grandma says, you don't burn Guy Fawkes. The Pope says you mustn't.'

Mitchell regarded him solemnly. 'But you're not a Catholic, and I'm not any more.'

Declan was in argumentative mood. 'Grandma says you still are at heart. That's why we've all got Irish names.'

Mitchell avoided the second question by reverting to the first. 'Call the guy John Smith then if you don't want to upset Gran.'

'He's a fine fellow, whatever he's called,' Virginia remarked. 'Who made him?' They all regarded the stuffed figure whose finery was not yet completely destroyed by the flames. He wore a huge tweed jacket and a long Dr Who scarf wound several times round his neck. The hat, with its pom-pom and stripes, Mitchell decided, was definitely more Smith than Fawkes. The face was a magnificent and luridly coloured mask.

A rocket shot up into the sky and distracted them, just a whoosh followed by a pathetic few stars but Declan and Caitlin were enchanted. The evening was cold and dry and smelt of many fires. Another rocket rose, flipped, shot out a trail of rather more impressive white stars and then subsided.

None of the bangs and fizzlings was sufficient to rouse the exhausted twins who now were snugly bundled into the sturdy buggy and sleeping, as far out of the smoke as possible, under Virginia's supervision.

DC Clement approached holding a fan of sparklers, which he offered to the children.

'Only one each. Don't be greedy,' Mitchell warned, and lit them. Caitlin, her mouth crammed with parkin, capered wildly. Declan wrote his name on the darkness with his sparkler, the vast final L threatening his sister's clothing. When the tips drooped to ash they duelled with the short wires that remained.

The fire suddenly gurgled and flamed and the guy slipped down into the heart of it. There were frantic cries of 'Stand back!' as those nearest removed themselves to safety. Clement was now nailing Catherine Wheels to a post on the edge of the open ground alongside the valley station, which was the site of the celebrations. Mounts Etna and Vesuvius twirled, sputtered and coughed, giving a poor imitation of their namesakes.

Another half-hour found Mitchell sternly reproving his first-born for the third time. Virginia touched his arm. 'Caitlin had a sleep late this afternoon but Declan's pride wouldn't let him. He's out on his feet. We'd better go.' Mitchell clamped Caitlin's hand to the handle of the buggy and swung his elder son up to ride on his shoulders. Virginia caught sight of Jennifer who was escorting her daughters towards the station car-park and dropped back to walk with her.

Mitchell strode ahead. 'We'll open up the car, shall we?'

Declan muttered sleepily in his ear. 'Daddy, what are tits?'

Mitchell grinned to himself. 'Who did you hear saying that?'

'A man on the phone. He said Mummy had lovely ones.'

Suddenly Mitchell was no longer amused. Tight-lipped, he helped his wife pack their offspring into the car and they drove home in silence. Sleeping children were placed in their beds and a tearful Declan patiently soothed.

The child recognised his father's rare anger – rare, at least, when directed towards his family. 'You're cross because I said that word, aren't you? I know what it means really. I won't say it again…'

Eventually Mitchell had a chance to demand an explanation from his wife. Disputes between them were always short and to the point. This one was cut even shorter by the shrill sound of the telephone.

Mitchell grabbed the receiver before Virginia could move towards it. When he

replaced it his fury was temporarily forgotten. 'That was the super. Who the hell
would have the nerve to dress a corpse up as
a guy and stick it on a police bonfire?

5

Apart from the humiliation of setting fire themselves to the evidence that was vital to their enquiry, Mitchell supposed that there were advantages in the murder scene being so close to headquarters. At least he had been able to park in his accustomed spot in the station yard and all the equipment had been at hand, so that, even before he arrived, screens had been set up round the pile of ashes and arc lights were dazzling the disgruntled officers gathered nearby.

Of course, it was unlikely that this stretch of waste ground was the actual scene of the victim's death. Mitchell indicated with a movement of his head that the officers, who were providing an audience for the search by the SOCO which was just beginning, should follow him into the station.

About to lead the first briefing of this new case, Mitchell was surprised at the diffidence he felt as he stood in front of his men. He tried to attribute it to anxiety about Virginia. He had proposed that he should ring her parents and ask them to take in their daughter and grandchildren until he should be free to look after the family himself. She had adamantly refused to disturb them at this hour of the night. Nor would she contemplate interrupting the stupor the children had fallen into after the excitement of the first part of the evening and the consequent trauma of knowing that their parents had been in serious dispute about a subject they did not understand. He could not even ask Clement to continue his voluntary surveillance. There was going to be more than enough to keep all his men busy here. He knew, though, that anxiety for his family was not the only reason for his present misgivings. He realised that, even after his promotion to sergeant, he had failed to co-operate with his superior officers and learn leadership. Rather, he had played power games with them, continuing to see how much insubordination he could get away with because he had a quick mind. He had depended on his promotion coming from his straight manner that had made witnesses talk to him and trust him. Now he needed the organisational skills he had failed to practise and had to deal with junior officers who might try the same tactics on him. He had earned respect in spite of himself because he had the qualities required in a good detective. Though he had been glad to move up in the force he had not sought advancement for its own sake. He preferred maximum freedom from bureaucracy to do a job as he thought it should be done rather than power over others. Did that mean, he wondered, that he was not happy with responsibility? He thought not. He certainly would not have changed places with any of the men and women in front of him, waiting for him to address them.

He was glad to see Jennifer amongst them. She, at least, had been glad about his promotion and was easy with it as she worked towards her own. He raised a hand, the chatter died away and, grinning, he began. 'Well, having all stood around for the last few hours, cheerfully watching all the evidence we need go up in smoke, we won't be surprised if our mugshots in the tabloids tomorrow are a bit eggy.' Mitchell remembered the precise moment he and his family had seen the upper body of the guy sink into the heart of the fire, sending out sparks and hot gusts that had driven all the spectators back. It had, after all, been not Guy Fawkes but John Smith. 'The up side is that the super can't blame the rest of us. He lit the fire himself before retiring to his office with friends' – and, Mitchell suspected, more of the whisky he had already imbibed. Later, Kleever had circulated, making sure he was seen socialising. He had stopped to admire the twins and tweak Declan's ear in a patronising way the child had resented. Caitlin had submitted placidly to having her

'Yes, I know. Sorry. Can you say when you left so I can pin down the times our customer might have visited?'

Clement looked embarrassed. 'It's funny you should ask that. I was there till after midnight. Then I got a call from HQ to go to a domestic at Heath Street. I said I was off duty but they said it sounded serious and they knew I was in uniform and handy in the car. No one else was near so I went, at about one o'clock.'

'So, what was funny?'

'Nothing was happening. All dark. All quiet. I went round the back of the house but there was still nothing. Then I tried the same number in Heath Avenue, Heath Lane, Heath Crescent and Heath Edge Road. Absolutely zilch so I went back to your place. I didn't look at the washing line and I never checked it out with HQ. I've been too busy with you being away and me trying to keep an eye on Ginny...' He flushed. 'I mean Mrs Mitchell. It's just that I've been talking to DS Taylor and, she being a friend, always calls her–'

'Yes, yes. If you manage to spy out whoever's hounding her you can call her what you like. You'd better get on with your house-to-house stint now. By the way, who suggested that you should put all this overtime in on our behalf?'

Clement flushed again. 'Well, the super

suggested it, but I'd already volunteered to Sergeant Taylor. I don't know if she mentioned it to him. It's just that ... well, I'm a free agent, no responsibilities off duty. You couldn't be there and, well, my kiddie would have been not a lot older than your twins, so, well...'

'I'm very grateful.'

'Like I said, it's a pleasure.' He departed, red-faced.

Mitchell decided it was time he made tactful enquiries of Superintendent Kleever about what he had or had not noticed as he applied his taper to the kindling at the base of the bonfire. Before he could leave, a tap at the door preceded the arrival of Caroline Webster waving a computer print-out. He grinned at the new DC, glad of the reprieve she offered him. 'Important enough to be consulted about the wallpaper now, am I?' He saw, as she handed over the roll, that it was a list of missing persons. 'This is the long version. Aren't we looking for someone local?'

Caroline shrugged. 'All I know is that the only Cloughton and district missing people are a four-year-old girl who was found safe and sound a few hours ago and an old woman from the geriatric hospital at Deepwell. Sergeant Taylor rang Dr Ledgard and he ruled both those out just from a preliminary glance at the remains so she asked me to get the whole list run off. When I gave it to her, she said you'd be interested to see it.'

Mitchell spread the roll out on his desk, swore as it escaped his fingers and curled itself up again, then ran his eye down the list, knowing Jennifer would have indicated where he should look. When he found the red-biroed asterisk he whistled. One person on the list, as from now, was missing no longer. He reached a hand towards the phone, meaning to ask for a line to the Millton station in Cumbria, then changed his mind. He ought to feel annoyed that the complications of his neighbour's private life were delaying his investigation but he had a personal reason to be glad of a pretext to interview Richard Lee Hillard.

DC Clement was not optimistic about what he would learn from his house-to-house enquiries. No street, not even an isolated dwelling, overlooked directly the patch of ground on which the bonfire party had been held. And his own allocated street was some considerable distance away from it. Last night the weather had been more reasonable after all the rain earlier in the week. It was still chill November though and the ground was wet. Households without children had either thankfully ignored the date or had watched their fireworks on television.

Clement considered that he himself would be better employed watching Virginia as the DI was out of the way. In fact, he decided he would visit the rest of the houses in his street but not report in when he had finished until he had driven past the Mitchells' house to have a look around.

Four more houses to go. At the first of them, he received no reply. He noted its number in his book. The second was opened by a fat-faced child who informed him that the family had held its own bonfire in the back garden.

'You didn't fancy the police one?'

The boy pointed to his face. 'Me an' Darren's got mumps. The other mothers won't let their kids play with us. Me dad said sod 'em, we'd 'ave us own fire.' Clement took a quick step backwards before sympathising. 'We seen all their rockets and stuff anyway,' the boy announced triumphantly.

At the third house, Clement was asked more questions than he managed to put. Seeing the police activity and being asked about the guy, the householder had formed the theory that it must have been stuffed with stolen property that someone had failed to remove in time. Clement sighed. 'Good story. Write it up and you'll get it on the telly.'

The man beamed. 'Hey, do you think I might?'

Half-way to the next house, Clement called over his shoulder, 'What have you got to lose?' He could never understand those officers who tried to avoid house-to-house duty because they found it boring. He knew most of his morning's efforts had been counter-productive but, as always, he had found the householders highly entertaining. He wondered what his last house would bring.

His rapping was answered by a ferocious barking and, when a man came to the door, Clement was glad to see he was restraining the large dog on a leash. However, the relative sizes of dog and man meant he still feared for his new chinos or even for his buttocks. He presented his warrant card and asked his first question, raising his voice over the continuous barking.

Immediately, the man nodded. 'That's where I walk Major every evening, about half six, soon as my shift finishes. Except that it's run rather than walk as far as he's concerned, and it's him that takes me.'

Clement could well believe it. Still shouting, he pointed out that conversation was rather difficult. The man apologised. 'The missus and I are used to it. We part hear and part lip read.' By now the man had backed and Clement had followed until they were up the hall and almost into the living-room. Through the open door Clement could see a gigantic television set, round which all the seating was arranged.

'How do you manage to follow a television programme?'

'He's in his kennel by the time we want to watch.'

'Could he go in now for a few minutes?'

The man considered this revolutionary idea. 'It's not his usual time, but he might do.' Obviously the dog ran the household. Nevertheless it proved unexpectedly obliging and lay down in the huge wooden structure that leaned against the side of the house. Back inside, Clement took Mr Foggin through his previous late afternoon's walk, first through the ginnel between the houses of two parallel streets and on to the waste ground. 'He usually runs free from there but I kept him on his lead till we were past the pile of stuff for the bonfire. I wouldn't have put it past him to run off with that dirty great half tree they had on it. Then I saw a man with a wheelbarrow coming out of the half dark and, as he got nearer, I could see that it was a great big guy he was bringing. The dog went at it, sniffing and nosing, so we spoke and I offered to help him lift it on. He refused at first and I thought it was because he was scared of Major. Anyway, he couldn't manage very well, so in the end I came back and gave a hand.'

'And the two of you managed?'

Mr Foggin grimaced. 'It weighed a ton. I said, "What's it stuffed with?" and he laughed and said, "Don't ask!"'

'Was it stiff or floppy?'

'What?' Clement waited, disdaining to repeat his question. Mr Foggin considered. 'I thought the top half might have come from one of those shop window models, the head and shoulders like. That part was solid but the legs as I had hold of felt floppy.'

'Anything else about it?'

The man shrugged and shook his head. 'It was getting dark.'

'OK, what did you notice about the man?'

Mr Foggin was becoming bored. 'That he were dressed for the weather, like me, so I didn't see much of him.'

'Bigger or smaller than you?' Clement considered this very tactful. The fellow whose description he needed could hardly have been smaller than the one who was supplying it and still capable of pushing the barrow.

'Good bit bigger but he still needed me to hold the legs. He warned me to be careful with the clothes, said he'd cobbled the guy together himself and stitched him up with a darning needle and twine. He didn't want the finery to come off till all the kids had seen him. By the light of the flames he must've meant. I thought he was a bit of a fool for a copper, pouring petrol all over the place, but I didn't want to argue with the law.'

'How did you know he was a policeman?'

'Asked him, didn't I?'

'Right, which way did he go when he was finished?'

Mr Foggin shrugged. 'Dunno. He's one o'yourn so why not find him an' ask him? Major was trying to get to the guy, jumping up on the branches and old furniture and so on, so I clipped his lead on and left yon chap faffing around arranging things...'

Clement left his questions there and arranged a time later in the day for Mr Foggin to come into the station and make a statement. As he scrambled into the car to make his check on the Mitchell household, he caught sight of Sergeant Taylor at the end of the street. She was probably looking for him. He drove off as unobtrusively as possible.

Mitchell, sitting in his office on Saturday afternoon, felt rather at a loss. He was not at home in it yet. He had no sooner settled in than the superintendent had shooed him off on this stupid course. Actually, some of it had proved to be more useful than it would be expedient to admit after all the fuss he had made. Fortunately, what with the bonfire and Virginia's problems, and now a burned-to-a-cinder corpse, no one had had the chance to ask questions about it and make a humiliating reply necessary.

Mitchell looked around him, liking the neat, functional little box that had been assigned to him. There was a place for everything he needed and no room for anything else, especially no room for that obnoxious ivy that spilled and trailed its leaves over useful shelf space and obscured the titles of his reference books. All his team members were busy. They would have the right, when they came to report, to complain as in the past he had done himself that a DI should teach by example. He was beginning to see, after just a month in that exalted position, that the best thing a DI could do was sit and wait, keeping a finger on the pulse of the case, knowing where each man was and what he'd discovered.

The realisation did not please him. What was best was not what he wanted. He wished he were out on the streets, asking questions of those who wanted to help and annoying and irritating those who did not until they lost their tempers and told him what he needed to know in spite of themselves. Resolutely he opened the file on his desk and read the few flimsy sheets that recorded his men's morning efforts. The telephone rang. The desk sergeant was in a panic. A missing person had been reported.

Apart from a civilian office girl, he and Mitchell were the only two officers presently in the little station. The desk couldn't be left. What should he do?

If the man were so easily flustered he would have to be dealt with. For now Mitchell soothed him. 'I suppose, in the circumstances, I'd better go myself.' He took down details. 'Can you let her know I'm on my way?'

In high glee, he grabbed his jacket and set off. Wasn't someone called Chase one of Jennifer's clients, in connection with her funny phone calls? Climbing into his car, Mitchell examined in retrospect his dealings with Sergeant Jerrold. He had had only a short time to estimate him but the first impression was not favourable. Should he have told him not to mention the charred corpse? It would have been insulting to an officer of twenty years' standing but perhaps it might have been advisable.

In ten minutes, the new DI was parking outside the Chases' house. He approved of its gleaming windows and sparkling paint-work. He approved too of the woman who opened the door to him. She looked well scrubbed and wholesome. No doubt the world in general considered her beautiful. She was blonde and blue-eyed with a good skin and a well-proportioned figure, though a bit on the solid side. She was not his type, though. Mitchell preferred women to be dark and vital like Ginny.

His second thought about Mrs Chase was that she could not have manhandled her husband's body on to a bonfire. However, the huge black man standing behind her could have done it easily. The word Nubian floated into Mitchell's mind. Wasn't that what those particularly tall broad Africans were called?

As he was driving, he had remembered more of the details Ginny had given him last night in their post-quarrel analysis of her situation. At least one of Jennifer's pregnant victims suspected this missing man of making their malicious calls and Ginny had a connection with him through writing the history of his company. Justin Chase linked the two cases and might, now he was missing, provide grounds for keeping Jennifer in his team until his own enquiry was completed.

To Clare Chase he revealed no prior knowledge of her husband's circumstances. He acknowledged her introduction of her husband's brother Warren and invited the two of them to explain the present situation. They looked at each other and each of them waited for the other to begin.

Mitchell prompted. 'How long has your husband been missing?'

Clare shrugged. 'I don't really know.'

Mitchell held his tongue, waited. 'I lost my temper with him yesterday morning. I went for a walk to calm down. When I was less angry, I remembered that Justin's hospital appointment was at eleven thirty but it was too late for me to take him. I knew he wouldn't miss it and I thought he'd have called a taxi, I knew he'd be even more furious with me for forgetting.'

'And when he didn't come back?'

'I assumed they'd admitted him.'

She glanced at her brother-in-law, who obligingly backed up the story. 'Justin thought he might be kept in after his next check-up. His doctor had promised to look into the possibility of trying a new drug he thought might help but Justin couldn't be given it at home.'

The two eyed each other again and, when the silence had lengthened unproductively, Mitchell asked, 'So, you discovered he wasn't there when you rang up to enquire for him?'

Clare sighed, got up and began to pace the room. 'I was still angry with him. I thought I'd teach him not to expect me to be there for him however badly he behaved. I expected a message from the hospital to take his things in. I was going to leave them at reception without going in to see him, to teach him a lesson. When no request came, I assumed he preferred using hospital things to asking me a favour. I decided to leave him without a visitor the first evening, to give him time to think things out.' She fell silent again but continued to walk up and down the same strip of carpet.

Mitchell turned to Warren Chase who took up the story. 'This morning, Clare rang me. I usually take Justin to the football match on Saturday afternoons and she told me not to come. I said I'd drop in anyway, give her a lift the hospital for the afternoon visiting. When we got there, they said Justin had broken his appointment and they hadn't seen him. Clare started to cry, the Sister made her some tea – well, told one of the nurses to do it – and I rang you people.'

Mitchell was amazed by the couple's obvious conviction that he would believe their unlikely story.

Returning to his office, Mitchell found the chair behind his desk occupied by a familiar figure, extremely tall, extremely thin and wearing a smug expression. The pathologist, he reflected, looked much the same as when, on his first murder enquiry, with only a few months' experience in CID, the great man had explained the basics of his science as the pair of them knelt beside the body. The aggressively red hair had faded a little but hardly showed grey. The face was deeply furrowed but, as far as Mitchell remembered, it had always been so.

The reason for the doctor's smugness lay on the desk between the two men, several neatly typed sheets which he had obligingly stayed to translate. Mitchell was both grateful and impressed. 'You've had your finger out. Thanks a lot.' He rang for coffee, then sat in his own visitors' chair and began to make notes in his personal shorthand as Dr Ledgard went through his report.

For the first time, his father-in-law not being in charge of the investigation, Mitchell could allow the pathologist free rein. DCI Browne had usually hushed him after only the necessary translation of technicalities, and just when the account was becoming interesting. He had then placed a copy of the report on file for the less squeamish members of the team to peruse for themselves. Mitchell had always done so, but in print the details lost some of their fascination for him.

Ledgard too was relishing his seldom-interrupted account. He settled further back in Mitchell's chair, took a sip of station coffee, hastily replaced his cup and continued. Mitchell, for whom the station coffee was an improvement on his wife's drank with relish and scribbled.

'…not fractured. It looks as though the liquid in the head turned to steam and burst the skull. The brain was exposed and

116

shrunken and burned on top. The skin on the face and ears was destroyed but the chest wall was relatively well preserved, protected by the thighs as the body leaned forward. The forearms and hands were completely destroyed. No chance of any kind of prints, just charred bone from each upper arm projecting as stumps.'

Absent-mindedly, Ledgard drank again, winced and continued. 'The legs below the knees were destroyed and the thighs deeply burnt.' The door had opened after a tap that Ledgard ignored. The face of the office girl appeared, convulsed and disappeared again without the purpose of her visit being explained.

'It all sounds a bit negative,' Mitchell remarked mildly. 'Was there anything useful?'

Ledgard nodded enthusiastically. 'Oh, yes. Bones, especially the pelvis, sacrum and femur, suggest a man. And, funnily enough, some scraps of clothing survived.'

Mitchell was not impressed. 'That won't help to ID him. I'd guess his own were removed and others substituted. Could give a lead on the culprit though. Are you saying you don't know whether the victim was dead when the fire was lit?'

The pathologist looked up in surprise. 'You think he was a masochist or something?'

'He could have been drugged or banged on the head.'

'I think he was dead.' Mitchell opened his mouth but Ledgard silenced him with a gesture. 'There was enough skull and skeleton left for us probably to have detected the work of a hammer or bullet but any indication of suffocation or strangling has gone. Have you powdered something from my lab to bulk out the instant coffee?'

'That's not instant. It takes Fiona half the morning to produce.'

'I can believe it. It's inimitable.'

Mitchell grinned. 'I'll buy you a beer when I knock off. Oh! Sorry, I can't.' Mitchell wondered how he could have forgotten the need to return home as soon as he could.

Ledgard was unperturbed. 'We looked for smoke particles in the relatively undamaged air passages. Nothing there.'

Mitchell nodded. 'What about–'

'Dental data's likely to be still usable.' Mitchell brightened. This was what he wanted to hear. 'From the teeth, I'd say the man was in his thirties, early rather than late. Some of the jaw was left and the size of it suggests large features. The teeth were well filled…'

Mitchell's pen continued to fly until Ledgard abruptly stopped speaking and stood up. Never one to socialise for long, his coffee undrinkable and his offer of beer withdrawn, he departed, passing Jennifer on the corridor on her way in.

Mitchell having hastily taken up his position behind the desk that Ledgard had usurped, Jennifer sank into the armchair in front of it, trying to remain impervious to its comfort as her new DI described his encounters with the Chase family and the pathologist. 'What did the Chases quarrel about?' she wanted to know.

Mitchell's gesture indicated ignorance. 'There's plenty of time to ask. It was interesting that she didn't say, didn't seem to regret it in the circumstances or wish she'd held her tongue.'

'Maybe she does but just didn't say so.'

'I got the impression that she's still just as angry with him, though she does seem genuinely worried about where he could be.'

'She thinks he might be my malicious caller. That would take a lot of forgiving. What impression did you get of the relationship between Clare and the brother?'

'Have you met him? Did you see anything to suggest–'

'No, I've just got a nasty suspicious mind.'

Mitchell considered the idea. 'I thought they might be in league for some reason but not that they were in love with each other. I didn't see any evidence of more fondness than you'd expect between relations by marriage. He certainly looked the right build to have done what was necessary if he had a motive. I waited till he was seeing me out before I asked about Justin's dentist. He was quick off the mark, wanting to know what we'd found. He said he wouldn't tell her I'd asked the question unless–'

'It's in all the papers.'

'She isn't reading the papers. She's trying to find out where her husband can be. We shall know before the end of the afternoon, one way or the other.'

'It's a ridiculously thin story.' Perversely, Mitchell now found himself wanting to defend it as Jennifer elaborated her remark. 'Clare begins every day by helping Justin downstairs and then supervises him until it's time to see him into bed. I don't think she'd be able to bring herself to leave him to his own devices for so long–'

'But she thought he was in good hands.'

'Only if he'd reached them under his own steam, which it seems he didn't.'

'Did you like her?' Mitchell trusted Jennifer's first judgement of a witness.

'I'm not sure. I admired her. I was sorry for her. I don't know.' Strangely ill at ease, Jennifer studied her fingernails before looking up to ask. 'Where's Clement been this afternoon? Where is he now, come to that?'

Mitchell gave her a brief summary of

Clement's report, telephoned from his car which was presently parked outside the Mitchell's house.

'I hope he stays awake longer than he did on Wednesday. If Ginny loses any more underwear he can keep her safe by running her in for indecent exposure.'

'He wasn't asleep!' Mitchell described the hoax call which had removed Clement from his watch. 'It looks as though Ginny's unwelcome friend is not only aware that he's being watched but he's also in a position to interfere with police communications.'

Jenny looked startled, but then shook her head. 'I doubt it. Anyone can make a bogus call and we have to act on them all. I'll check with the switchboard though.'

Mitchell re-read the scribbled notes he had made on Clement's call. 'If this Mr Foggin is to be believed, and I don't see why he shouldn't be, we're a bit nearer the time of death. Rigor in the trunk and shoulders but not in the legs means he met the man with the wheelbarrow about seven to ten hours after the "guy" met his death. Mr Foggin walked the dog in the dusk so it must have been about half-past six. That means it's likely that death took place during the later part of the morning.'

Jennifer nodded. 'And, if it's Justin Chase, that means he was killed as soon as his wife left him.'

'If she did.'

'You think she killed him?'

Mitchell shrugged. 'I've no idea. She could have, I suppose. Certainly her hulking brother-in-law could have.'

'Well, he'd have a motive.'

'So you think there's something going on between those two...'

Jennifer shook her head. 'I've no reason to, but I know Justin was to be left all the family money when the parents died, on the grounds that Warren could fend for himself.'

'What does he do?' Jennifer shook her head and Mitchell noted down yet another question to be asked. He saw Jennifer's surreptitious glance at her watch. 'Yes?'

'I've got to meet the girls from school and nursery. Jane's spending the day with a friend and won't be back till half-past five. I'll have to go but I'll be back for the debriefing.' She got up but lingered at the door. Mitchell raised an eyebrow, awaiting another comment or question. 'I'm not sure who's in charge of which case. Is the body yours or Kleever's? And where do I come in?'

'Good question. The super's main duties are at Cloughton headquarters, as everyone knows. This body belongs to Hubberton and I'm the senior detective, in fact the senior officer of any kind in this little station, so I'm nominally in charge.'

'Only nominally?' She came back into the room, wandering towards the window to check the weather, speaking to him over her shoulder.

Mitchell grinned. 'He's got it all worked out. If I think I'm not coping, he'll send a DCI. If he thinks I'm not coping, he'll do the same. Meanwhile, I get on with it. How long have I got you?'

'That's probably something else friend Kleever has worked out, but it looks to me as if my investigation and yours are about to come together, so with luck I'll be here for the duration. Did you say Mr Kleever was sending a DCI if you looked like making a pig's ear of things?' Mitchell looked up startled as Jen made for the door again. 'I'd say you were in deep trouble. He's just arrived himself.'

Jennifer sounded cheerful but left, more worried about Virginia now than when she had arrived and firmly believing that it was not Clare Chase who had told Mitchell the tallest story.

6

When the superintendent failed to make an immediate appearance, Mitchell decided to redeem the time by a further study of the PM report. He was exceedingly glad he had done so when Kleever eventually appeared with his own identical copy tucked under his arm. He settled in Mitchell's visitors' chair.

'You have the advantage over me. I haven't had time to open mine. Anything useful?'

Mitchell grinned. 'The sternal body is more than twice the length of the manubrium.'

Kleever's face remained deadpan. 'Well, we're grateful to Dr Ledgard for sharing that with us. What does it mean?'

'That the skeleton was whole enough for him to know the victim was male. The measurements here are all metric but I reckon he was about six feet two. There was a small scrap of scalp with hair. The texture was negroid but not necessarily pure blood. Because of technical things to do with the clavicle they've decided his age is over twenty-four and because something on his skull hasn't closed, he's probably under

124

forty. Dr Ledgard suggests early thirties and the jaw is whole enough to be useful with most of the teeth still intact.'

Kleever was smiling broadly by now. 'Forgive me for not being too impressed but I'm afraid your desk sergeant told me that the doctor made these helpful suggestions in person.'

Mitchell nodded complacently. 'Yes, but I've remembered it well, haven't I? There's a lot more. There were no soot particles in the lungs so he was dead before he was burned and there was no indication of the cause of death.'

'I suppose if he had MS it wouldn't have been too difficult to strangle or smother him. It's good about the teeth. We'll have to find the dentist to prove it, of course, but common sense says this is Justin Chase's body.'

Mitchell agreed. He offered his super-intendent a slip of paper. 'Dr Ledgard put a dental chart with notes in my copy – and Chase's brother gave Jennifer the dentist's name. I've sent someone who's seeing him right now. With luck we shall know for sure before the debriefing.'

The flow of conversation had not yet revealed what Mitchell wanted to know. He asked bluntly, 'Are you here because you think I'm messing up this investigation?'

Kleever looked surprised. 'No, you're

doing everything right. In fact, I think the team's working flat out as much to please you as to get a killer his just deserts. It's your home situation I wanted to discuss.'

Mitchell became wary. 'What about it?'

'Well, first I'm profoundly thankful that Virginia has told you herself about this chap. It was becoming damned embarrassing knowing about it when you didn't.' Mitchell gave a curt nod and the superintendent expanded. 'I'm coming round to agreeing with Sergeant Taylor that there might be a connection between the nasty calls to the pregnant woman and your murder, through the person of Justin Chase, but that your wife's harassment is of a different kind. Of course,' with the shark's smile that seemed to Mitchell to belong to all ranks above his own, 'that may be wishful thinking. If we had good reason to think that Virginia's problems are connected to your case, I'd have to take you off it.'

Suddenly Mitchell was prepared at least to pay lip service to his sergeant's and his superintendent's opinion. His attention snapped back to what Kleever was saying. '...and I'd like to know more about what we're up against. I had a word with the ACC in the hopes that he'd send us a couple of extra men. In vain, of course. He did make another offer, though. A friend of his, a clinical professor of psychiatry at "a well-established and respected US university"–'

'Are there any?'

'I think he said Harvard but I'll check if you really want to know.'

'Skip it. Go on.' It struck Mitchell that his manner was becoming less than respectful. He endeavoured to arrange his features into a more subservient expression.

'This chap's coming to lecture to the cadets at Wakefield. I was about to fish for an invitation when, knowing how busy we are, the ACC promised to arrange for the chap to come to Cloughton, talk to us and have a look at what we've got. He's a top world authority on stalkers and a consultant to a lot of big US companies, helping them ID potentially dangerous employees. The US press call him the FBI's premier shrink. I've gathered already that you incline to scoff at theorists.'

Mitchell held up a hand to indicate the withdrawal of his prejudice. 'I'll try anything that might lead us to this bloke.'

'Right, I'll let you know the arrangements. What do you think about bringing your wife in on this?'

Mitchell nodded. 'Good idea – and as many of the team as can be spared.'

'Depends on how many of them you're prepared to cover for.' Mitchell looked thunderstruck. 'Think about it, man!' Now Kleever was looking less than friendly. 'You shouldn't need me to tell you, you can't be in on any of this. Think yourself lucky you're at least being told what's going on,' He cut short Mitchell's vigorously expressed objections by walking to the door.

Before he disappeared, Mitchell stopped him. 'I shall only ask Ginny when she gets home.'

'Of course you will.' The superintendent grinned. 'There's nothing in the rule book to stop you behaving like a husband.'

'And, by the way, you're a witness in my case and none of the rest of my shift has the balls to ask you. Why the hell didn't you report the smell of the petrol that Mr Foggin saw our bloke pouring over the guy?'

Kleever shrugged. 'I'll give you a straight answer to a straight question. I was off duty. The bonfire was a social occasion and I was holding a small party in my office. I freely admit that all I could smell on that occasion were whisky fumes.' He smiled sweetly at Mitchell before closing the door quietly behind him.

Clement had further ingratiated himself with the new DI by volunteering to speak to Lee Hillard. Until the offer was made, Mitchell had been too busy to reflect that taking his neighbour to task might make his wife feel awkward in her future meetings with him. Clement arrived back in Fulton

Road some minutes before five.

The morning had been sharp but the afternoon had turned mild with some sunshine. There was no sign, however, that the Mitchell children had used the garden. No pram, toy or carelessly discarded garment marred the regimented neatness of the lawn. Maybe Virginia had cleared them all away, but Clement feared that the children, barred into the house, were suffering just as much as their parents.

Turning his back on the Mitchell house he knocked on the door in front of him. It was opened by a man in his thirties and the pair scrutinised one another before he greeted Clement with a resentful 'Yes?'

'Sorry to disturb you,' Clement announced, insincerely. 'Are you Richard Lee Hillard?'

'Who wants to know?'

Silently Clement displayed his warrant card and Hillard stepped back grudgingly. 'You'd better come in.'

This seemed to mean only as far as the narrow entrance hall where the pair continued to take the measure of each other. When Clement repeated his question, Hillard nodded.

'Formerly of 26, Lakeland Gardens, Millton, Cumbria?'

The man scowled. 'What is this?' Patiently Clement repeated his second question, eliciting a reluctant 'Yes.'

'Your parents are looking for you.'

Hillard dropped into the only seat, alongside the telephone, leaving Clement standing. 'Surprise, surprise!'

'Aren't you at all concerned for them?'

'No.' As if his reply, unqualified and uncompromising, marked the end of the interview, he got up again and wandered off to a room at the end of the hall.

Doggedly, Clement followed and spoke to the man's back, which was silhouetted against the french window and a rapidly dimming view of his garden. 'Your family will be informed that you are alive and well.' Clement saw the man's shoulders slacken and relax.

Hillard turned round. 'Is that all?'

'It's all I was sent to say.'

'I mean is that all that the old dears will be told? Not that I'm here, living in sin?'

'No, just the two facts that I mentioned.'

Hillard became comparatively hearty. 'Look, sit down. Have a coffee – if I can find the things with Gill at work. I didn't mean to be rude but, when I'd just managed to get a life back for myself, I thought you were going to hand it back on a plate to my mother again.'

Clement grinned. 'A bit possessive, is she?'

'You don't know the half of it.' Clement

saw he had unleashed a whole multitude of grievances. 'She took me shopping on a walking rein till I was past the age to start school. When I did go, she got Dad to take me and collect me in the car till I got to the sixth form. It was only after World War 3 that she didn't go to Manchester with me for my university interview. She invented a heart condition for my father to bring me home again after my degree and, under the maternal roof again, she just literally followed me around.' The complaint seemed to have been many times rehearsed.

Hillard plugged in the filled kettle and searched cupboards until he had produced a cafetière and mugs. Then he turned to Clement, casting his eyes to the ceiling. 'If I went to the sodding lavatory she stood at the bottom of the stairs shouting, "What are you doing up there? Will you be long?" She wouldn't allow any middle way so I just suddenly upped and left. I pretended to be away studying to give myself time to get settled. Now, presumably, she's discovered I'm not at the cottage.'

'Couldn't you have left a letter or telephoned to say you were all right?'

Hillard's laugh was unpleasant. 'That wouldn't be what she wanted to hear. The message she wants is that I'm not all right, that I can't manage without her so I'm coming home again.'

Though he could feel some sympathy for him, Clement found himself unable to like the man. 'I take it,' he remarked, 'that you are an only child.'

'No, I've a brother four years younger but you can't dominate two children. While you're busy domineering over one the other has time to escape, so whilst she concentrated on me, Nathan grew up with more freedom than a lot of other boys. He could never understand why I was so angry, why I resented her so much. There was hardly anything she stopped him doing and he wouldn't believe what a hold she had over me.'

'Maybe he will now that you've gone and there's only him.'

Hillard shook his head. 'No, he won't. He got married at twenty with their blessing, but maybe they'll believe me when she picks on one of the grandchildren and starts her tricks again.'

Clement drained his cup. 'Well, we shall do our little bit as I've explained. No mention of your girlfriend or your address.'

The man shrugged ungraciously. 'It wouldn't matter too much, I suppose, if she did find me now. My job with Cantrells isn't to be in Cloughton. When the three-month induction course is over in three or four weeks I'll be sent to their subsidiary company in Hamburg. She won't follow me there. She doesn't hold with abroad, can't rule the roost there. When I leave England I'll be safe.' His tone suggested that his escape would be from a lethal danger.

Clement shook his head. 'In that case, why not see her again, part on good terms...?'

Hillard's expression became thunderous. 'Why not piss off and stop poking your nose into what isn't your business?'

Clement was startled. Had there been some kind of abuse that Hillard was not prepared to admit to? He beat a hasty retreat, noticing as he unlocked his car that the Mitchell household was hidden away behind closed doors and drawn blinds.

By eight o'clock Virginia had tucked the last child into bed. Declan's behaviour today had been exemplary. He had been rewarded not only with half an hour of his mother's undivided attention after Caitlin had fallen asleep but with a lesson from her in two forms of patience. He was not fooled by her apparent enthusiasm. 'Do you have to play patience all by yourself? Well, I think it's more fun to play rummy or pairs with another person, like a mummy for example.'

Soon, he too was in bed and asleep. Benny was busy at his desk at the station, collating reports. Clement's car had driven away twenty minutes earlier.

Virginia began typing up a history of James Cantrell & Company Ltd. And wondering to whom her proof should be submitted for approval now that Justin Chase was no longer her contact.

Outside and thirty yards short of the Mitchells' house a large car drew up opposite the ginnel that separated numbers thirteen and fifteen Fulton Road. A man climbed out and used the ginnel to reach the narrow lane that bounded the back gardens of the odd-numbered houses. Gaining the Mitchells' plot from there the man silently looked about him. The doors were shut, the blinds down, the line empty.

The man was growing annoyed. Virginia was keeping him waiting too long. She needed a sharp reminder. It was time he had a satisfactory reaction. He eased his dark woollen hat further over his face and pulled on a pair of old black leather gloves. Then he delved into the compost heap with his hands, hurling chunks of rotten vegetation and kitchen scraps across neatly shorn grass and weedless borders.

Harriet Bradley's parents were both out. One was helping with an unofficial, hopefully unobtrusive supervision of a student disco. The other had disappeared much earlier to play golf with a potential client and was not expected back by either his daughter or his wife until the clubhouse bar closed down.

Harriet always did her homework on a Saturday evening. It helped to close her mind to her lack of invitations to join in the activities that kept her fellow fourth-formers occupied at that time of the week. She had read quickly through the relevant chapter in her history textbook. The causes of the Hundred Years' War were not at all apparent to her but the test scheduled for the following Monday held no fears for her. In the last few weeks she had taken on a totally new scale of values in which the passing or failing of a history test figured hardly at all.

She had left her English assignment till last. She enjoyed Shakespeare and was interested in Lady Macbeth, whose character was the subject of her essay. She knew that the rest of the class was going to paint a very black picture of a wicked woman driving her virtuous husband to a life of crime. Harriet saw the situation differently. She could not see much good in Macbeth at all. He was a weak-willed man getting cheap popularity because he had not sufficient intelligence to see danger in battle. Harriet had no patience with people who let other people make up their minds for them. She knew she was one of them herself and she despised herself most of all. Macbeth didn't have the courage of his convictions. He wanted all that was best for himself and hesitated to take it not because he was virtuous but because he was...? She sought the word she needed and her mind came up with it. Feckless!

That was what her mother called her father on weeks when he failed to earn the commission she expected. Macbeth knew that to obtain what he wanted, he needed a woman like his wife behind him to keep him up to the mark. She began to write and discovered that, for the first time for at least a month, she was enjoying herself. Her handwriting became a scrawl as it always did when she became lost in her subject. She scribbled fast and for a while she felt almost like the old Harriet. Then the telephone rang.

She wanted to ignore it. She turned back to her essay and finished her sentence but the ringing went on. Harriet knew she would have to answer. It was probably a friend of one of her parents and she would have no excuse for failing to take a message. She reached out and picked up the receiver. She knew at once it was her tormentor as he maintained a nicely judged silence, breaking it as she was about to hang up. 'Just to remind you, Harriet,' the voice whispered. 'You won't know whether lover-boy shared his fate with you until Christmas. It takes a few months, you know, before the virus can be detected. It won't be much of a Christmas present, will it?' After a couple more seconds of silence her caller hung up and, like an automaton she did the same.

Crazy thoughts chased each other round her mind. Maybe Macbeth had made his wife pregnant and she hadn't dared tell anyone. That might have been why she'd given suck and then dashed her baby's brains out against a rock. No, wait a minute, she didn't do that. She only said she'd rather do it than be such a coward as Macbeth was. The idea was in her mind, though. It wasn't in Harriet's. She could never hurt a baby. The only person Harriet ever hurt was herself. It was all she could do and why not do it now? Her mother had collected a new prescription for her sleeping pills only a few days ago. The bottle in the bathroom cabinet was nearly full. She could take her time. Neither of her parents would be back until late, certainly not her mother. And if Daddy arrived before he was expected he wouldn't dream of coming into her room and risk finding her less than respectably covered.

Her hands were shaking. She'd do what Daddy did to steel himself for an ordeal. He thought that neither of his womenfolk knew but Harriet had seen the bottle and glass behind the two-volume encyclopaedia when she'd taken it out once to check some homework. The glass was a large tumbler. Harriet filled it, wondering if her father did the same. She spilled some whisky on her white jumper and she made a plan to change before she took the pills. Mummy would be mortified if she were found in a dirty jumper.

Harriet had intended to drink the whisky in several large gulps but the first one took her breath away so that she lowered herself on to Daddy's chair, gasping. She finished the rest more circumspectly, but then, to prove something to herself that she couldn't quite remember, she half filled the tumbler again. When she had consumed the second draught, Harriet knew she was incapable of replacing the bottle and glass without breaking them. She giggled to herself. It was hardly going to matter if Daddy found her out. The giggle took control, shaking her body with laughter. Pushing herself upright by her arms, she found she could not stand. Continuing to laugh she crawled across the study, through the hall and slowly upstairs. At the top, she realised that, with the study as it was, it was Daddy who was going to be found out. Half-heartedly she thought about going down again but the abyss of the stairwell whirled and swam in front of her and she gave up her rescue attempt. She knew she had to go into the bathroom but she was finding it difficult to remember why. It came to her after a while. She needed to take Mummy's pills. Maybe that was to stop the room whirling round her.

She used the towel rail to steady herself as she jerked open the wall cabinet and grabbed the small bottle, knocking several others to the floor in the process. One thought she kept a firm grasp of. She must get to her own room because Daddy wouldn't come in there.

Still grinning, though she had long since forgotten the joke, she crammed the pills into her mouth before beginning the crawl to the bedroom next door. By the time she reached it the sweet taste of the pills' sugar coating had been replaced by an offensive bitter burning in her throat and on her tongue that made her heave. Instinctively she grabbed for the jug of water that stood by the bed. The glass rolled under the bed but Harriet managed to drink from the jug, pulling it towards her and letting the water spill into her mouth. She swallowed thankfully before falling across the sheepskin bedside rug, her head propped up against the side of the bed. She had forgotten to change her jumper but at least the remainder of the spilt water dripping over the edge of the bedside table on to her shoulder diluted the whisky stain.

Sidney Hillard's blue-tinged lips quivered as he faced his younger son. 'After all we've done for him, I can't believe he'd do this to us.'

Nathan Hillard paced his parents' living-room, equally unable to credit what he was being told, whilst his mother sobbed convulsively, her vast girth filling the settee.

'Look, Dad, start at the beginning. I didn't even know he wasn't at the cottage.'

'Neither did we till a couple of weeks ago.'

'So, why didn't you tell me than?'

Mrs Hillard removed the handkerchief from her mouth. '…More people you tell … more gossip … people talking … undutiful children … never like to worry you … either of you … that's why we never wrote to tell him about Charlie … poor boy … didn't like him … never deserved that … completely disappeared … thought he was killed too … then a message like that…'

He husband, lost in his own hurt and bewilderment, seemed unable to stem the flow. Nathan turned his back on his mother after handing her the cup of tea he had poured for her.

'Dad, sit down and let me ask some questions.' His father sat down obediently, his breathing alarmingly wheezy. 'How did you find out Lee wasn't in Grasmere?'

His mother drew a deep breath but a glare from each of her menfolk kept her silent.

'We'd sent three letters. He hadn't answered any of them. Your mother wanted to go when he didn't reply to the first one.' Nathan could imagine. 'I persuaded her to

140

let him be but now it turns out she was right. Anyway, it wasn't like him so we went to the cottage.'

'And?'

'No one had seen him. He hadn't bought anything at the village shops. The cottage was locked and there were no books or work papers there. The bed wasn't made up.'

Nathan nodded. 'It must have been a sudden decision on Lee's part to go. He was with us the weekend before and he didn't say anything. He's always got on all right working in his room or in the library, hasn't he?'

Mr Hillard shrugged. 'He didn't discuss it with us. We'd been having a day's shopping in Lancaster. When we came back, he said he was finding it distracting trying to work here. He said he'd got behind with his thesis and he was going to try a change of scenery until it was finished. It was a bit sudden but it sounded reasonable enough.'

'...Funny ideas ever since he went to that college ... met that Charlie ... didn't wish him dead, of course ... now Lee's got no manners either ... glad he's gone...'

The men talked over the mutter. 'She means Charlie. She doesn't mean it. She got a bit jealous if he spent a lot of time with his friends.'

'You're going to have to tell me about Charlie.'

141

His father shrugged. 'Not much to tell really. Lee had two friends he spent a lot of time with at university. One was a nice chap but he got married and Lee lost touch. Neither of us was keen on the other but we didn't wish him any harm. He only lived in Barrow so Lee saw him occasionally but they weren't as close as before.'

'So, what happened to him?'

'He was killed in an accident just after Lee went away. He was already worried about his work so we thought it would upset him even more if we told him about it so we didn't mention it in our letters.'

'As he never got them it's academic.'

His father stared at him, puzzled. 'Charlie wasn't academic. He got into trouble for not going to his lectures and not finishing his projects. Had to leave college in the end.'

Nathan sighed and refilled their cups before asking, 'So what now?' Both parents looked enquiring. He tried to hang on to his patience. 'Well, are you wanting me to look for him, or what?'

Both parents spoke at once. 'There's not much point if he doesn't want to be found.' 'Of course we want you to … naughty boy … should be back here…'

Nathan sighed. 'Look, you two need to talk to each other.' Suddenly he felt pity for his mother. 'I've got a couple of ideas, things I could try. I'll see what I can do.'

142

'What are they?'

'Let's see if they work, Mother, before you start building up your hopes.'

The tears began again. '...Now both my boys are keeping secrets from me ... we've got a right ... not fair to keep us in the dark...'

Nathan retired to the bathroom, less from need than from a desire to take a few breaths of less emotion-laden air. As he left the room his mother's voice followed him. Was he leaving them as well? Where was he going? For the first time, Nathan began to have some sympathy with the action his brother had taken.

7

Jennifer was the first to appear at Mitchell's six-thirty debriefing. She perched on the corner of Mitchell's desk to ask, 'How did you get on with friend Lee?'

'Hillard? Clement volunteered for the job so I was glad to let him do it.'

'Benny!'

'Well, Hillard lives across the road from us. As he pointed out, it could have ruined our reputation as neighbours if I'd seen him.'

'Since when has that bothered you?'

'Oh, let the lad feel he's done us a favour.'

'He seems to be doing rather a lot of them. Do you trust him to pick up pointers to Hillard possibly being Ginny's stalker?'

Mitchell thought about it. 'He's a bright lad. Anyway, I can keep a better eye on Hillard by meeting him socially when he's less on his guard. I don't think he's a serious contender actually, having seen them together now and then.'

'He's hardly likely to choose moments when you were around to look at her lecherously.'

The arrival of most of the rest of the shift

in a bunch put a temporary end to Jennifer's objections. Mitchell rose to address them. One of the more timorous DCs was left in the silence that fell remarking, 'I saw the super a minute ago. That's all we...' He caught his DI's eye.

Mitchell answered the unspoken question by shaking his head. 'Having admitted his nose and taste buds were too occupied with whisky fumes to be aware of any rival ones from petrol when he ceremoniously lit the fire, he's keeping a low profile. You must have seen him retreating in shame to head-quarters.' A gasp went round the room as he hurriedly continued, 'The dentist on Royd Road has identified the records we sent him as being those of Justin Chase. Taking that together with other evidence from Dr Legard, we're happy – perhaps it would be better to say fairly sure – that he's our victim. Sergeant Taylor has been to see his wife and has one or two points to make.'

Jennifer ignored his offer to give place to her and spoke from the centre of the group. 'Mrs Chase was very distressed, of course, but not shocked. She'd been expecting the news.'

'Does she realise you'll still have to continue your enquiry into the malicious calls?'

Jennifer turned to answer Clement's question. 'She's anxious that we should. His death seems to have turned her round, made her unable to accept that he's responsible, and she's hoping we'll clear his name.'

'Where are we on the malicious calls exactly?'

Jennifer turned back to Mitchell. 'I've discovered another victim.' She passed on, briefly, the information Clare Chase had given her about Harriet Bradley's ordeal. 'I'll see the girl tonight if I can.'

'Right, what else is there?'

'We haven't,' Clement suggested, 'given any thought to Faye Weston's brother. He's a man involved…'

Mitchell was pleased. 'Good thinking, Clement. You've got yourself a job, but work through your action sheet first.' He let his shift question one another and discuss the answers until their suggestions became ludicrous and unlikely to throw up any more useful ideas. Then he drew the meeting to a close. 'Jennifer, you're scheduled to see Clare Chase again. See what you can find out about Warren Chase's job and financial position. And watch out for any clues to their relationship being more than sister and brother-in-law.' Seeing her face, he added, 'Tactfully, of course,' then saw that he had not improved the moment. 'Most of the rest of you will carry on with the house-to-house. In particular try to find anyone who saw Clare leaving, returning, walking about at the times she claims she did. We need to see this Mr Foggin again and ask him if the person with the guy and the barrow could possibly have been a woman.'

Clement raised a hand. 'He's here now, making his statement. I spoke to him as we came in.'

'Right, get down there and ask now then, if he hasn't left.'

Clement disappeared at the double, taking his action sheet with him. Mitchell distributed the rest of the pile. The shift glanced at them with varying degrees of enthusiasm. 'Whilst you're all enjoying yourselves,' Mitchell added, 'I shall be seeing the Chases' GP to get some social and medical background. I hope he's not one of those pompous ones in league with Hippocrates. Caroline, I've sent you to Cantrells. Can you ask some general questions about Chase's work? You might see what they have to say about Lee Hillard as well.' He raised his eyebrows as Clement came back into the room. 'Well?'

Clement adopted a not very successful attempt at the local accent.' ""'Course it weren't a woman. It weren't a bloody darkie neether."'

When Mitchell dismissed them he gestured to Jennifer to stay behind. 'It was good of you to break the news to Mrs Chase…'

She smiled. 'I'm glad you didn't think I was treading on your toes. It was better coming from the one of us she'd met before. If that's all, I'll get off to see the Bradley girl.'

Mitchell knew that Jennifer's daughters were spending a couple of days with her parents. She was probably anxious to put in as much of the intervening time as possible on the job to make up for the times, rare enough, when her duty to them overrode her paid duties to the force. 'Jen, you don't have to put in twenty-four hours a day just because–'

She grinned at him. 'Yes I do, but it's more for my sake than yours.'

Mitchell scribbled in his notebook before asking, 'Did you pick up anything on Warren Chase, or about Justin's work?'

She shook her head. 'It was just a call to break the news and pick up the pieces. I'll go again soon. By the way, Faye Weston and Megan Scott have had no more calls since they made it widely known that there's a trace on their line. Gemma's seem to have stopped too. And I consulted the computer about her boyfriend.' She glanced at Mitchell, hoping he would not be offended by the implied criticism. 'Did you realise you'd already come up against him twice? Drugs offences. The second time, he was sent down.'

Mitchell blinked. 'Steve Thacker? I hadn't thought. Steve's a common enough name. Anyway, that wouldn't make...' Jennifer watched the implications of what she had said dawn on her DI. 'Are you suggesting that he's hassling Ginny to get back at me and all the other calls are just a blind?'

'Gemma could have given him all the information he needed about the other girls, probably quite unwittingly.'

'I'm saying it wants looking at.'

Jennifer's red Fiesta had a chip of paint missing from the bonnet. She had been meaning to deal with it for the last nine or ten months and the spreading area of rust annoyed her afresh as she made her way up the curving drive and parked in the lee of a white Mercedes. For a moment or two she contemplated the large and gracious house on her right and the large and well-laid-out garden all around. She pitied the youngster whose home it was and whose plight she would endeavour not to reveal. She was glad now that she had not rung to announce her visit. She wondered to which parent the white monster belonged. Clare Chase had thought the father would be marginally the more sympathetic. What Jennifer would really have liked would be to find the girl in alone but she might have to wait for ever for that. If only Harriet were a couple of years older so that she could be taken off to the station. She sighed and made to get out of her car to knock on the door.

She had been seen, however, from a large bay window, so that the door opened without a knock. The man who approached was immaculately dressed and punctiliously polite. She assured him that he could indeed help her by allowing her to speak to his daughter. She smiled at him ingratiatingly. 'I realise she's only fifteen years old and I have no right to insist, but I would very much appreciate speaking to her alone.'

The sight of a warrant card brought about a slight change in the man's manner. It was no less courteous but more formal. 'I would need to know what the interview was about.'

'It's a matter of incriminating some people she knows. I really do only want her to help with our enquiries quite literally. Harriet has done nothing to bring herself to our notice except as a witness. She might just be more willing to tell what she knows if–'

'Yes, yes, I take your point. Give me a moment to think about it.' He led the way into the house and climbed half of the grand staircase leading up from the spacious hall before calling his daughter's name in a measured tone. Turning back to Jennifer, he explained, 'She'd returned to her room before I came in. I thought she was doing homework but she may have

150

gone to bed. Is it urgent?'

'I really would like to speak to her. Are you sure she hasn't gone out?'

He looked affronted. 'I'm sure she wouldn't have without asking permission.'

Jennifer blinked. The man stood, irresolute, on the top stair. 'Could you just check the room?' she prompted. She was beginning to be alarmed.

He shook his head. 'I never go in, not now she's so big...'

'Then perhaps you wouldn't mind if I...' She came quickly up the stairs and pushed past him as he continued to stammer. Rapping hard on the door he indicated and getting no reply, she pushed it open and looked in. She was across the room in two strides and by the time the girl's father appeared in the doorway she had checked the almost non-existent pulse. 'Ring for an ambulance quickly.' She spoke calmly and quietly and prayed that he was not too shocked to respond. She reached to pull the girl's padded quilt down from the bed to cover her and heard Mr Bradley's voice carrying out her order.

The girl was still breathing though shallowly. The straight blonde hair fell across half her face and lay in swathes on the rug. Jennifer gathered the two or three pills that lay on the floor beside her and put them in a plastic bag from her pocket. She

151

handed it over as Mr Bradley reappeared. 'Give those to the ambulanceman. What are they?'

'They look like my wife's sleeping pills from the bathroom cabinet.'

'See if you can find the bottle whilst I carry her to the door to save time.'

He shook his head and tenderly gathered the girl's slight form, his scruples about her developing body forgotten. 'I'll do that. Bathroom's next door.'

Jennifer nodded. 'Tell them,' she added over her shoulder, 'she's had whisky too. Where's her mother? When you've gone I'll fetch her and bring her to you at the hospital.' She lowered her voice as she emerged from the bathroom, the bottle in her hand.

He was breathless from descending the stairs with his daughter's dead weight. They reached the hall and stood together with the door open ready. 'Why did she…' he began, after a minute. 'Was it to do with what you…?'

'Lay her on the floor now. She's too heavy.'

Tears rolling down his cheeks, Mr Bradley shook off Jennifer's hand. 'No, I'll hold her. I can't imagine… Can you tell me…?'

Jennifer told him enough for the present. 'I think she did it because she's pregnant.'

He was silent for some seconds and when he spoke his voice was hardly audible. 'And she couldn't tell me?' He turned eagerly as he heard the siren of the ambulance.

As Jennifer drove off to keep her promise to collect the mother and deliver her to her family, she noted that Mr Bradley had not said 'couldn't tell us.'

Virginia knew that Benny would come home for half an hour at teatime if he possibly could, so that the twins would remember that they had a father. Tonight, as they flung themselves on him and he swung them in turn over his head and set them down again, she was reluctant to spoil the moment for him. She had promised, however, to keep nothing else concerning her harassment from him. When Sinead and Michael had been bathed, dressed in pyjamas and put in the playpen to drink their milk she led her husband out to view the back garden.

He regarded it stonily for a moment before asking, 'Why didn't you tell me this morning?'

'I didn't draw the curtains back till after you'd left.'

He nodded, then blinked at her as he demanded, 'Why are you carrying your handbag about?'

Even more reluctantly she opened it, drew out an envelope and handed it to him by its corners. 'There's this too.'

Wordlessly, he slipped it into a plastic bag before folding it into his wallet. He wandered out into the garden and Virginia left him to himself for a moment, returning to the living-room to check on the twins. She was on her way upstairs, a child on each hip, when he returned.

'I had arranged to see Jennifer in fifteen minutes. I'm late already. I'll read this later. What does it say?" Having followed her he took Michael from her and plopped him into his cot. Virginia's voice came, muffled, from the depths of Sinead's.

'It'll keep. There are six pages of it. It keeps referring to next time he sees me, begging me to arrange to meet him face to face.'

'What!'

Virginia shrugged. 'You'd better not follow it up. You could mess up your whole career if you don't obey the rules and keep out of this. Maybe I should have handed it straight over to the super. It'd better not be you who delivers it to him.'

'You don't think I'm not going to read it?'

She smiled wryly. 'No, that isn't what I think. I wonder...'

'Yes?'

'Leave it. It's not your investigation.'

'Ginny!'

'All right. I wonder, since he seems to know so much about me, whether he knows

154

about police protocol too and whether part of his enjoyment is this dilemma.'

'You mean he's getting an extra kick out of putting you in a position where, whatever you do, you're going to be in schmuck with either me or Kleever? Because you're supposed to keep me out of it and–'

'You've got the idea. I don't mind you putting it into words but you don't have to bloody spell them for me!'

He could not remember ever having heard her swear before. It was not through virtue or good manners so much as her view that an English graduate ought to be able to express every possible shade of meaning from the resources of that language. She recovered herself quickly. 'Look, it's romantic drivel, cleaner than the phone messages but it's more aggressive and frustrated in tone.'

Part of Mitchell's mind was amused by her objective description. This professor the super was going to introduce her to would be meeting his match.

'He says he's bought a video camera with a powerful lens. He says I belong to him and when will I admit it and that his patience is running out...'

With the letter safely in his pocket, Mitchell stopped listening to his wife's actual words. Instead he heard the desperation of their tone. It occurred to him

155

that she must have read the six pages many times to give him this neatly tabulated list of their contents. He made a decision. 'That's enough, Ginny. I'm not going out.'

He waited for objections but she seemed pleased. 'Well, if it was just Jen you were meeting and the girls are away, she may as well come here.'

Jennifer, when summoned, hesitated only to ascertain that Mitchell would be making the coffee. When she had viewed the vandalised garden she apologised for her levity then she was silent for some moments before announcing, 'You need cameras.'

Virginia looked puzzled. 'Surely he did it in the middle of the night.'

Jennifer threw her hands in the air in mock horror. 'These arts people! Even in the sixth form, if you're doing three sciences they think you need a dollop of culture and you get it under various high-sounding titles. There's no science for the English/History/French lot though. They think they know it all.' She appealed to Mitchell. 'Are you going to explain infrared rays to her or shall I?'

Virginia regarded her calmly. 'The arts are a patchwork quilt. You can have a few patches sewn together to make something small and useful. Science is all built on what went before. If you cut a patch out it unravels and is useless.'

'Did you have to start her off? Give her

some coffee quickly to shut her up.'

'To get back to the point,' Jennifer observed, passing the cup Mitchell had just filled, 'I can't think why you didn't suggest it.'

'Because,' Mitchell retorted, 'I'm apparently not allowed to suggest.'

Virginia grinned. 'Now you've started him as well.' After a struggle with herself, she added in a casual tone that fooled neither of her companions, 'He gave a number I could ring to arrange to meet him.'

Mitchell whistled. Jennifer said, 'What was it?'

'I've rung it.' Virginia listened to the eloquent silence that fell.

Her husband broke it with one word. 'And?'

'It's a mobile number and the mobile was switched off. You'll find the number in the letter.'

Arriving at the medical centre the next morning, Mitchell found all the patients sitting tidily on rows of chairs. He found out why when he joined the queue at the reception desk. Debbie Johnson informed each patient who accosted her which doctor he could see and when and indicated where he should sit. A table covered in magazines was pointed out and each patient obediently selected one and at least made a pretence of reading it. The reading matter provided offered a wide selection. Mitchell could see the *Financial Times*, for that day judging by the headline, nestling against *People's Friend* and half covered by that week's *Cloughton Clarion*.

Being seven minutes early for his appointment with Dr Simpson, Mitchell too was allotted a chair but, perversely, he chose his own. His neighbour, anxious and heavily pregnant, spoke in hushed tones to the small child on the other side of her. The little girl was amused by her mother's game and replied in a penetrating stage whisper.

Mitchell grinned at the mother and nodded towards Debbie. 'I bet her kids are the best behaved in West Yorkshire.'

The woman sniffed. 'Would be if she had any. Too inconvenient for Debbie, having kids is.'

Mitchell was amused to see that the buzzer and light flashing beside each doctor's name were not synchronised. By the time the sound had alerted the waiting patients to look at the list of names over the door the light beside the relevant name had stopped winking and no one dared rise and go towards the consulting room till given permission by Debbie's sharp, 'Doctor hasn't got all day, Mrs Jones!' Flushed with guilt the string of Mrs Joneses thankfully scurried away.

Mitchell was quite pleased when the receptionist came over to say Dr Simpson was running behind with his appointments and that his wait was likely to be extended. 'You're keeping me well entertained,' he told her. She knew this was not a compliment and marched haughtily back to her station, shapely hips bustling.

The practice nurse appeared in search of a missing patient. 'Is Gavin Peters here?'

Debbie glanced up from the appointment book. 'That's the second time he's failed to turn up this year.' It being now into November, Mitchell marvelled at her memory.

The nurse protested. 'He was only late last time. He'll probably turn up today.'

'Then he'll have missed his appointment and he'll have to make another. Mr Greenwood is a little early. You can see him now.' Mr Greenwood and the nurse retreated together to the nether regions.

Mitchell's neighbour turned to him again. 'She's trained him well enough anyway.'

'The nurse? Yes, she seems to have got him well in hand. I expect he's thankful when his stint here is over.'

'It's her husband. She takes him home with her.'

Mitchell raised his eyebrows. 'I thought my woman was bossy but I'd better count my blessings.'

When he was eventually admitted to the

surgery, it cheered Mitchell to see that Dr Simpson looked more tired than he felt himself. The voice in which he answered, however, was brisk. 'I dare say there are various ways I could help you. What exactly do you want from me?'

Mitchell liked a straight-talking interviewee. 'I want to know something about Justin Chase's disease, the mental as well as physical effects. I want to know if you think there's any chance that he might have committed suicide and if his wife might have taken the opportunity of a convenient bonfire to remove the evidence and hide the shame of it. Then I want to know how his condition affected his marriage and general family relationships, how well he could do his job and whether his wife was sufficiently fed up with looking after him to have put him out of his misery either for his sake or for her own. Will that do for starters?'

When the doctor blinked, taken aback, Mitchell paused to draw breath and smiled. 'I'm not either as detached or as callous as all that sounds, but, if I'm honest, I'm hoping you can answer all of those questions.'

'Clare is still my patient.'

'And one of my suspects, unless you can persuade me to remove her from the list.' The doctor nodded reluctantly. 'So, something about the disease – briefly, please.'

Dr Simpson settled back in his chair. 'Multiple sclerosis means many scars. It damages the sheathing of the nerves so that messages from the brain don't reach the muscle. In time the unused muscles waste away. Symptoms vary greatly between both different patients and between one day and the next in a particular individual.'

'And in Justin Chase's case?'

The doctor blew out over steepled fingers, giving himself time to consider his responsibilities to all the people concerned. 'Excessive fatigue, the very beginning of speech and sight difficulties, bladder problems and overweight because of his inactivity and his drugs. Having been a sportsman, he minded being overweight as much as, perhaps more than, all the rest.'

'So we had a very frustrated man. Would he, in your opinion, have contemplated suicide as a way out?'

The doctor shook his head. 'Clare was the one who was depressed. Justin was angry. He hadn't sunk to total hopelessness. When patients get past that, things sometimes look up. They become resigned. I think things would have got better within the marriage if Clare could have hung on just a bit longer.' Mitchell's ears pricked up. Was the implication that she hadn't been able to? 'As for Clare disposing of the body, I don't think she could have brought herself to burn it however he died. Considering his profession, I don't think Warren would either.'

Mitchell blinked. This man had followed him all the way. Fearful of stemming the flow of information he refrained from asking the obvious question and went on listening.

'I was becoming increasingly worried about Clare. Practically, she was coping very well but she couldn't share the strain. It didn't help that Justin found sympathy intolerable so that Clare felt she had to conceal as much of the situation as possible.' The doctor stopped speaking and sat back with an expression that told Mitchell that the medical man had revealed as much as he thought proper.

Mitchell switched his questioning to more factual matters. 'What was Justin's job?'

'I'm not sure exactly. He worked for Cantrells and had a sophisticated computer system at home. He was coping well, according to Clare, with whatever was required. He was completely undamaged mentally and his hands seemed to function fairly well most of the time. The musculature of the lower body was intermittently inadequate for mobility and becoming worse.'

He paused and Mitchell watched patiently as he struggled with his scruples. He was disappointed when the doctor continued, 'I think that's all. I do have a long list of house calls.'

Satisfied for the time being, Mitchell thanked him and rose to leave. He reached the door before the doctor called him back. 'There is just one more thing. Last time Clare consulted me was just a couple of days before Justin disappeared. She was very tense and even more button-lipped than usual but she did ask me about the possible mental effects of her husband's illness and whether it could make him act out of character. I wondered if he might have lashed out at her physically instead of just verbally.'

'No, it wasn't that. We know what she thought he'd done.'

The doctor too kept back his question. 'I was crassly trying to cheer her up, knowing there were more than a dozen other patients waiting for me. I told her how much we admired her for taking on marriage to a man with a degenerative disease. Others do it if it becomes necessary not many take it on in full knowledge of what's to come. She looked thunderstruck.

'Thinking about it afterwards, I strongly suspect that he married her without telling her so that she only found out about his illness when the symptoms became notice-able. To tell you the truth you're so anxious to hear, I think I'd just snatched from her her last reason for soldiering on.'

Clement had found his quarry in a tiny house in the middle of a terraced row in a run-down area of Cloughton adjacent to a 1960s estate where his uniformed colleagues patrolled only in twos. Warren Chase's house was stark and clean and so extremely barely furnished that Clement decided it must be his choice rather than the result of circumstances. Clement had been impressed by the powerful physique and gentle manner of his host. Host he had certainly been and the DC, as he asked his questions, drank Warren Chase's excellent coffee and consumed scones rich with sultanas and butter, had felt like a very impolite guest. When the man revealed that he was the pastor of a non-denominational church, centred on the building like a small hangar in the middle of the estate, it seemed to Clement the ideal occupation for him.

Satisfied that he had obtained the information that the DI required, Clement now set off to follow up his own idea. Faye Weston's brother proved to be a beautiful young man. Clement viewed him with a suspicion that verged on contempt and that was more obvious than he knew.

Weston stood back to let him in. 'No, I'm not gay if that's what you're wondering. Ask my wife if you don't believe me.' He led the way into an untidy sitting-room. 'Have you come about this nutter who's running up a huge phone bill by pestering Faye and Megan? There's nothing I can tell you. I don't know why you think I can. I've never spoken to him.'

Clement supposed he would get a word in eventually. The man's tone changed. 'You haven't come because you think it's me?'

'The possibility occurred to us but it was nothing personal. We're having to talk to any man who has any connection with the victims and you have to admit your connection is fairly unusual.' In spite of himself, Clement added, 'Didn't your wife object – or doesn't she know?'

He paused, staring at Clement, then decided not to be offended. 'Yes, she did, and yes, she does. She gave her unwilling consent because she likes Megan. She was sorry she was also agreeing to oblige my sister. She doesn't like Faye.'

Since Weston seemed not to resent his curiosity, Clement gave in to it. 'Aren't you worried about the family complications you're causing?'

'Which ones?'

'Like feeling responsible for your child when it arrives. Like having your wife – and maybe other people – suspecting a relationship between you and its mother. Like what the child will be told about its origins.'

Weston nodded soberly. 'Yes, I am. I thought I could just step aside when the deed was done, leave all the rest to the two girls, but you're right. I can't and it's a relief to talk to somebody about the mare's nest I've created. I can't talk to Lisa. She'd only say she told me so. I used to be a good friend of Megan's and now we have a very strained relationship. And Faye keeps me at arm's length too. Maybe she's one of your "other people".'

'Megan told us the baby will go in a factory crèche whilst she's working. I don't suppose you're thrilled about that.'

Weston waved this suggestion away and gave a mirthless grin. 'That doesn't need to happen. I hope it won't. It's just Megan's gesture.'

'A gesture that means what?'

'Megan doesn't need to work at all. She's got money her grandmother left her. She probably wouldn't have if the old lady had suspected. Most of the family have refused to have anything to do with her since she came out and they hate Faye. They think she's after the money. So do I. I mean, I don't hate her but I've noticed that she's never had a partner who was hard up.'

'So she swaps and changes? The baby won't even be brought up in a settled relationship?'

'It'll be safe with Megan.'

'So why does she work in a factory?'

He shrugged. 'Why does she spend all her

166

time play-acting?' Clement looked puzzled. 'Well, the white make-up, the black and white clothes, the veggie diet. I think she lost herself when her family threw her out. Then she tried to redefine herself. She's hoping "This is what I do" will substitute for "This is what I am".'

'Maybe the baby will help.'

'Maybe it will. And now I've told you how mixed up I feel, you'll trot off to tell your boss that you're certain I'm getting my kicks from making Megan's life a misery with threatening phone calls and ringing all the others to add verisimilitude—'

'To an otherwise unlikely circumstance,' finished Clement desperately. 'We must do a G&S together one day.' Weston had predicted precisely Clement's intention and he was glad of the silly joke to cover his confusion. 'Whatever I tell my boss, he'll make up his own mind. And, by the way, how did you know about all the others?'

Jennifer looked forward to her interview with Harriet Bradley with some misgivings. Was this what life would be like when Lucy and Judith became adolescents? Surely not. Harriet was the product of her upbringing and Jennifer had no intention of becoming the same sort of mother as the woman she had driven to the hospital on Saturday night. The problem that lay most heavily on

Mrs Bradley's mind had been how likely the news of her daughter's predicament was to reach the ears of her colleagues and friends.

At least Jennifer would be able to reassure Harriet that it was very unlikely she would be harassed on the telephone again. By now the hospital might well have done tests to lay some of the girl's other fears to rest. If not, they would sort things out at the appropriate time.

Jennifer made a courtesy visit to the nurses' station to obtain permission to speak to their patient. Sister volunteered the information that Harriet was young and strong and so was recovering fast. She had lost her baby.

Harriet's appearance confirmed Sister's optimism. In spite of the application of a stomach pump, the effects of the pills her system had already absorbed and bleeding from the loss of her pregnancy the girl looked healthy and cheerful. Her secret had been shared and most, at least, of her worries had been removed. Jennifer added her own reassurance that the phone calls had stopped for good. The caller was not in a position to repeat his offence.

Harriet grinned happily. 'There's nothing left for him to threaten me with now. I'm not pregnant any more. I haven't got AIDS and Daddy's forgiven me.' Jennifer noted the omission. 'It was only that when he rang me on Saturday I was just beginning to realise that no amount of furniture removing was going to shift the baby, and Kate, my cousin, had asked me to be a bridesmaid. I got the letter that morning and Mummy was going on and on about the beautiful dress she'd make me and I knew I'd be too fat and pregnant to wear it. So, I was feeling really miserable when he phoned me and started going on about AIDS again and it all got on top of me... What's the matter?'

Jennifer asked, as calmly as she could, 'You had another malicious call on Saturday?' The girl nodded and Jennifer pulled her chair close to the bed. 'Harriet, I want you to describe that call to me in the minutest detail, second by second.'

'But you said it wouldn't–'

'For you, no. But you weren't the only victim. There's still a danger that someone else will get as desperate as you did and they might not be found in time.'

'All right.' The girl frowned in concentration. 'I was writing an essay on Lady Macbeth.'

Jennifer listened with waning patience to a summary of the unfinished essay. 'And the telephone rang.'

'Yes, and I was cross because I'd just begun to enjoy my work. For once, I even didn't think about the man as I picked the receiver up.' She stared into space, obviously reliving the experience.

'What did you hear?'

'I heard silence at first, so I knew it was him.' Jennifer nodded. 'Then I heard his whispering voice.'

Jennifer gritted her teeth and asked patiently, 'Can you remember his exact words?' It was obvious that Harriet could but that she could not bring herself to repeat them.

'He just said that I wouldn't know till Christmas whether I had it or not.' Her voice sharpened. 'Is that right?'

'How far on with the pregnancy were you?'

'Three and a half months.'

'Then, if you've been tested, the result will be valid. If Sister says you have nothing to worry about then you can trust her. What else did the caller say?'

'That it took a few months before – I remember this bit – the virus could be detected.'

Jennifer scribbled in her notebook. 'Right, and then?'

'He said it wouldn't be a very good Christmas present. Then he shut up and put the receiver down.'

'Straight away?'

'No, after a few seconds.'

'Harriet, shut your eyes and go through it

170

again in your mind. Did you hear anything at all besides the man's voice?'

The girl obediently shut her eyes. After a moment she opened them again, grinning proudly. 'When he'd finished and was waiting to see if I'd say anything, I heard another phone ringing. I didn't know I'd heard it till I played it through again in my head just now. And there was something else. I've just realised there was no buzzing. In the other calls there was buzzing in the background. It sounded like that thing on Mr Cooper's door that tells him there's somebody in the shop.'

'Mr Cooper?'

'The chemists in the precinct. Mummy goes there a lot.'

Jennifer took her notebook up again, jotting quickly so as not to hold up the conversation. 'Can you tell me anything about the voice?'

'It was breathy, as if he wasn't using his vocal chords at all. When he first rang I wasn't even sure it was a man until he started saying rude things about...' She blushed furiously.

'About your body?'

Harriet nodded without looking up. A startling idea occurred to Jennifer and she scribbled again. When she eventually rose to leave, Harriet caught her eye, pleading. 'You won't tell Mummy I've talked to you, will you? She said I wasn't to, that the less anyone was told, the less chance there was of it getting in the papers.'

Jennifer winked at the nurse who had been standing at the end of the bed in her capacity of chaperone. 'I won't tell her, but if she finds out you can tell her that she herself gave me even more help about quite another matter.'

8

Having been several times reminded by his mother of his promise to find Lee, Nathan Hillard had at last made contact with his ex-schoolmate, Sergeant Marcus Duck, out in the wilds of Millton. It had been an awkward telephone call. Nathan was embarrassed to be asking a favour from someone who, in the past, he had teased unmercifully about everything from his name, through his red hair and the gaps in his teeth to his low exam results.

The man he had grown into seemed to bear no grudge as he strode, hand extended, from the pub doorway to the corner table where Nathan waited for him. 'Hillard! You haven't changed much.'

Nathan saw that Marcus Duck had changed a great deal. 'Hello – er, Marcus. Good of you to make time for–'

Duck waved away the polite formulae. 'The whole station wittily calls me Donald so you might as well go on doing it. I'll have a pint of Guest, please,' he added as Nathan got up to go to the bar. He smiled to himself as he waited, Nathan noticed, then received his glass with a nod of thanks. He swallowed a third of its contents in one long draught before facing his host across the rickety table. 'Well, I don't suppose this session is for old times' sake, so what can I do for you?'

Ruefully, Nathan gave an account of his brother's disappearance and the onus on himself to find him, ending hopefully. '...so I wondered if you could help me.'

Duck placed his empty glass on the table. 'What makes you think that I'd want to?'

'Look, Donald, I'm really sorry for making your life such hell as a kid.'

'You toughened me up to do what I'm doing now. What I meant was that Lee's probably quite happy where he is, where your mother can't go on plaguing him. From what I remember of him, he's not likely to learn to stand up to her. I reckon that running away is about the best that he can do for himself.'

Nathan went to refill the glasses and think out a reply. 'It isn't, you know,' he announced, coming back and placing brimming glasses on the table and continuing the conversation as though there had been no interruption. 'I agree that Lee probably needed to find himself, wherever he is. But now, to regain his self-respect he needs to come back and prove that he can stand up to her. And surely he owes them something for supporting him financially for all this time.'

'I think you should leave well alone.'

'I'm not going to. If you won't help it will just take longer, but I shall find him in the end.'

Duck sighed. 'I believe you. I said you hadn't changed. Did you have something particular in mind that I'm suppose to do for you?'

Nathan brightened. 'I thought you could find out which force it was that notified Cumbria that Lee is alive and well. Will you?'

'You're not Lee. If I say no this time, you'll just keep asking. I may as well give in now as later.' So Donald had not changed as much as Nathan had thought. 'If I do it, what will you do next?'

Nathan had already given much thought to this. 'Well, he must be working. He didn't receive any of the money Dad sent to the cottage. All the letters were found unopened on the mat. Lee likes his creature comforts. He's not going to be satisfied with what he can buy for himself on the dole. His degree's in computer science so the obvious thing seems to be to get in touch with all the computer firms in whatever area he's living in.'

'It'll be a big area. I won't be able to give you a district or even a town. Anyway, Lee could work on computers for a firm that makes anything. All firms use them nowadays. It'll be a very long haul.' Duck pushed back his chair. 'I'll see what I can do, but you might be old and grey before you find him by this method.' He left with the same energetic stride that had brought him in, leaving Nathan reflecting on ugly ducklings and swans.

As DC Caroline Webster was missing when Mitchell began his briefing, he had to begin his 'Ladies first' policy with a report from Jennifer. She spoke without reference to her notes and her fellow officers regarded her, half depressed, half offended, as the news sank in that the malicious calls were continuing though Justin Chase was dead.

'Are you sure,' a uniformed officer asked hesitantly, 'that the girl isn't just attention-seeking?'

'And swallowed most of a bottle of Mogadon when she'd no idea that I'd be coming to rescue her, just to make it more convincing?' The constable retired, scarlet-faced.

Jennifer could find no one to back her theory that the breathy voice that had made 'rude' observations on Harriet's anatomy might be female. She had become fascinated with her theory and spent some time wondering which of the two girls, Megan or Faye, was sufficiently dissatisfied or maladjusted to resort to harassment of girls

176

who had become pregnant in a slightly more socially acceptable way.

It was some minutes before she realised that the case was being thoroughly worked over without her. She tuned into the discussion, trying to pick up the information she had missed. No one so far seemed to have seen Clare Chase out on the walk she claimed to have taken. Nor had anyone been observed approaching the Chases' house.

Caroline Webster slipped into the room just as Mitchell was summarising his conversation with Dr Simpson. He made much of the latter's suspicion that Clare Chase had found out only a day or so before the murder that Justin had tricked her into becoming his nurse as well as his wife. As she settled herself on the chair enthusiastically offered by a hopeful uniformed constable, the one Jennifer had recently crushed, Caroline observed, 'If she wanted revenge on him, she should have let him go on living. The state he was in meant he'd already got his come-uppance.' The lovelorn constable nodded in agreement.

The conversation passed to Warren Chase, his physical strength, his fondness for his sister-in-law and the loss of his inheritance in favour of his brother making him Caroline's choice of suspect. Clement, who had discussed his work and his church with him, strongly disagreed.

177

This topic came to a dead end and Mitchell turned back to Jennifer to ask, 'How did you get on with my friend Steve?'

She grinned, thankful that she had come out of her daydream in time to have her answer ready. 'When he finds the bastard who rang Gemma and made those suggestions about him, he'll lay into him good and proper – but only in a manner of speaking like! And he doesn't know who's messing about with the bloody DI's wife but it's a pissing good idea and he wishes he'd thought of it.'

Mitchell, the only one present who knew Steven Thacker well enough to appreciate the flashes of clever mimicry, laughed, then sobered quickly. 'How did he know about that?'

There were blank looks all round before Clement suggested, 'Perhaps he did think of it and then did it.'

Jennifer shook her head. 'It didn't strike me that ideas were Steve's strong point. And he might share the lewd hopes of Ginny's stalker but, from what she's told us about the calls, I shouldn't think his vocabulary is in the same class. Anyway, I would think telephone harassment is a bit subtle for him. He seems to prefer a hands-on approach.'

Mitchell nodded agreement. 'That's right, preferably when they're balled into fists.' He glanced at Caroline. 'I suppose you were late because you saw a man you fancied and picked him up for a drink.'

Caroline grinned but blushed too, still never quite sure whether Mitchell was teasing or reprimanding her. 'Well, yes, I did, actually.'

'You know debriefing means confession time.'

Caroline relaxed. 'Right, I shall reveal all. I had to wait to see Mr Cantrell himself. One of his employees was ill and he'd driven him home. He was very anxious to co-operate when he came back but he didn't help much. He said Justin Chase had been a co-founder with him of the firm and did one-off jobs for them as he was able. One was to put together a tome of techno-babble, optimistically called a handbook. He gave me one and I tried to read it.'

'What does the firm do, exactly?' More than one of the officers present were glad of Clement's question, permissible on his part because he was relatively new to Cloughton.

Caroline explained. 'Amongst other things, they started trading in other people's PCs about ten years ago and began playing with the idea of producing their own almost immediately. They've two on the market at the moment. I had their technical superiority carefully explained to me but I hope I'm not expected to pass that on. Since I didn't understand a word, I just

179

tried to stem the flow. Checking with the handbook I told you about just confused me more.

'Another job they gave him was preparing the material for the article Ginny was writing about the firm for that "Memories of Cloughton" book. She'll be able to tell you quite a lot about them from that.'

'So, where does your date come in?'

'As I went in I spotted a chap I met at the training college in Wakefield. He didn't stay the course. Left after six weeks. I'd forgotten he went to Cantrells and I hadn't seen him for a couple of years. He winked at me going out so I thought I'd spend half an hour seeing what he could tell me.'

'I've no problem with your duty taking you into a pub with a handsome young man, so long as he came up with the goods.' Mitchell's tone was silky.

Caroline sniffed. 'That's what he thought I was going to do in exchange for his helping with enquiries.'

'So, what happened?'

'He had to settle for a couple of drinks instead. He told me Justin Chase taught him his job two years ago when he first went to Cantrells and Chase was in much better health. Jonathan thought he was a good teacher so long as he was in a good mood, but even then he resented not being trusted to do the pioneering work any more, not being the firm's kingpin. Mr Cantrell told me that all the impetus for launching their own PC came from him.'

'Which university?'

'UMIST,' Jennifer supplied, when Caroline shrugged. 'Clare told me.'

'Anyway, Jonathan told me Cantrells would have offered Justin work for as long as he was capable of doing anything and a good pension after that. It was his work that put Cantrells on the map.'

'I'm surprised they could afford it,' Jennifer observed. 'It's only a tiny place.'

'Well, I gathered it isn't making small profits. I suppose if everything's done by microchips you don't need all that many people or very much space. Chase was scheduled to be responsible for giving Lee Hillard his three-month induction course before he went abroad but he went through a bad patch at the time. Hillard did his first month with Jonathan and then a week or two with Mr Cantrell, the MD. He was supposed to do the final month with Chase, beginning this Monday.'

'That's very interesting. Any more?'

'Not about Chase. He went wittering on about Hillard but I thought you'd still be interested.' Mitchell indicated that he was. 'Hillard was the one who'd been taken ill. The MD didn't know but Jonathan had taken him home twice before with the same trouble. Jon thought he had a grumbling appendix. He was afraid it would burst whilst Hillard put off seeing a doctor. Hillard was afraid of losing the job if he wasn't fit when it was time for him to go to Germany and was hoping to stave things off until he'd got there. He told the MD it was the curry he'd had the night before.'

'So, when the MD knew he was ill, he drove him home himself.' Jennifer sounded impressed. 'They must think a lot of him then.'

'Jon said the MD called him a second Chase. From his tone of voice I suspect he's jealous.'

Mitchell was hardly listening. A horrifying idea had come to him. Was his first murder investigation as a DI going to prove just an attempt to cover up a computer fraud? There'd be a fight, he promised himself, if Kleever tried to hand it over to the computer boffins or the Fraud Squad.

Virginia waited less than patiently in Kleever's office at Cloughton headquarters for Professor Klein to appear. Kleever had chatted to her pleasantly when she arrived, being tactfully and inoffensively sympathetic. However, she knew she was keeping him from his work. She produced a packet of documents from her bag and announced her intention of filling in the time by reading some of the material her employer had sent her for the next article she was to write. It was obvious that neither of them was finding it easy to concentrate but Virginia had done away with the necessity for further talk and she was free to review her situation.

She had always taken a quiet satisfaction in her role as Benny's wife, coping as a student and then a working mother of four. She believed she was level-headed. Her friendship and advice were often sought. She remembered a recent Dutch uncle talk she had given Jennifer and blushed as she reflected on the way she had received reciprocal advice from her friend.

Virginia had been pleased when she had overheard a remark of Caroline's to the effect that, if this had to happen to anyone, then the DI's wife was the person out of everyone she knew most likely to take it in her stride. She had admitted to no one, least of all to Benny, that she was quite terrified. Of what, she was not quite sure. She was not especially afraid of physical harm, except on behalf of her children. Chiefly she was afraid of her enemy's underhand approach, his insistence on secrecy, his waiting till he knew no one else was there. He knew her better now and it was only a matter of time before he found her alone.

The worst thing was hiding everything from Benny. Her instinct, like his, was to be perfectly straightforward in all her dealings. Their quarrels, occasionally vigorous, were always brief because each said exactly what the problem was and the other understood. Benny knew the facts now but he still had no idea of the dread that flooded her on waking each morning. He had no conception of her almost uncontrollable anger when she refused to let her children run free in the park, play hide and seek in the garden they'd chosen for just that purpose or even answer the telephone.

She was grateful for the expert advice she was about to be offered but she knew she would resent the measures that she expected this specialist consultant to recommend. Keeping always with other people she found irksome. She was as gregarious as most people but at the same time she was a deeply private person. Dearly though she loved the large brood she and her husband had produced, she sometimes resented them too. She needed to be alone from time to time and she always welcomed the long evenings when Benny was on duty, the children asleep and she had her mind and imagination free for herself. Now, until this fiend could be apprehended, being alone was something to be dreaded and something that was forbidden. She had not decided how much she was prepared to admit in his meeting, apart from the bare facts. Probably little more. She wished that Kleever would be suddenly called away. She knew that this was ungrateful, considering how much he had organised for her protection, the services of Clement and the other two officers, the infra-red cameras in the garden, the presently awaited consultation. Nevertheless she could not feel free to parade her fears in front of her husband's superior officer.

She was very conscious that if Jennifer was right in her assessment then her stalker had no connection with either the harassment of the pregnant girls or the murder of Justin Chase. So her own plight was holding up and obscuring the progress of both those cases. She took another sip of the rapidly cooling coffee that Kleever had asked someone to bring in and covertly watched him watching her.

She had found him much more understanding than she had expected. He had described to her briefly his encounter with another stalker when he had been a superintendent in his last posting. Virginia had been surprised to realise he had made a sideways move to Cloughton. Then, recognising her own reaction, she had felt glad that she had not succumbed to her fears to the extent that she couldn't take an interest in someone else's affairs.

Suddenly, she decided it was good for her

to be here. Especially good to be out of the prison of her house. She had travelled the short distance from it in a taxi. She despised herself for this as well as regretting the pleasure of striding out on the short trip as she would usually have done. She needed a few hours away from home. For her the atmosphere in the house was poisoned and she felt that in future she and Benny would never be happy there. She knew that never before had she experienced such neurotic feelings or behaved in such an illogical way.

The superintendent stood up and she forced her attention back to his moving mouth. He had seen Professor Klein, escorted by Jennifer, arriving on the station forecourt outside his window. A minute later, Jennifer came in alone, her dark hair ruffled, her expression as she glanced at Virginia concerned but a little distracted by all the other things on her mind. Virginia was chastened. Jennifer was responsible for two fatherless children, and was part of two serious investigations, yet she was taking time to attend this session to see if there was any way she could assist in finding the man who was harassing her friend.

The three of them made stilted conversation until Professor Klein made his entry. Virginia glanced at him. The lank dark hair, large square black-framed glasses and slightly abstracted, almost bewildered expression immediately brought to her mind the front man of her parents' bygone heroes, the Shadows. Her spirits having been lifted by Jennifer's proximity, she mouthed 'Hank Marvin' in her friend's direction and was disappointed when Jennifer looked puzzled.

They both shook hands soberly with the great man and Virginia settled herself in Kleever's most comfortable chair to give a fair hearing to whatever he had to say. At Kleever's request, he began with his celebrated – in the USA at least – stalker profile. The first type he described seemed to Virginia to be relatively harmless, someone with a rather extreme 'crush', someone known to the victim and just making a nuisance of himself. She thought she could have coped fairly easily with someone like that.

Professor Klein leaned back, well launched on his exposition. 'It's stalking by a complete stranger that's the most unpredictable and unnerving.' She had not needed an expert to tell her that. 'It's beyond any attempt at rationalisation. This kind of stalker has some impression of his victim, distorted but real to him. He sees her, becomes attracted to her. Then, he projects his own fantasies on to the flesh and blood person, ascribes to her all the characteristics he wants in an idealised partner.

'When he pursues her, she fails to live up to his standard and then he becomes dangerous and threatening.' As he continued his lecture, Virginia began to feel some confidence in him. He seemed to have a fairly accurate understanding of what was happening to her and, for the first time, she felt there was a possibility that the man might be apprehended. Kleever broke in from time to time, bearing witness from his own experience – just one case, Virginia suspected – to the soundness of Klein's theories. She was amused by his obsequious manner and tried to imagine Petty, his predecessor, deferring to this American 'expert' whose casual manner, informal attire and extreme likeness to one of her mother's idols made him seem incomplete without a guitar.

Now the professor had moved on to his third stalker type. 'Of course, if he's selected his victim completely at random, trawling through the phone directory till a female voice answers, his motive is different.' Virginia's relief that her harassment was about to be competently dealt with began to evaporate. 'This type, who sometimes never sees his prey, wants power, not love. He gets his sexual thrill from knowing he's terrorising his victim. He gets a kick from the fear and confusion he can cause. Like a rapist, he gets sexual stimulation from subjugating and petrifying his victim.'

Jennifer glanced at Virginia, saw that she was offering no comment, then volunteered, 'Our man didn't use the phone book. Ginny's number's ex-directory.'

'My stalker's victim,' Kleever put in, helpfully, 'had her number changed. He hung around her young son's school, offering a bribe to any child who would tell him the new number.' Virginia was too perturbed by the content of his remark to be amused any longer by his childlike attempts to obtain his distinguished visitor's attention.

Klein eventually tired of his lecture to the extent of asking if Mrs Mitchell would kindly describe exactly the form her own harassment had taken. Virginia enumerated the various ways her persecutor had annoyed her and he commented on each. 'Spreading the rubbish heap around the garden is his way of letting you know he's still around.'

'He needn't have bothered then. I hadn't forgotten. What about my underwear? That's what bothers me most – not losing it but, well, it means he's getting close up to the house where I thought the children could play safely.'

Klein's answer was merely to begin on the next instalment of his theories. The facile American tags were beginning to grate on

Virginia and she had no more interest in the man's pontificating. When he at last finished his peroration, she sat with minimum good manners through Kleever's account of the steps that the Cloughton police had taken, the co-operation of the telephone companies, the installation of night-time cameras and the subsequent disappearance of the stalker from the garden.

As she thankfully contemplated her imminent release Virginia was surprised to hear Jennifer ask, 'Is this "stalker personality" you keep referring to something that's inborn, or is it caused by something that's happened to him?' Both men looked startled. Virginia thought they had forgotten Jennifer was in the room.

Klein recovered himself. 'That depends.' Yes, Virginia thought, it always did.

'What if a perfectly normal man,' Jennifer persisted, 'had a tragedy in his life? Could it give him this kind of warped personality?' Virginia was surprised that Jennifer put any more value on the man's opinions than she did herself. 'What if he lost his lover or his wife or children? Would it turn him into this kind of a monster?'

Klein thought not. 'This personality,' he averred, 'is born. Of course, it's usually well disguised. The stalker is often an intelligent man who may hold down a responsible job and give every appearance of being well adjusted until something triggers the stalking activity–'

'Isn't that more or less what Jennifer's asking?' Virginia had had enough of listening with polite respect.

The session, now it had been restarted, gathered strength. Virginia had stopped listening and spent the rest of it hoping that whatever theory was firing her friend was worth the waste of the nicest afternoon, as far as the weather was concerned, for several weeks.

9

Debbie Johnson muttered to herself as she gathered up magazines, dropped into the appropriate box the toys that were scattered around the surgery waiting-room and shut down the playpen. Then she mopped up the spillage from an overturned vase, refilled it and rearranged its crushed blooms. She looked up as her husband came in, still folding the white coat he had removed when his last patient departed. 'I don't know what we have cleaners for. I've done most of their jobs for them before they arrive.'

'Well, don't then.'

She tutted. 'You know perfectly well I'm incapable of looking at a mess and not doing something about it. Why do people, even women, become such sluts when they get in here? They wouldn't have their own places like this.'

'Oh yes, they would. And far worse. I have to visit them. Some of them have carpets that stick to your shoes. You should be thankful they're in here for so short a time. They aren't kept waiting long enough to make it positively insanitary.'

'If you're referring to the loos, that's where

I draw the line. That's definitely the cleaners' job.' She vented her indignation on attacking the fingermarked door with a damp cloth. 'I see we had Mummy in to-night.'

'We had a host of mothers, didn't we?'

'Yes, but only one with a captial M. Is Little Miss Prim still in hospital?'

'How should I know?' Damian watched as Debbie turned over the huge pages of three appointment books, one for her husband and one each for the two doctors, ready for next morning. 'Now Mummy knows she's not going to become a grandma in the near future, maybe we'll hear less about her nerves.'

'From what I've heard she didn't know it was likely to happen to her till the danger was over. Where's Derek?'

'Don't be familiar. You wouldn't call him Derek to his face. Dr Simpson has gone to visit Mrs Chase.'

'I don't see why. She's not ill.'

'Oh, come on, her husband's been murdered. I shouldn't think she's feeling too well.'

Debbie tossed her head. 'We aren't social workers, you know.'

'Dr Simpson says we are.' Damian was always embarrassed when Debbie talked about themselves and the doctors as if they were equals. It left them vulnerable to the put-down that Dr Fowler, at least, was always ready to provide.

'I don't suppose you got anything out of either of them about what that great slab of a copper came about?' Damian shook his head. 'Good job he was CID. Not exactly built for chasing criminals.' She banged the telephone down on the counter, having cleaned every crevice. 'I thought about giving him a diet sheet but I wasn't sure he could read. Ignorant type, he was.'

'I expect he'd come about Mr Chase.'

Debbie sniffed, not finished yet with Mitchell's personal and social shortcomings. 'No conversation either. I only passed the time of day and asked how things were going. He slapped me down and went to sit in the far corner by the playpen.' She grinned. 'Wait till he's ill.'

'He might not be on our books.'

'Oh yes, he is. And his wife and a houseful of infants. He'll find I've got a long memory.' She surveyed the waiting-room smugly. 'It's about ready now for what that lazy crew call cleaning. Gemma Platt missed her ante-natal appointment. I bet it's because she doesn't want Janet to see she's covered in bruises again.'

'Dr Fowler,' her husband corrected, knowing he was wasting his time. 'There's no privilege in being familiar when you haven't been invited. Anyway, there aren't any marks on the little girl. I check her out regularly. Gemma knows that and so does the brute who hands it out to her.'

Debbie nodded vigorously. 'And she'll never be free of him. He's never touched the kid so no one can stop him seeing her or the new baby. Thank goodness we didn't bother.'

'That's the reason, is it? So that when you run off it'll be a clean break without any access-to-the-kids arrangements to mess things up?'

She gave him her sweetest smile. 'Silly!' She blew him a kiss that caused him to blush painfully as Dr Fowler came through reception on her way out. 'Goodnight, Janet,' she continued, addressing her employer.

Dr Fowler paused at the door. 'Goodnight, Mrs Johnson. I see you've waved your magic wand in here and all is as it should be again. Well done.'

Even the peaceable Damian was needled. 'Patronising sod thinks we're a couple of chars!'

Angela Hillard was incensed. She had been delighted when Nathan told her he had taken a week of his annual leave in the middle of November. While the fog and sleet competed to see which could ruin most days in England, her heart had leapt at the thought of a few days in the sun on the other side of the world to help them survive the rest of the winter. Then she had learned that the purpose of this free time was for Nathan to ring round the major computer firms in West Yorkshire in search of his brother.

Outbursts of temper were not Angela's way. She undermined her husband's efforts with a series of sweetly helpful suggestions. 'I brought you these throat sweets from the supermarket,' she told him now as she served his lunch. 'I thought you'd need them with all that talking to do.' At breakfast, it had been, 'I need to speak to my sister but I realise you have a better claim to the phone. I'll go next door and borrow theirs. I'm sure Mrs Cohen will understand.'

Nathan was now on the third day of his phone-marathon and he felt quite sufficiently discouraged without any hassle from Angela. He was also beginning to become worried about its cost. Obviously Angela's talents included telepathy. 'I'm so glad,' she told him, whisking away his plate before he had mopped up his gravy, 'that when the next phone bill arrives you won't be cross about all the calls I've made. It's very good for me not to be able to pick up the telephone on the spur of the moment and at such expense to you. Maybe I won't trouble Mrs Cohen. I could write to Karen. They say the art of letter writing is dying – perhaps I should do something about it.'

Why, Nathan wondered, were women so childish? There were no spoons set on the table. Obviously 'no pudding' was also part of the punishment. Ignoring his wife, he went back to the phone, dialled the next number on his list and asked for Lee Hillard.

'Which department, please?'

'I'm afraid I don't know.'

'Just a minute.'

Fearing it would be several minutes, Nathan sighed over the waste of time as well as money. His temper was not improved by the metallic rendering of a selection of classical themes that was beginning its second time round before the dulcet tones informed him that the company did not employ a Lee Hillard. He was about to remark that the company owed a humble apology to Mr Beethoven, but thought that might elicit another 'Which department?'

He proceeded to the next number and made his request again. A voice mumbled. 'Sorry, I didn't catch that.' Angela crashed plates together as the girl on the other end of the line repeated her remark. Nathan groaned. 'I'm very sorry. This seems to be a very bad line. Did you say you don't have a Mr Hillard working for you? I'm sorry to have troubled you.'

He waited to try again until he had helped his wife to carry the dishes from the table to the kitchen. As she ran water into the sink, he closed the intervening door quietly. It remained shut. Thankfully he began dialling again. As the number rang out a loud burst of pop music startled him and he saw that Angela had dragged one of the speakers from the CD player that entertained her in the kitchen to a new position on the floor behind the dining-room door.

He was surprised that stretching the flex so far had not dragged the wires out of the plug. There would be little point in arguing with her or in putting the speaker back in its usual place. It would be just his luck to pull the wires out himself and be accused of having broken the damned thing. Anyway, he was sure she had half a dozen more plans in reserve. He slipped the list of companies and their numbers into his pocket, grabbed his anorak from its hook as he passed through the hall and slammed the front door as he left the house. He'd have a couple of pints at the Drum and Monkey and make a few calls from there.

After his second pint, he could almost see Angela's point of view. The phone bill was going to be enormous and he probably wouldn't find Lee this way. Angie could do with a winter break. He could himself, come to that. Still, he'd asked the landlord if he could use the phone now so he might as well just try the next firm on the list. Then he'd call at the travel agents in the precinct and book a weekend away for the pair of them. He could spend some of the time dreaming up new tactics.

He had taken this current list of numbers from the Bradford directory but they had the codes of the small towns that surrounded it. His right index finger throbbed as he punched, another reason to call a halt. By the end of the week he would be suffering RSI. He waited for the inevitable engaged signal now that it was well past lunchtime, but the number rang and was answered promptly by quite an efficient-sounding girl. He asked for his brother.

The girl conferred briefly with a colleague and he was not treated to tinned music before she returned to him. 'I'm afraid he's out at lunch still. Can he ring you back or should I take a message?'

Nathan had not really believed he would reach this stage and wished he had prepared for it. 'No, thanks. I – er – need to speak to him. I'll try again later.'

'Who shall I say rang?'

Nathan overrode this with a brief, 'Thanks anyway.' He replaced the receiver. Now he deserved a real drink.

When Clare Chase appeared in response to her knock, Jennifer was pleased to see signs that she had been weeping. It was important that she question the woman closely, but as long as her ominous calm continued, Jennifer feared being the trigger of a complete breakdown.

Clare was wearing some kind of inappropriate sports outfit, knitted cotton top and trousers in grey and white. When she was at her best it probably enhanced her fair prettiness and drew attention to her lean, athletic build. Now it just added to the colourless dejection of her drained face and bedraggled blonde hair. The clothes were scrupulously clean but looked as though they had been dragged from a pile of garments waiting to be ironed. Jennifer was not unfamiliar, on her own account, with the sort of situations that drove elegant women to look like this.

It was difficult to decide whether or not Clare was pleased to see her. She was invited in with a listless gesture that indicated no curiosity about what the police might have discovered nor about what they might require of her. Jennifer admitted immediately that her call was not to say that the police were any further forward in discovering Justin's killer. 'I do have some good news for you, though.' Clare appeared neither cheered nor interested. 'Shall I make us some coffee?'

On the strength of Clare's languid 'If you like,' Jennifer made free with the Chases' kitchen to the extent of producing strong instant coffee and opening tins until she discovered a hoard of ginger biscuits. She put some of these on a plate on the table, where both women ignored them, and placed a steaming mug in front of Clare, before asking, 'Do you want to hear the good news?'

The dispirited 'If you like' was repeated and Jennifer wondered how many of her words were being assimilated. She began to describe what had happened to Harriet.

Clare kept her eyes on her fingers which she alternately interlaced and freed. Twice, she remarked, 'Poor little kid,' without seeming either involved or concerned. When Jennifer finished speaking, she raised her eyes to the sergeant's face and asked, 'So?'

'So,' Jennifer repeated desperately, 'you can remember Justin with respect as well as love. He didn't make the call that drove Harriet to attempt suicide and so he almost certainly didn't make the others either.'

Now Clare was defiant. 'I already knew that.' When Jennifer remained silent the defiance soon crumbled and the tears reappeared. 'All the time I was yelling at him, I knew he couldn't really have done anything like that, but I was so angry with him for what he's done to me. I could hardly believe that. And sometimes I thought, if he could be so cruel to me, why not to them? I wanted to hit him hard with anything that would really hurt. And, for some of the time, on and off, I really did suspect him.'

Her bent head and the application of Jennifer's clean handkerchief to her mouth made her words difficult to discern. She shook convulsively but was sufficiently aware of herself to recoil when Jennifer reached out a hand to her. She waited. When Clare spoke again her words were clear, calmer and coherent. 'I was hoping, when the police came back, that it would be you.'

'Why was that?'

'Because it'll be easier with someone I know ... to confess, I mean.'

Angela Hillard's already black mood was not improved when Nathan returned home, almost four hours later and definitely not sober. She employed her usual method of expressing displeasure until her husband's uproarious laugh at her every feeble sarcasm showed her she was wasting her time.

She mellowed a little when he announced that he would be taking her out for dinner that night and a lot when he proposed a weekend away. 'Well, all right. But I'm not going out with you in that state. You can have an hour to sleep it off, then a whole pot of coffee and a cold shower – well, cool then.' He appreciated the concession. 'So, where will be going at the weekend?'

Most of Nathan's wits were still scattered but some sixth sense warned him not to reveal at this point that they would be going to Cloughton, in West Yorkshire, to see what Lee was up to. She smiled indulgently when he told her, 'It'sh a … shecret!'

Benny Mitchell was sitting in his office, reading, for what seemed the hundredth time, through the current case file. His concentration was less than sporadic and none of it made sense. The scant three and a half hours of sleep he had managed the previous night had little to do with his inability to think constructively about the case. Mitchell was fortunate in needing little sleep, which was just as well, he realised, considering that he had had four babies in the last seven years to disturb his rest.

The questions that were troubling him personally were easier to dwell on. In fact, they were insisting that he dwell on them. For a start, why was the super giving him so much rope with this big case? It was, in fact, more a string of connected cases. And how long was it going to be before Kleever's efforts nailed this animal who was daring to harass his wife?

For the first time since he had met her, he knew that Virginia was frightened and neither he nor she knew what to do about it, besides what had already been done. Ginny thought that because she had not admitted to any of her fears he didn't suspect them. It wasn't the first time she had underestimated his sensitivity. He knew too that she almost felt she was to blame for the whole situation. That, in some way, she had inadvertently attracted this man's unwelcome attentions and that, therefore, she was the one who had brought the children into danger, maybe into physical danger. Certainly, into an upsetting atmosphere of apprehension and parental discord.

He had been assured that Kleever now had Virginia's protection well in hand and he was not quite so concerned for her physical safety. Even so, he could not wait to see her persecutor behind bars. It irked him that he was not allowed to bring this about personally, though he well understood his embargo.

Mitchell was worried too about the suggestions Jennifer had been making about young Clement, to Ginny rather than himself. According to her, Jennifer had asked some very odd questions at the session with Professor Klein. Putting these together with certain other of his sergeant's remarks made over the past week, he was getting the impression that she believed the lad was responsible for the stalking. In particular she had warned Ginny about encouraging the DC to station himself outside their house.

Of course, Clement had been through a personal tragedy that would have threatened the sanity of some men, but Mitchell thought the young officer seemed to be of very sound mind and that his grief, though profound, was normal. If Jennifer had had any dcfinite grounds for her suspicions, she would certainly have brought them to him. Or would she? He was off the case. For all he knew, she had reported to Kleever and Clement was their chief suspect.

Ginny herself was traumatised. Maybe her own judgement about this was not of its usual keenness. Perhaps she had read into Jennifer's remarks more than had been intended. Surely, otherwise, Clement would have been given duties that kept him away from Fulton Road.

On the other hand, if their man should turn out to be Clement, it would explain how he came to know such a lot about Ginny's circumstances and habits, knew when her husband would be safely out of the way.

Mitchell shook himself mentally. This was foolishness, last-resort thinking. Clement was as fond of their four children as he would have been of his own young son. He massaged the tight muscles at the back of his neck and looked across the room, then leapt to his feet. This was the last straw. That all-encroaching ivy had put out new leaves all over the top of his bookcase again.

Closing the file with an irritable slap, Mitchell took a pair of scissors from his drawer and chopped the stems to within an inch of their lives.

Clare Chase began her confession with a question. She had got over her tears, had obviously made her decision about what she intended to reveal and regained her usual calm, even suggesting that they made more coffee. 'We'll drink it this time,' she announced, reaching for and biting into one of the ginger biscuits. Turning from refilling and switching on the kettle, she asked. 'Am I right in my impression that your relationship with your own husband is a painful one? I'm not,' she went on hastily, 'asking impertinent questions about the details. It's just the impression I get, because your kindness to me was as much in what you refrained from asking and saying as in anything more positive. I felt you understood my mixed feelings.'

Now Jennifer stared at her hands, which she kept perfectly still. When Clare embarked on an embarrassed apology, however, she held one up to silence it. 'My husband was killed as the result of a car bomb. He was a policeman too. My first reaction was to be furious with him for cheating me out of my chance to get back at him for something we had been quarrelling about. You're right, I'm not going into details, and you're right too that I perfectly understand your ambivalent feelings about Justin.' She picked up her coffee cup and began to drink, averting her eyes from Clarc.

As she began her account, Jennifer had the impression that she had prepared it carefully. 'We had an old-fashioned, fairy-tale church wedding. I said "for better, for worse". I even promised to obey him. I knew he wasn't the type to boss me about unreasonably. In return he promised to endow me with all his worldly goods, though they consisted of his share of the house deposit and a clapped-out Austin van.

'Apart from failing to get pregnant, for the next three years I had everything I'd ever wanted. Then, in the autumn of the following year, Justin began to suffer from blurred vision and severe pain in one eye.'

Jennifer sat perfectly still. Caroline Webster, who had said no more than 'Hello' since she came in with her sergeant, tried not to fidget on her upright chair behind the other two women. She scribbled as unobtrusively as possible. Clare's voice seemed to come from a long distance. 'The doctor gave him pain-killers and he soldiered on, but towards Christmas he was having dizzy spells and twice, in December, he wet the bed. I couldn't understand why he wasn't having hospital tests. He'd already had them, of course, but he pretended to go. Now I know why he wouldn't let me go with him.'

Her manner was becoming agitated. To hide it, Clare got up and continued her narrative, pacing the room. Knowing what it must cost her to describe her husband's deception in its sordid details, Jennifer was careful not to catch her eye. 'He gave me the news, said the doctor had called whilst I was out. Over Christmas the symptoms died down and he seemed very cheerful but I'd been to the library and read up the progress of the disease. The black depression came in February when his speech became slurred and walking difficult. He had to give up work for a while and he was confined to a wheelchair. Then, suddenly, most of those symptoms went away and ever since he was better on the whole.

'None of it made any difference to how I felt about him – though, of course, I got tired and worried. Then, last week, I saw the doctor myself, about something trivial but it mattered because I had to stay fit to look after him.' She seemed to feel it was in bad taste to trouble her GP with any complaint that was less serious than Justin's.

'Of course you did.'

'He said how much he admired my brave choice. I thought he meant sticking by Justin now he was ill. Then he went on talking and I realised–'

'That he'd known all the time that you were taking on more years of sickness than health?'

Clare was silent for so long that Jennifer bitterly regretted her impatient interruption. She had tried a different approach. 'What would you have done if he'd told you?'

'I don't see how I can know for sure, but I think I'd have done exactly the same, pushed the wheelchair willingly, had the house adapted. But he hadn't let me make that decision. I was so angry I couldn't contain myself. I didn't know you could love somebody and hate them at the same time. I felt used and insulted. I'd given things up because he couldn't share them, including lovemaking. Now I felt he'd cheated me out of them. I'd gone without them willingly but now I was determined to have them.'

Again, there was a long pause, separating her explanation of her motives from the account of her crime. This time Jennifer waited patiently. Clare came back to the table and drank the rest of her cold coffee before resuming her story. 'Warren was the only person Justin would allow to help him besides me. My sister often offered to sit with him for an evening but he wouldn't have her. I could understand it, but I didn't care any more. Last Thursday night, I asked Susan to come over. I told her I wouldn't be back till morning. I went round all the clubs till I found a good-looking bloke.

'He was obviously on the prowl and I asked him to spend the night with me. We went to a really grotty bed and breakfast place and I couldn't bear to let him touch me. I paid him the money for the room before I left in the morning. Susan didn't ask any questions. She never liked Justin from the start.'

Clare collapsed back into her chair as though the account had used up all her strength. 'Then it really did go on just as I've told you already.' She sat on in silence for some moments.

'And that's your confession?' Clare nodded once. Jennifer wanted to laugh. Then she wanted to cry.

10

Nathan Hillard thought he had been very clever. He learned that Bradford had been doing quite a lot to shine up its image as a tourist centre. By dint of making a few more calls he had found a very comfortable hotel, booked a show for Saturday evening at the Alhambra Theatre and reserved a table at an Indian restaurant recommended by the tourist information office. Then he discovered, to his delight, that, though he had never heard of it, Bradford contained a famous National Museum of Photography. Photography was Angie's particular interest and hobby.

By another happy coincidence, the school friend who had persuaded her to join the school photography club, which had taught her almost all she knew on the subject, now lived in a place called Queensbury, quite close to where they would be staying. Though Angie did not allow him to claim credit for this last pleasure of seeing Sarah again it certainly added to her generally positive attitude to their little trip.

Their meeting was quickly arranged by more phone calls, Angie being quite happy to run up the bill again now that peace was established. She and Sarah would visit this museum together, leaving him to his own devices on Friday afternoon. So, he could visit Cantrells without disobliging her.

Just before they left Barrow, the arrangements improved by yet another degree. Angela was invited to lunch with Sarah. Of course, Nathan was invited too but Sarah's husband would be working and Angela was relieved when Nathan assured her that he would not dream of inhibiting the flow of 'Do you remembers?' with his embarrassing presence.

Late Friday morning, therefore, found him accosting the gate-man at Cantrells, Cloughton, to be shown where he should park his car whilst he visited Mr Hillard. At the reception desk, he assumed his most charming manner. 'Not an appointment exactly. Are you the young lady I spoke to on Wednesday? From Barrow in Furness, to speak to Mr Hillard but he wasn't in. I was going to ring again, but then I realised I had to be in Bradford this morning, so, when I'd finished my business at Novell' – he'd done his homework on Bradford computer companies too – 'I came along in person.'

The girl's expression was apologetic. 'I'm afraid you're unlucky again. I'm terribly sorry but he's busy just now. This autumn and winter the mayor's taken it into his head to do a systematic tour of the town's businesses and it's our turn this morning. He turned up, complete with his chain of office, for a conducted tour and Mr Hillard volunteered to take him. The rest of us were very grateful. They shouldn't be long. They've been at it for nearly an hour and the mayor's easily bored. Besides, people who don't work here find it hard to understand what goes on.

'Tell you what, I'll just make out a visitor's badge for you and then I'll take you down to the canteen. At least I can guarantee you a decent cup of coffee. Can I have your name?'

'Neil Harvey,' Nathan told her quickly. He felt, uneasily, that the name had a familiar ring. He had an idea it belonged to a well-known sportsman and waited for some comment. The girl merely wrote it on a piece of card which she fitted into a plastic case with a clip for attaching it to his jacket. Nathan was not sure of the reason for his extra small deception. Maybe he expected Lee to make himself unavailable if he knew his brother had come looking for him.

Arriving in the canteen, the girl insisted on fetching his coffee on a tray, adding a sandwich and a chocolate biscuit. She presented it with a smile. 'I thought you might have a long wait. No, you can't pay for it. It's the least we can offer you for keeping you waiting twice.' Nathan was impressed. Lee had obviously found employers who could afford to pay him well.

'Oh!' Nathan looked up at the girl's startled little exclamation. 'I was going to say I'd let him know you'd arrived and send someone down to get you but here he is. The mayor must be sampling all the canteens too. Perhaps this whole idea is to economise on his housekeeping.' Chuckling at her own rather risqué little joke, she hurried away, heels tapping on the tiled floor.

From the shadow of the plastic palm under which he sat, Nathan watched the two men, the one still wearing his flashy gilt chain, as he ate his food and drank the coffee which more than fulfilled the receptionist's promise.

Beginning his Friday night briefing, Mitchell was not in the best of moods after an exchange with Kleever on the subject of the stalker. Apart from reporting no significant progress yet, Kleever had refused to be drawn on who was suspected, what measures were being taken or even who was deployed on the case. It had been a second repetition of an argument he had lost the first time round.

It didn't help that Ginny was on Kleever's side. 'I can imagine just what you said and how you said it,' she had retorted when he complained. 'You just convinced him that if you knew the men you'd hassle them till they'd told you everything. Then you'd muscle in, trying to do things your way and get yourself and probably half your shift in trouble when you lost your temper with whoever you suspect.'

She'd seemed to enjoy rubbing salt in the wound. 'He's quite open with me and he's doing all he can. There are a couple of uniforms temporarily in plain clothes, who've taken over from Clement.' Mitchell was deeply hurt when she omitted to name them, and deeply suspicious that Clement had been relieved of his turns at play watchdog. 'The super's got to work according to the rules and so have you,' she'd finished sententiously.

His team began to arrive, interrupting his orgy of self-pity. He could see they mostly felt discouraged and all felt exhausted. He invited Jennifer to report first.

She gave a modified version of her interview with Clare, appealing frequently to Caroline for confirmation of another point of view.

'There doesn't seem to be any incontrovertible evidence either way for Clare as the killer,' Caroline decided, 'but I don't think she did it. She's obviously gutted, not so much by the aborted one-night stand that she embarked on in a furious temper so much as by her last words to Justin. It was such a foul accusation to make and, if he listened in to Harriet's call, as she believes he did, he'd have understood quite well what she thought he'd done. I really think she loved him.'

Jennifer shook her head. 'I believe she loved him too, but loving him or being eaten up with remorse don't necessarily mean she didn't kill him. Violence seems to go against her nature, but then, so does behaving like a common prostitute.'

A fraction of the forensic report that he could not remember having absorbed rose to the surface of Mitchell's mind. 'SOCO found mucus on a pillow case pushed into the washing basket in the bathroom.'

'But he probably dribbled in his sleep or something. It's hardly evidence that she smothered him with a pillow.'

'Or that anyone else did.'

'At least we know what that final quarrel was about now. Anything else, Jen? Apart from the general weakness of her story.'

'I think the night on the tiles strengthens it.'

'How on earth?' Clement's was not the only puzzled murmur.

Jennifer tried to explain. 'When she'd done everything for him since his illness first became apparent, I found it hard to believe that being angry with him, whatever he'd done to deserve it, would cause her to neglect him. But, if the fault was on her side and she didn't know how to face him because of something she'd done, then I can understand.'

Clement still looked mystified as Jennifer passed on to the rest of her jotted notes. 'Two small points. First, we already know that Lee Hillard was supposed to begin the last month of his induction course with Justin on Monday. Apparently, Justin said to Clare that Mr Hillard would get a surprise when they met.'

'What do you think he meant?'

Jennifer shrugged. 'I only met him once. In fact, I wouldn't even describe it as meeting him. I talked to Clare in the kitchen and he went off to his study. It could mean they met before, I suppose, and that Hillard had forgotten about it, or didn't realise it was him.'

'It's not a common name. Wouldn't he have asked for details if he'd heard it, known someone of that name in the past?'

'Maybe Justin Chase considered himself the brains of the outfit. He might just have meant that Hillard would be surprised how hard he would have to work under him compared with the other two.'

'Anyway, Clare didn't know what he meant. Mr Hillard might have an idea

217

himself, I suppose. The only other thing was that Clare said Warren Chase is extremely hard up. There's family money to come, which will be his now, I suppose, but the parents aren't dispensing it freely whilst they're still alive. Any money he does have goes straight into the church.'

'I bet the parents will love that!'

Jennifer overrode the interruption. 'Clare says it's falling to bits. I went to look at it. It looks as if it's made of old bits of Anderson shelters that are rusting away. And his car's given up the ghost. The church is supposed to provide him with an income but he lives on social security which he mostly gives away.'

'So, where's the money willed now?'

Jennifer shook her head impatiently. 'I suppose it's still as it was. The parents won't have a new will as first priority before there's even been a funeral.'

Mitchell nodded. 'All right. What else have we got?'

A series of negative reports followed that left them all even more depressed. Mitchell began a summary of their findings. 'The chap who's calling the pregnant girls knows somehow when their phones have been tapped. Faye and Megan haven't been bothered since the trace was put on their line. Neither, incidentally, has my wife, at least by telephone. Someone knew it was still safe to ring Harriet Bradley's number.'

'So, are we looking for someone who works for BT?'

'Maybe, if he's also psychic and knows who's pregnant as soon as they do.'

'Or we're looking for the sort of person other people confide in, or some sort of figure like a social worker whose job or whose nature it is to know a lot of other people's business.'

'I think, if I were pregnant, whether or not I was glad about it, I'd confide in a woman friend rather than a man,' Jennifer opened her mouth to disagree with Caroline but she was interrupted.

'You mentioned your wife, sir.'

Mitchell blinked at the young uniformed officer. After nearly 6 weeks 'sir' still felt strange. 'Yes?'

'We haven't found out yet how Steve Thacker knew about Mrs Mitchell's problems. Do you think we should–?'

'I'm afraid,' Mitchell told him stiffly, 'that's been put outside my jurisdiction. You'll have to ask Superintendent Kleever.' His telephone rang. He listened, then smiled. His shift waited for him to relieve their curiosity. 'There's a Nathan Hillard downstairs. By devious means he's traced his missing brother. Since the said brother was going to get a surprise from our victim, I'd better go and have a word with him.'

Gemma Platt rolled away from the middle of the bed to the extreme edge before letting her bulky body relax. The bigger she got, the more she wished Steve would leave her alone but she daren't refuse him. She had plucked up courage a couple of weeks ago to suggest it was uncomfortable for her and not good for his baby. He had not been angry but neither had he had any sympathy. 'Tough,' he'd told her. 'I said to get rid of it and you wouldn't so you'll just have to put up with it.'

'But it's yours, Steve,' she'd protested. 'How could I?'

He'd been mollified until another thought had struck. 'So long as you're not suggesting I have to pay for it.'

'You don't pay for Kayleigh.'

'No, and I hope you know better than to try that on an' all.'

His arm muscles flexed and she changed the subject hurriedly. 'What were you looking so pleased about when you came in?' He told her. Gemma's eyes widened. 'That mucky beggar who rang me is trying it on with an inspector's missus?'

Steve nodded. 'Bloody good thing. They won't get their fingers out for us but if he's beggaring about with one of theirs they'll be shooting with all their guns.'

'That lady sergeant was very nice with me

last week.' She glanced at Steve to check that this had not annoyed him. He was lying on his back, grinning at the ceiling. 'How did you find out?'

'Worked it out for meself, didn't I? That young copper's car's been parked outside the Mitchell house on and off for ages. I'd been wondering why. Then when your nosy sergeant came round it suddenly came to me. Why were they making such a fuss about a few phone calls and nobody getting hurt? It was a shot in the dark but I could tell from her face that I'd hit target.'

'You are clever.' He wasn't but she knew she was clever enough for them both. Clever, but not brave, otherwise she'd have taken Kayleigh and left him long ago. A thought stuck her. Could he? Possibly? She was certain he wasn't the caller who had upset her. Steve used shorter, ruder words for what that caller had had to say. But would it have entered his head to get his own back on that copper Mitchell while he had the chance? Had he made some copy-cat calls to his missus? That was easier to believe than that he worked things out like he said, just from seeing a parked car. He wasn't without his share of cunning. He had an eye to the main chance. 'Steve, it wasn't you that…?'

She'd spoken without thinking. She couldn't be as clever as she'd thought or she'd learn from experience to keep a rein on her tongue. The duvet cover wasn't much protection against his fists, but, after a couple of blows, the attack stopped. After a moment she stuck her head out from under the covers. Steve was getting dressed to the accompaniment of her father's voice echoing in the stairwell. 'Gemma! Why the hell have you shut the bloody shop?'

Her father was in his forties now but he was still fit and a big man. A fair bit bigger than Steve.

Nathan Hillard's reply to Mitchell's polite greeting was, 'Look, I've got to be away from here by four.'

'Got another appointment?'

'Sort of.' Nathan explained why the DI's enquiry had to be fitted round the convenience and appeasement of his witness's wife. Highley, the desk sergeant, smiled to himself at the expression on Mitchell's face.

Deadpan, Mitchell suggested that a call could be made to the Museum of Photography.

Nathan shook his head. 'That would give the game away. She'd realise I came to Bradford for my purposes and not as a treat for her.'

Amused, Mitchell drew him back to the point. 'I hear you've been clever enough to locate your brother. I hope you haven't come here expecting us to force him to return to the family fold.'

Nathan was shaking his head. 'I haven't found my brother.'

'Not found him?'

'I went to Cantrells and found the mayor having lunch, complete with chain that kept clunking against his plate.' Mitchell leaned against the reception counter, quite happy for the younger Hillard to wring the last drop of drama from the situation. 'He was sitting with a man whom everyone at Cantrells calls Lee Hillard. It wasn't my brother.'

Megan Scott waved her visitor goodbye as Fay Weston came downstairs.

'Did I hear Colin's voice?'

'Yes, he came to see how his infant was doing. Did you finish your chapter?'

Faye scowled. 'No. That wasn't part of the bargain.'

'I'm not trying to rush the book. It was only a friendly enquiry.'

'Stop deliberately misunderstanding me. Friendly is about all we've been lately.'

'Sorry. I just don't feel like anything else. I'm sure we'll be back to normal when the baby's here. I didn't know being pregnant would be either so tiring or so absorbing.'

'I meant having Colin around wasn't part of the bargain. This infant will have the two of us. It's not going to need a father.'

'That's what I've just told him, which I think is why he didn't return my wave.'

Faye's glower faded a little and she allowed Megan to make her a cup of tea.

Harriet was back in the surgery waiting-room. It felt familiar to her. She was beginning to feel more at home here than anywhere else except her classroom and her own bedroom, which now had its furniture back in the normal position. She reached across to the table for a copy of *Fast Forward*. Then, seeing Mummy's slight frown, reached a little further and picked up a copy of the *Dalesman*.

She leafed through it idly, pitying the folk who had submitted these jokes if they really found them funny. She wondered who in the world could be interested in a step-by-step account of some old dodderer as he dragged himself up Pen-y-ghent. Keeping the magazine open in front of her she listened to the gossip of several mothers-to-be behind her. She'd heard one of the other people behind the counter mutter to Mrs Johnson that it was tactless of Mummy to bring her today when there was an antenatal clinic. Mrs Johnson had merely sniffed.

A surreptitious look behind her told Harriet that the size of the baby bumps was various and that none of the women was known to her. She could sympathise with the gory details they shared of their morning sickness, haemorrhoids and backache. She was pleased and grateful to have been spared the latter two.

Exhausting their symptoms at last, the ladies fell to speculating on the sex, potential characteristics and chosen names of their forthcoming offspring. Harriet had never reached the stage of believing that the thing growing inside her was a person. She had thought of it more as a malignancy, growing and poisoning her life and her future. She'd evidently been expected to feel some grief for the loss of her child. She had heard the hospital nurse telling Mummy not to hesitate to consult her GP if she thought Harriet would benefit from counselling.

That was not the reason they were here, however. Mummy thought Harriet would benefit from being on the pill. 'It would make me feel easier in my mind after the shock you've given us. You mustn't think of it in any way as licence to go on misbehaving yourself, but you've fallen once and we must think about your reputation.'

Harriet was thinking about it too. It would improve her street cred no end if she could produce from her pocket a pack of contraceptive pills, labelled with her own name. The buzzer for them to go into the surgery broke into a reverie in which

Melanie Patchett was clapping her on the back and inviting her to 'Join the club, kid.' She almost jumped out of her skin and it took several moments for her to collect herself and follow Mummy out of the waiting-room.

'I think,' Mummy observed grimly, 'that we'd better get you something for your nerves too.'

Nathan Hillard was now sitting in Mitchell's office, glancing ostentatiously at his watch before he replied to each of Mitchell's questions.

'What did you say when you accosted him?'

'I didn't accost him.'

'Why not?'

Nathan gave Mitchell a pitying glance. 'I would have thought that was obvious. I want to know what the hell this chap's playing at, masquerading as my brother. If he knew I'd sussed him, he'd be quite likely to do a runner.'

Mitchell regarded his witness with a little more respect. 'Good thinking. Any more suggestions?'

'Yes. I was sorting things out on my way here. I think somebody with a zoom lens should take pictures of him. Then they could be shown round to see if anyone recognises him.'

'What's your job? Ever thought of being a detective?' Mitchell could see that this was the most exciting thing that had ever happened to Nathan Hillard and that his enthusiastic efforts to solve the puzzle might well obstruct the official enquiry.

'I'm an accountant – well, training to be. It's more boring than I expected. Are you offering me a reference if I decide to change course?'

Mitchell grinned. 'Does this man look like your brother?'

Nathan thought for a moment. 'If you wrote down a description of Lee, this chap would fit the bill. He's about five feet nine, with brown hair, brown eyes, sallow skin... It would fit me too, wouldn't it? But, if you mean could anyone who knew Lee possibly mistake this man for him, even from a distance, then no. His manner's different. He's a flashier dresser than Lee. His face is fatter and he's, well, completely different. Since he doesn't know me, I moved over to the next table to his to finish my coffee and had a good hard look at him. I'm pretty sure I've never seen him before.'

He looked at his watch again, making Mitchell feel suddenly irritable. 'For Pete's sake, man, stop it! Do you want us to find out what's going on here or not?'

'I want to know what's going on. Yes.'

For the moment Mitchell ignored the

implication of this form of reply. 'Then fix your woman now and then give me the whole of your attention.'

Nathan finally chose to risk Angie's displeasure rather than risk having no part in this only adventure ever to happen to him. He accepted the invitation to use Mitchell's phone and left a message at the café where she and Sarah were supposed to be meeting him for tea. He grew quite bold. Would the proprietor please tell Angela to carry on with the meal and not wait. He would pay for it, of course. He was helping with police enquiries. He was not in any trouble and when he met her back at the hotel – by the way, she must ride in a taxi at his expense – he would explain.

Mitchell tried and failed to imagine Ginny's reaction at receiving a similar message from himself.

Proud of himself, Nathan pulled his sweater sleeve firmly over his watch face and announced himself to be at Mitchell's disposal.

'How do you know,' Mitchell demanded, 'that you're not in any trouble?'

'I came here of my own accord to report.'

'That's just what you'd have done if you'd bumped Lee off yourself and infiltrated this other chap...' The expression of alarm on Nathan's face almost persuaded Mitchell that he had hit on the truth. Then he pulled himself together. For goodness' sake, he was supposed to be a DI now! 'Forget it. It wasn't very funny. I suggest you start as far back as you can remember and tell me everything about Lee that you can think of.'

'School and so on, you mean? How could that–'

'Trust me.'

'All right. He was four years old when I was born but he didn't grow up very fast. I soon overtook him. Once we were of a height, people thought that I was the older one.'

'Why was that?'

'I think because of Mother. She doesn't make friends very easily so she became obsessed with Lee instead.'

'Why not both of you?'

'After four years she'd got used to concentrating on him and left me alone. So much so that I often felt left out. I thought he was the favourite, especially when he went to university and I wasn't encouraged to go as well. I was quite bright too. I think they wanted to stop him becoming an independent adult. If he became a student, it would be longer before he had any money of his own and was in a position to make a permanent move away. To please himself.'

'Go back a bit.'

'Yes?'

'How was he at school?'

'Clever. Always top of his class. Useless at games.'

'Did he find it difficult to relate to people too?'

'He never went around with a crowd like I did. He had special friends – not that I'm implying what that suggests nowadays.'

'You don't think he was gay?'

Nathan looked surprised. 'I'm fairly sure not, thought I can't remember him ever having a girlfriend.'

'So, who were these special friends?'

'At school he spent most of his time with Stuart Pearson. Why?'

'Carry on for now. Did the friendship last?'

'Not after school.' He anticipated the next question. 'Lee went to UMIST. Did Computer Science there.'

'And then who were his friends?'

Nathan looked alarmed at the battery of questions. 'I suppose he got the nearest he'd ever been to belonging to a gang for those three years. Maybe it was because Mother wasn't around to embarrass him. He never brought them home while he was a student, but one of them lived just over in Barrow and my parents met him later.'

'Did your parents know the other boy, Stuart Pearson?'

'Yes, he lived nearby. Lee talked about his university mates. Two of them especially.

230

The Barrow one was called Charlie something, Potts maybe, or Potter. Occasionally
Lee came over to see me and always looked
Charlie up. We didn't mention it because
the old dears didn't like him. Mother didn't
like Lee having friends at all, but even Dad
said Charlie was a bit of a slippery
customer.' Mitchell noted the change of
tense. Did he think Lee was dead? Did he
know he was dead? 'I can't remember the
name of the other. He lived miles away. I
think he got married. Why do you want to
know about his school and university
friends?'

'Because we've already heard all this stuff
about his mother dominating him.'
Nathan's face asked the question. 'From the
gentleman you're so interested in. So, he's
someone who knows all about your family
circumstances. Move on now, tell me
something about the people Lee worked
with.'

'In Cumbria?' Mitchell nodded. 'He never
really had a job. He did his Master's degree
after finals and then various bits of research,
on grants. He's very clever but not a lot of
use, if you get me. He didn't seem to have
any mates, just Mum and Dad and a lot of
bits of paper to prove who he was.' Again
there was a slip into the past tense.

'And you never met Charlie?'

Nathan shook his head. 'No, but it isn't

him. He was killed in a big fire at his firm a few months ago. Come to think about it, I do have a vague idea what he looked like. His picture was in the paper.'

'And you can't tell me anything about the third member of this trio?'

'Not at the moment. Something might come back to me.'

Mitchell handed over a small white card. 'You'd better have my telephone extension number then, just in case.'

Nathan's hand froze in the air as he reached out for it. 'That's it!'

'What's it?'

'You said "just in case".' He had sprung up from his chair and now slowly subsided on to it again. 'That was the other man's silly nickname. His real name is Justin Chase.'

11

With several new aspects of the case opened up by Nathan Hillard's visit, Mitchell was rather sorry that he had dismissed his shift when he left them. He considered calling Jennifer in again, but then pictured her delightedly joining her daughters for tea. Was that a good reason for a DI to do without his sergeant as a sounding board for his plans and theories? It occurred to him that he had an even better sounding board at home as well as a bigger crowd of children to have tea with.

Returned to the bosom of his family, Mitchell found himself in the role of referee as Declan and Caitlin argued about whose turn it was to choose the book for their bedtime story. Having been missing at this hour for several days, and Virginia being presently busy with the twins, he had only his wits to rely on. He decided to cast his vote according to his own preference and asked, 'Which books are you wanting, anyway?'

'*The Owl who was Afraid of the Dark*,' they chorused.

'So, if you'd discussed it quietly instead of

screaming at each other, you'd have realised there was nothing to quarrel about and we'd be half-way through the chapter by now,' he told them smugly.

They settled, one each side of him, on the settee. Caitlin found the page for him and smiled ingratiatingly. 'It's still my turn, and we're having this book because I choosed it,' she whispered audibly.

Mitchell winked at Declan who raised his eyes to the ceiling with an exclamation. 'Women!'

Mitchell began rather laboriously on chapter three, 'Dark is Fun', in which a baby owl visited a bonfire. After two paragraphs, Caitlin complained. 'You aren't doing all the bird voices like Mummy does.'

Mitchell was offended. 'No, I'm doing them like Daddy does.'

Declan shook his head. 'No, you aren't. You're doing them like an ordinary person.'

'It's my way or no story.'

They subsided and Mitchell read on. As the chapter ended, Declan almost burst his father's ear drum with a remarkably accurate owl screech. 'I've been practising,' he announced, proudly.

Mitchell rubbed at his assaulted organ. 'Well, it's perfect now. You needn't practise any more.'

Virginia came in grinning. 'I've run their bath. They'll get themselves clean. You can just supervise to make sure there isn't a flood.'

Mitchell sent the two older children to undress whilst he went to play with the twins. He knew he was risking his wife's wrath but he got away with it and, by the time he went downstairs, Sinead and Michael were asleep and the other two children very nearly so. 'Mr Kleever came to see us,' was Declan's last remark, the thumb in his mouth muffling his voice. Mitchell felt reassured that the hunt for his wife's stalker was being given its due importance.

Giving her husband the opening he wanted, Virginia kicked her shoes off and settled where Caitlin had been, tucked her feet beneath her. 'I'm ready for my story now.'

Obligingly, he regaled her with an account of the day's developments and, as usual, she heard him out without interruption.

'So, what now?' she demanded as Mitchell reached Nathan Hillard's departure.

'Well, someone will have to do a general check in Cumbria – go to Millton and Barrow as well possibly. And then someone will have to go to Cantrells again.'

'Who will it be safe to see there? This impostor chap might be in league with some of his colleagues.'

'In league to do what?'

'I don't know. If this impostor is in the

MD's good books he might be given a warning to disappear.'

'I suppose so, but we'll still have to go. I'd like to have this bogus Hillard tailed but I don't suppose Kleever will stump up for that. It seems logical to me to assume he has a connection with Justin Chase's death but we can't prove it and, whatever the technical crime he's committed in impersonating Lee Hillard, it doesn't rank with murder.'

Virginia gave him a hard look. 'You're not telling me you won't do exactly what you want and let the powers that be shout about it afterwards?'

Mitchell ignored the question, busy recalling each stage of his conversation with Nathan Hillard. Virginia eventually broke in on his musings. 'You only have the brother's word that it isn't Lee.'

'He'll be found out pretty easily if he's having us on. He didn't strike me as that type of nutter and he did suggest taking photographs and showing them round. What about your day? Declan tells me you were honoured with a visit from his lordship. I'm glad you're getting some information. He refuses to discuss anything to do with your problem in front of me. It's ludicrous that he doesn't at least keep me informed about what's going on!'

'It's your own fault. You're your own worst enemy. You never stop asking him and he knows you'd interfere if you were in on all his plans, not that there are any to speak of. He came to tell me there were no prints on that card that came with the flowers, except a small one of mine.'

'You let them have your prints?'

'Of course.'

'You didn't tell me.'

'I didn't think you'd need telling that I would co-operate by submitting to standard procedures. I'm very surprised, though, that they found a print of mine. I picked the card up very carefully by the edges.'

'I shouldn't have to get this from you!' Mitchell banged his fist on the back of his chair. 'It's stupid!'

'It isn't stupid. It's protocol. You're happy enough when it's working for you. I'll tell you what, I won't cook any supper. I'll ring for a takeaway and you can make the coffee.'

Mitchell managed a half-hearted smile. The evening was looking up in some ways.

With the telephone in her hand, Virginia paused. 'By the way, a warning.'

'Yes?'

'Declan's teaching Caitlin to do the owl screech.'

Mr James Cantrell insisted on being addressed as Jim. Then, having enquired for DC Webster's forename, he peppered his conversation with 'Carolines' as good business training demanded. His handshake had left her wondering if she would ever play the piano again and his deliberate, unrelenting eye contact made her want to laugh.

To give herself time to weigh him up, she asked what had brought him to England, and he described his early career in a deep south American accent. He had been with an American company called Doctor Design, 'kind of a cute name.' It had prescribed for whatever ailed the electronics community.

'We designed circuit boards in practically no time, dealt with problems firms' own engineers couldn't solve, showed them how to manufacture and market people's ideas for products.'

Caroline interrupted to repeat her question. He shrugged. 'Well, a hell of a lot of us were doing it back home. My company got squeezed out. Over here it wasn't all so far on.'

Caroline tried to avoid the dazzling smile. 'So, what does your company here do?'

'The idea is, Caroline, that companies with good ideas but inadequate engineering resources can contract for services. We offer cradle-to-grave solutions, from engineering phase, through prototype to pilot run to full volume production.' He was obviously quoting from his company's promotion material and Caroline wondered if he had written it himself. 'Our success is based on a simple formula. "Do it quick. Do it right first time".' He began to enumerate successful projects.

It occurred to Caroline that, apart from a single conventional expression of shock and sorrow at the death of his colleague, Cantrell had made no mention of him. 'I get maybe twenty calls a week from people who think they have an idea. There's the rocket scientist with the off-the-wall, half-baked scheme that sounds cute, Caroline, but when you look at the feasibility of implementing it at a reasonable cost, when you look at the market challenges, Caroline, you see this guy doesn't have a clue.'

The door opened to admit an employee who asked a question that Caroline made no attempt to understand. Cantrell wrinkled his nose. 'You need Lee to tell you about that, Neil, but he's sick this morning. Try Jonathan.'

The door closed and Cantrell turned back to his visitor. 'Ninety per cent of these people, Caroline, are in the rocket scientist category. There's something fundamentally flawed in what they're trying to do, but they don't know because they don't have a broad enough background. They say, Caroline, that they have lots of friends who would spend ten thousand pounds for their whizzmobang but it doesn't work that way. Would your enemies buy it, is what you've got to ask. I've seen so many people who've sunk thousands of hours into a project that has absolutely no chance because they didn't have a multi-disciplined view, Caroline, of what it is their project needs to get to the market place. And make somebody a million–'

'How did Justin Chase fit into all this?' Caroline cut in desperately.

He wagged his finger at her. 'I'm coming to that, Caroline. We hatched the plan between us. He had his UMIST degree–'

'But, where did you meet him?'

'Back home. He'd been head-hunted by a guy in my company but it folded soon after. He decided to become an industrial consultant because he'd watched some guys he thought weren't very good making forty and fifty dollars an hour. He thought, Caroline, if he was a good consultant he could make eighty thousand dollars in half the year and spend it in the rest. He approached me because I'm a good marketing man. Plus I had a bachelor's degree in electrical engineering with minors in computer science and economics.

'It was my idea to bring it over here,' he went on, anticipating Caroline's question. 'We got so much business we became workaholics. Justin was working ninety hours,

Caroline, cut back from a hundred and ten when the MS hit him. Work was pouring in. Too much. We put the rates up and there was still too much. We began to subcontract to friends. Justin's garage was the lab and assembly area. He had a massive library in his bedroom. The living-room was the office, the bedroom was the living-room and the conference room was a corner of the dining-room where the table was! The copy machine was in the entry foyer. You had to stand sideways, Caroline, to get in and out.'

'You lived together?'

'Only for a few months. Then Clare came on the scene and there was plenty coming in so I got my own place. Clare did the accounts on the first PC we bought. We came here in early '92. We had fifteen employees by then and a stable of sub-contractors and a state-of-the-art lab. Three years before, we'd still been trying to pick up freelance consultant jobs to pay the bills.'

'And now?' Caroline listened to a torrent of facts and figures supporting Cantrell's assertions that the company was expanding rapidly in Britain and on the verge of establishment on the Continent. When he paused for breath, she asked the question that had been puzzling her for some time. 'I don't understand why you're entrusting this new venture in Hamburg to a man who's done nothing commercially successful since he qualified.'

Cantrell beamed. 'Good question, Caroline. Neither had Justin till he met me. Justin was an ideas man and so is Lee. I'm the market expert, Caroline. I was behind Justin and now I'm behind Lee.'

'But he'll be in Germany.'

Cantrell shrugged. 'What's a few miles, Caroline, when you've got airplanes and computers? Lee's the new product I'm selling!'

On Saturday morning Jennifer tapped on Mitchell's door before opening it in her usual manner. She checked herself as she saw he was using the telephone. Tight-lipped, he motioned to her to come in and to sit down. The call finished without his speaking another word and he replaced the receiver with deliberate restraint.

In no mood for treading carefully, Jennifer demanded, 'Who's upset you?'

'Bloody Kleever has!'

Jennifer was startled. Benny was no bootlicker, was often slightly less than polite, but, even in police company where the air was often blue, he rarely swore. His Irish Catholic mother had refused to countenance it in his early teens when most boys first learned and practised this section of their vocabulary. She waited for some clue to the reason for his displeasure. When none came, she asked, 'What's he done?'

'Sent me to Cumbria to follow up this Lee Hillard business.'

'It's your case. What did you expect?'

Mitchell shrugged and held up a hand as Jennifer drew breath to berate him. 'I've heard it all already from Ginny. I've got a job to do and she's being well looked after. Actually, if we're picking bones…'

'You've got one to pick with me.' Unruffled, Jennifer waited for his complaint.

'It's about Clement. I'm getting the distinct impression that you seriously suspect him of being Ginny's stalker. For goodness' sake, why?'

Jennifer sighed. 'I haven't any grounds for it that would be news to you. When I try to follow up the idea, it seems a nonsense, but when I try to ignore it, it won't go away. Losing his wife and baby is quite enough to unbalance anybody. He spends all his spare time hanging round your house. Ginny says she spent a lot of time talking to him at the super's party. What really sticks in my gullet is that fake call to a non-existent domestic…'

'We get plenty of those, surely? And what following up have you done? You haven't mentioned anything to me.'

'Because I knew you wouldn't take it seriously. All I did was find the switchboard girl who took the call.'

'And?'

'She said the caller was breathless. The message was given in a whisper. When she asked for a repeat, whoever it was hung up. She thought it was a hoax even at that stage but she didn't dare ignore it.'

'But that call could have been made by anyone who wanted Clement out of the way.'

Jennifer shook her head. 'No member of the public would expect Clement to be the officer chosen to be sent.'

'I suppose not. Who did pick him?'

'She doesn't know.'

They were both silent, contemplating the unpleasant consequences of taking this particular enquiry further. Each respected the other's judgement and was nonplussed by their present disagreement. Finally, Mitchell got up and irritably pushed his ivy plant further along the top of the bookcase. 'Who put this thing there?'

'How should I know?'

Mitchell pushed the pot back to its original position and sat down again. 'There isn't enough to pass it on to Kleever. If anyone else had to come to me about it, I'd have kicked them out of my office and preferably off the case. I'll keep my eyes skinned and I'll be careful where I send him.'

Realising the size of the concession Mitchell had made, Jennifer nodded and changed the subject. 'Did you get anywhere with the mobile number in Ginny's letter?'

Mitchell looked up guiltily and Jennifer grinned. 'You'll just have to hope they don't tell whoever Kleever puts on to it that they've been asked that already. Fat chance! Whose was it, anyway?'

'I haven't heard anything yet.'

'Is he getting bolder – or just more reckless because he's not managing to rattle Ginny enough?'

'How much rattling is enough? Anyway, he might think the number isn't going to be any help to us.'

'Or he's showing off. You know, "You can't catch me even when I give you huge clues." By the way, I checked out the chemist in the precinct that Harriet mentioned.' Mitchell blinked. 'She thought she heard something like the warning buzzer on his door during some calls. His name's Threlfall. He made some telling comments on the Bradleys but I didn't get anything useful.'

Mitchell was not pleased by the sudden change of subject. It seemed Jennifer was going to heed Kleever's warning not to discuss the stalker with him. Still, he could not envy her predicament, and it occurred to him that she had been the one who had introduced the subject this morning. His manner thawed as he described to her his session with Nathan Hillard.

'He kept using the past tense when he was talking about his brother but I suppose that could be because it's three months since he saw him.' He described Nathan's suggestions for identifying Lee's impersonator. 'The only difference between him and us is that he thinks the third or fourth person approached will say, "Oh, yes, I know him!" We know that we've got to go through the whole charade and that it'll achieve sod all.'

Raucous laughter on the stairs heralded the rest of the shift. They crowded into Mitchell's office and he grinned round at them. 'You all went off early last night. Knowing how dedicated you all are I know that those who didn't stay up to solve the case all on their own last night will have got up early this morning to do it.'

They eyed one another until Jennifer broke the silence. 'Since you'll be away in Cumbria, we thought we'd all take one off so as to be totally refreshed when you come back.'

Clement looked alarmed. 'I did have one idea,' he offered. The rest eyed him suspiciously, Mitchell and Jennifer carefully did not. Clement's idea was that he should approach a pub acquaintance who worked for Compaq to see if he could pick up any Cantrells gossip.

Mitchell thought that he was unlikely to pick up anything germane to the case. There was a childish mutter of 'Creep' from the middle of the room and Mitchell wondered if his constable's only problem was that he was a boss-botherer. For the moment he merely observed that it could do no harm and Clement subsided. Mitchell continued his briefing. 'The biggest problem is that we don't know how many villains we're chasing. Someone is frightening pregnant women, someone killed Justin Chase and someone is stalking my wife. Are we looking for one perpetrator, or two or three?'

'We've also got some sort of a fraud case,' Jennifer reminded him.

'Impersonation, actually,' put in a PC whose name Mitchell could not remember but to whom he had taken a definite dislike.

Mitchell ignored him. 'Go on, Jennifer.'

She spoke more slowly than usual, thinking aloud. 'It seems reasonable to me to assume that Justin Chase was killed because he would have called our Mr X's bluff. Mr X had an income at risk of...'

She glanced hopefully at Caroline, who shrugged. 'Jonathan was a bit jealous, I think. He guessed at forty-odd thousand and was certain that there was the potential to double that and more if the Hamburg business was properly developed.'

Jennifer nodded acknowledgement of

Caroline's contribution and turned back to Mitchell. 'Are we going to arrest him?'

Mitchell found he had made his decision without realising it. 'Yes, we are, but not quite yet. I want him interviewed once more without him realising we're on to him. I just want him asked general questions about Justin Chase and why he didn't volunteer his previous acquaintance with him when he learned of his death. Whoever goes will have to be careful. We've no evidence they'd ever met since college. I want something definite established before we bring him in.'

'It's easy to see why a Lee-impostor would keep out of Chase's way,' Caroline remarked, looking puzzled, 'but it seems odd that Chase didn't make a move to arrange a meeting with an old friend.'

Clement looked anxious to be helpful. 'What if no names were mentioned, just a "Could you help us out with the new man?"'

Jennifer shook her head. 'I think it's more likely that he didn't want to be seen in a wheelchair by someone who had thought of him as something of a sportsman.'

'Maybe,' put in the pushy PC, 'he was offended because it would have been far easier for Hillard to have visited him and he didn't.'

'Quite likely!' The constable glanced at Mitchell, suspecting irony. 'Caroline?' Mitchell invited, seeing from her face that a theory was brewing.

'I think they were possibly not such good friends as Lee pretended. Nathan Hillard has said – well, hinted, anyway – that his brother wasn't very popular at school. Maybe he came back from university claiming a big friendship with someone clever and sporty, as Justin Chase was then, to bolster his own image.'

Now tongues were loosened, and theories, likely and unlikely, came thick and fast. Delighted, Mitchell sat back to listen.

'What if something had happened in the past, some injury that Chase had done to Hillard, so that he knew he was in danger from him?'

'But we don't think it was Hillard who killed him, do we? It was Mr X pretending–'

'Just a minute. Did Justin Chase already know it wasn't Lee, so he didn't expect the impostor to recognise him and...'

This theory suddenly ran out of steam and there was silence until Clement was inspired again. 'Did Chase know this man wasn't the real Lee because he was in on whatever deception was being practised–'

'Surely not.' Mitchell was irritated by Jennifer's interruption. Clement had a right to finish making his suggestion. 'He was never left alone for more than ... well...'
Aware of Mitchell's displeasure, Jennifer

thought better of her objection.

Clement returned to his theory in triumph. 'Ah, but he's left in his study with his computer all the time. His wife doesn't seem to have interfered when he was shut in there working.'

Mitchell let his team's imaginings go on for a few more seconds before demanding loudly of no one in particular, 'Does everyone think I've offered a prize for the most far-fetched notion to be produced?' The suggestions ceased.

Mitchell grinned. 'I'm afraid no award will be made in this section as no entries reached the required standard. Seriously, any one of them might be the key to the case but we haven't time for any more. Keep thinking but make sure your theories fit the facts we already know and remember there are a lot more that we haven't discovered yet. Let's get foraging soon, but, whilst you're in the mood for brainstorming, see if you can find me a few reasons why a malicious caller might want to harass pregnant women with this specially nasty suggestion.'

'He thinks he has a religious call?'

Mitchell turned to the uniformed man who had spoken. 'Voices, you mean? Like Sutcliffe claimed? I suppose I've heard worse ideas. What else?'

'He's frustrated because he's sterile.'

'He's had a one-night stand and picked up something nasty and he's venting his anger and fear?'

'Someone who does have AIDS so his marriage is doomed.'

Suddenly and guiltily, Mitchell remembered Dr Simpson describing a miserable morning surgery during which he had listened to Clare Chase's troubles and confirmed that one of his patients was HIV positive. He scribbled a note to himself to see Dr Simpson again which had the effect of drying up his shift's second flurry of theories. Time was getting on. He reached for his pile of action sheets.

'Clement, see if you can have lunch with your Compaq friend. We might even put it on expenses, provided you see Steve Thacker first. We want to know everything he can tell us, and especially how he knew about my wife's harassment. Whilst you're doing that, Caroline can keep his lady friend entertained. We want to know everything she can tell us about the afore-mentioned Thacker.'

Caroline grinned. 'If we can prise them apart.'

'Drag her in if you have to.'

'Sir, she's six months pregnant at least!'

'Then you'll have to think of something else. Jennifer, I want you to organise a tail on our impostor. He mustn't be alerted so make it a lot of people doing short stints.'

'Should I ask...?'

'Friend Kleever? Yes, you'd better. He's going to moan about money so get it all sorted first, then ask him to do it and make helpful suggestions till he's confirmed all you've done.' He raised his voice to drown a couple of suggestions that this was an unfair comment on the new super. 'I know he's not another Petty, but Jen will never reach DI until she's learned to manage a super. I'm passing on my five weeks' experience. Once you've arranged to have him followed – the bogus Hillard, I mean, not Kleever – I want you to go and see him.'

'He won't be at work on a Saturday, will he?'

'The photographer presently hiding behind my bedroom curtains rang to tell me he's obligingly clearing out his garden shed. When he got a bit warm, lifting heavy things, he even more obligingly took off his anorak so we'll get a good look at him. If he's going anywhere after he's finished, he'll presumably need a shower first so if you hurry you'll catch him in. You can get off now.'

'Right.' Jennifer went to the door but paused there. 'I've been wondering...'

'Don't keep us in suspense.'

'Well, whether Lee meant to leave home and take the job and the bogus Lee took

252

over at interview time. Or did he get rid of Lee in some way and then look around for a job some distance away so that he could use his stolen qualifications?'

'Mr Cantrell may help us there.' Jennifer nodded and departed. 'Caroline, how well did you hit it off with him?'

'Well enough. Have I to go again?'

Mitchell amended her sheet and passed it to her. 'Ask him for the job application and anything else with what purports to be Hillard's handwriting and signature on it. We can show them to his parents and maybe his university teachers.'

'Could we be putting the blame on the wrong person?'

Mitchell frowned. 'Sorry?'

Caroline clarified her question. 'What if Lee really is going to Germany, but for some reason can't show his face at Cantrells' Cloughton headquarters? This bloke might be holding the fort here until Lee can take up the position in Germany where no one knows him.'

'That's stupid! Why on earth...' The bumptious PC subsided into the unfriendly silence and Mitchell was grateful for a just reason to rebuke him.

'Go on, Caroline. I'm not sure I'm with you, though. Persuade me.'

'You said that, according to Nathan, Lee had "special friends" and had never had a girlfriend. What if he's gay and his substitute is his partner? Suppose Lee stole something, not money or goods but perhaps an idea or some information from a computer. He can't turn up at Cantrells because someone there knows about it.'

'Wouldn't they know his name, in that case?'

'I suppose so. I haven't thought it through. It's only just occurred to me that it might be Lee rather than our Mr X who's organised what's going on.'

'What about when he has to come back from Germany? Or what if pictures are taken at company dinners and social occasions?'

'Well, there'd be risks. All criminals take them and a lot get away with taking pretty daring ones. Presumably his partner would go to Germany too. If Lee kept him well informed he could probably take over again for trips back here. He's obviously holding his own at the moment.'

'Right. See what you can find out to support any of these far-fetched fancies, without asking any leading questions. I should ask Cantrell to meet you at his office. That way there'll be less chance of someone spiriting documents away.'

As Caroline noted down her instructions, Clement asked, 'Who are we showing the pictures of the bogus Hillard to?'

'I'll take them with me to Cumbria if they're ready in time. Or I'll get them sent on. If that doesn't get us anywhere we can bang him up here, once we've unearthed something specific against him to justify it. Then we can stick his face in all the papers. Now it's high time we were all moving.'

His telephone range. Mitchell lifted the receiver, waving to his shift to take the rest of the sheets and start following the instructions on them. Then he asked the desk sergeant to repeat his message.

Sergeant Bird did so, adding, 'Sir, is something wrong?'

'Nothing you can help with,' Mitchell told him gloomily. The telephone company had answered his question promptly and let him down. They had traced the mobile phone, the number of which Ginny had been asked to ring. It corresponded with the phone belonging to Justin Chase, which he had reported to Cloughton station as having been stolen from their car. Now the case he was not allowed even to know about had a connection with the cases he was busy following up. He was about to have to hand over his first murder case as a DI to another officer.

12

The stalker was becoming very angry with Virginia. The immediate cause was her family's obvious removal from home. Doors were locked and there was no answer to his knock. There was no car in the garage which was filled instead with the large toys which he usually saw standing outside on the patio at the back of the house. This too annoyed him. Police children, of all children, should be taught not to put temptation in the way of thieves.

He stood in the shelter of the hedge and peered through the small window at the far end of the garage. He could make out a huge red plastic capsule that held sand and buckets and spades. Then there were one small and one larger bicycle, a dolls' pram and the twins' large pram.

Virginia's actual absence was not the main cause of his annoyance. What really galled him was her failure to react to him. Her flight to whichever relative or friend was taking the family in until Mitchell returned was not a result of Virginia's fear of him. Her fear was of worrying her husband. When she had not been affected by his phone calls, nor grateful for his flowers, he had been offended and rightly so. Now he was angry because she was refusing to be afraid. Who did she think she was? Did she think she was under some sort of divine protection? Or did she think, as a police wife, that she was immune to physical harm?

Hurting her physically was not what would give him most satisfaction. It was Virginia's air of always being in control that challenged him and breaking that control was what he was determined to do. If she was physically harmed in the process, then so be it. Why should she feel safe and happy in a dangerous world? Why did she believe and expect that everyone she met would like her? Whatever had she done to be held in such high regard?

She was physically attractive, certainly, slim and lithe in her movements even after bearing four children. She would wear any odd combination of clothes and make them look right for her. He had seen her dressed elegantly and wearing cosmetics, even jewellery, but not often, and she always let her hair curl wildly. She ought to take more trouble.

He regarded his own neat tailoring complacently, then felt angry again. Last time he saw Virginia in his everyday persona, she had known he would be visiting. And yet she had opened the door to him wearing jeans and a sweatshirt and insulted him with instant coffee in a mug with a childish cartoon on it that presumably belonged to the boy.

He had deliberately refrained from harassing her during the last few days, letting her build up the hope that he had abandoned his crusade now that things had been made so difficult for him. It was time now for some more dramatic move. He'd drive her to crack up if it killed both of them.

Mitchell had begun his drive to Cumbria in a cheerful frame of mind. He loved travelling because it left him free from all immediate responsibility save that of arriving. It put him in a state of suspension between one situation and another. It was time out to reflect and consider.

He had quickly become reconciled to his trip. He was less anxious about his wife now that she was in the care of her parents. The case seemed to be developing quickly. Perhaps he would trap the stalker before anyone else realised that he had access to the murder victim's phone.

Meanwhile, he was looking forward to seeing Nigel again, to sinking a few pints as they exaggerated the triumphs of the old days and considered their present problems. When Nigel had decided to get his promotion by returning to uniform, Mitchell had scoffed, but things had turned out well for him in back-of-beyond Barrow.

Mitchell examined the country roads along which he was driving with interest. It was obvious that he had left Yorkshire behind and yet he could not quite work out why. Here, as there, the hillsides were scruffy and scrubby and there was nothing refined or sculpted about the shape of the wind-stunted trees and shrubs that were further dwarfed by the sudden drastic rise and fall of the land on which they grew. The difference couldn't only be in having left behind the dry limestone walls of Yorkshire and seeing the fields and roads bordered instead by millstone grit or thorn hedges.

After a further half-hour, Mitchell had decided it was only short journeys he enjoyed. He could do his thinking on his feet and he itched to begin on this next branch of the enquiry. A further couple of miles and he was finding cause for concern in everything that had cheered him little more than an hour ago. During the last few days he had made enquiries, tactful, devious and finally direct. He had discovered, apart from two uniformed constables who had given a few hours to keeping watch on his wife, no one who claimed to be deployed on the case. Surely, the officers Kleever was using had not been told to lie to keep him out of things?

Suddenly, Mitchell realised he had missed his turning. He studied the map to find the quickest way to regain his route and completed his journey with his mind on his driving.

Saturday evening's debriefing was taken by a tight-lipped superintendent. The shift all felt his tension and sat unnaturally straight on the chairs in Mitchell's office. Without Mitchell, it seemed a different place but Jennifer did not blame Kleever for the unhappy atmosphere. Half the unease at a debriefing led by a detective superintendent was a legacy from Superintendent Petty who had tended to use such occasions as an opportunity to throw out veiled criticism of the team, not excluding their DI.

Kleever did not criticise Mitchell either overtly or by implication, even though Jennifer suspected the tight lips expressed his disapproval of Mitchell's precipitous departure without the benefit of his superintendent's advice. Kleever was built on the same lines as Mitchell. Slightly above average height, he seemed shorter because of the breadth of his head and shoulders. Benny, though, was built like a tank whilst to Jennifer, Kleever seemed made of softer stuff. Flesh was beginning to lodge round his jaw and under his chin, though only an enemy would say he was running to fat.

When she had first met him, her impression had been that he was bald but he actually had quite a lot of fine hair. It was greying from mouse-brown and cut very short in a style imposed on his generation of young constables and which he had probably never changed. He was like Petty at least in the respect that he dressed formally.

After surveying each member of the shift in turn he sat in Mitchell's chair, filling it just as generously as its owner and giving the officers in front of him their usual freedom to express their views on the development of the case as each reported on the day's activity.

He nodded to Jennifer to take first turn and she gave an account of her interview with the self-styled Lee Hillard. Jennifer wished she were giving it to Mitchell. She hardly knew most of the officers who had been pulled on to this case. She could work with them well enough, but preferred a familiar listener as she juggled with her ideas before they became opinions.

As her report finished her tone became more tentative. 'Whoever the man is, he's a keen gardener. He'd done a tremendous amount of work and he seemed to feel a genuine satisfaction from it – especially when you remember that he's expecting to leave the garden behind in the near future. He's quick-witted too. I suppose he knew we'd be seeing him again and he'd prepared himself, but I didn't manage to catch him out.' She omitted to mention that she had used Mitchell's mobile number to warn him to listen out for gardening enthusiasts amongst the real Lee Hillard's friends.

'What was your impression of him as a man?'

Jennifer wished Caroline had asked her question less publicly. She was not prepared to say here that she had found him very attractive. He was not conventionally handsome but his features expressed a kind of charm. Charismatic was the word that came to mind. Part of her had been tempted to take him up on his mocking offer.

She tried to give an answer that was relevant to the case. 'The picture of him hovering on the fringe of Justin Chase's set didn't ring true. The man I spoke to this morning lives on his wits. He'd have been the centre of his group, manipulating the people in it, not trying uneasily to keep in with them. I couldn't believe in his description of himself as a hanger on, but he knew that that was how Lee was. Whoever he is, he knew Lee in Manchester.'

Mitchell's phone rang. Kleever picked up the receiver, said 'Thank you' and put it down again. 'The message was that Harriet and Mummy are downstairs. Is someone going to explain?'

Answered by a chorus, he pointed to Caroline, who offered, when she had identified the visitors, to go down and deal with them. Whilst they waited for her, Kleever produced the photographs of their mystery man in his garden and handed them round. 'I suppose no one here recognises him?'

Heads were shaken. Clement asked, 'Has the DI got copies?' and had his toes stamped on by the DC standing beside him.

Kleever merely shook his head. 'I've had one taken round to Mr Foggin, the old chap who met the guy on the way to its cremation. He only produced a "Could be".'

Having something to do with their hands loosened the team's tongues.

'Who do we show these to?'

'Can we bang him up and then publish it nationally?'

'Can he be put on trial without a name?'

The officers who had been tailing the bogus Hillard reported that he had attended his place of work, taken his girlfriend to the pub and transformed his garden.

Kleever scowled. 'We can't afford to go on with that, especially with such negative results.'

Clement looked alarmed. 'But if we keep interviewing him, won't he realise we're after him and disappear?'

Kleever's frown grew deeper. 'He's only three weeks to see out and then he thinks he's safe. He's got too much to lose to abscond now.'

With the superintendent in such a parsimonious mood, no one asked about Clement's lunch with his friend from Compaq.

Kleever was about to break up the meeting by the time Caroline reappeared. 'I got them to the point as soon as I could,' she offered by way of apology, 'but not before I'd heard all about a music exam result, a dreadful sore throat and a tribute to Harriet's powers of observation.'

'And what had she observed?'

'She'd already told us about a buzzing noise that interrupted her malicious calls. This morning she attended the medical centre and it dawned on her that the patients had a buzzer signal to go into the surgery. I think we ought to ask some more questions there. It's the obvious place where people would know who was and wasn't pregnant. We should examine the phones there and work out where the buzzer can be heard from.'

'Would anyone dare make malicious calls with the place full of staff and patients?'

Jennifer considered Clement's question. 'It would be rather clever really. There'd be plenty of background noise going on. I dare say a lot of calls made from the surgery are confidential so someone speaking in a hushed voice wouldn't be thought odd. At the same time, being at work there sounds like a good alibi. You think of funny phone calls being made in private. Could we put someone in?'

Kleever looked less than keen on the idea. 'It wouldn't fool anybody. The place has functioned for a good while with the present staff. They all know they don't need anyone else.'

'And who would we liaise with?' Caroline asked. 'It's the sort of offence that could have been committed as easily by one of the doctors as by any of the lesser mortals. We couldn't be sure we were arranging things through an innocent person.'

'Has a recording been made so we can do a voice trace?' Everyone turned to the blushing PC whose maiden speech this was.

Kleever shook his head. 'The calls have always stopped by the time the telephone company steps in to help us. Besides, it's difficult to do anything with whispers.'

Caroline put in, 'The surgery's just the place where the girls could be asked if they've taken any steps to protect themselves. They'd admit it readily if the question came from a concerned GP who was anxious for their pregnancies to go smoothly. And if the girls don't come in to answer, a doctor can always pop in to see them when he's in their neighbourhood.'

'It doesn't have to be a doctor,' Jennifer objected. 'Officially everything's confidential but I bet there's plenty of gossip going on outside surgery hours.'

'That receptionist's a nosy-parker,' one of the uniformed men volunteered. 'By the time she's finished cross-questioning you, there's nothing left to say to the doctor when you eventually get to see him.'

'You're registered there?' The PC nodded. 'How many males are employed there?'

The PC ticked them off on his fingers. 'One of the practice doctors, Simpson, and a locum they have a regular arrangement with, Carter. There's a male nurse, Johnson, husband, poor beggar, of the nosy receptionist and the cleaner's husband is a sort of general handyman. Got made redundant from that place called Domestic Décor. Does the garden, puts shelves up, slaps paint around and so on. They're friends of my wife.'

Into the discouraged silence that followed, Jennifer remarked, 'He wouldn't know we can't do a trace.' Her grin infected the rest of the assembled officers.

Kleever looked doubtful. 'You're suggesting we invite them to make a recording in order to eliminate themselves and then study their reactions? I don't like it.'

Jennifer was undismayed. Benny would be back in a couple of days and he'd like it very much. Kleever turned back to Caroline. 'I was about to ask you about your visit to Cantrells before the Bradley child distracted us.'

Caroline described her session with 'Jim', stressing his admission that Justin Chase had had the ability to bring the company to its knees, had he felt so inclined.

'Should we be looking at him, then?'

'He'd hardly present us with his motive if he'd killed Chase.' Caroline's tone was withering.

Clement's was sulky. 'It could be bluff.'

Kleever interrupted, asking for Caroline's general impression of Cantrell. She considered for a moment. 'In the firm, he's the hard seller with the commercial contacts. He's not the ideas man as far as the company product is concerned. He promotes the ideas men. He likes finding unknown ones, backing a winner and then exploiting him. But he's afraid of him at the same time because he knows too much. That explains, maybe, why he's prepared to send such an untried man to start the daughter firm. Apparently Justin Chase had read the real Lee's papers and been interested in them. He hadn't mentioned to Cantrell that he knew Lee. It could be that he had personal reasons for keeping quiet. On the other hand, it could be that they weren't such good friends as Lee claimed and he really didn't remember him.

'Cantrell wasn't very helpful about samples of handwriting.' She produced the two signed documents that he had lent her.

'Trouble is,' grumbled an elderly PC from the back of the room, 'kids reared on computers never learn to write.'

Kleever beamed at him. 'You're showing your age, Alderson, but I'm inclined to agree.' He turned back to Caroline. 'You've spoken to Gemma Platt, haven't you?'

Ignoring a mutter of 'Busy little bee', Caroline described this interview briefly. 'She only had old bruises this time. Thacker knows to hold off. Gemma has a theory about how he knew about Virginia's problems.' She nodded to Clement. 'He's told her he worked it out because of your car being outside their house. Gemma says she thinks one of Steve's big mates is a police snout. She says he might have heard a radio message in one of our cars, or overheard a scrap of conversation and told Steve about it.'

'Anyone like to confess?' Kleever invited. He had become much more relaxed as the debriefing proceeded but now his lips tightened again.

Caroline went on, hurriedly, 'It's probably

just surmise on Gemma's part. Anyway, Ginny says her caller's very well spoken. That doesn't sound like Thacker.' With nothing further to report she withdrew thankfully into the body of the group again.

Kleever ended the proceedings soon afterwards, after delivering a message from Mitchell. He had persuaded Dr Simpson to reveal that the patient he had confirmed as HIV positive was Colin Weston, the father of Megan Scott's child. Most of the shift, as they departed, felt that, though there were nasty moments in the lives of all policemen, there were evidently comparable moments in the experiences of every GP.

13

His courtesy visit to DCI Nigel Bellamy provided Mitchell with addresses for the people he wanted to see, directions for reaching them and an invitation to an evening meal with his old colleague. He mentally reviewed his aims before driving out to meet Hillard's parents. On his way, he called at the little Millton sub-station and found that the officers there already knew all that Nathan Hillard could tell them.

Nathan was apparently awaiting further developments before upsetting his parents any further with news of his brother's impersonator. Until now, the police attitude had been to let Lee escape if that was what he wanted. They had discouraged the interference of his parents. Mitchell hoped they would be willing to co-operate with him now that he really did want to trace their son.

The Millton sergeant who had suffered at the hands – or rather the tongue – of Mavis Hillard had warned Mitchell to see her husband alone. However, it proved impossible to move her from his side without causing her great distress and she resisted all the efforts of the WPC the Millton station had lent him to persuade her into the kitchen. Her rambling speech had now become not only disconnected but inaudible, a mere moving of the lips. Mitchell could see that she had become clinically disturbed. She shook her head distractedly, refusing to make cups of tea.

Sidney Hillard apologised and confided that she would neither cook nor eat and was losing weight fast. Mitchell decided the woman could lose several stones before she would be in any danger of starvation. Nevertheless he could see that she urgently needed medical treatment and advised Hillard to call in their GP.

He nodded. 'She's depressed. I know that. But a doctor won't help much. He can't alter the fact that one of her sons has gone to work away where we can't find him and he doesn't want to be in touch.' He gave Mitchell a bitter smile. 'The other is looking for him because he doesn't want to be the only one forking out for an old people's home for us. He needn't worry. I've made all the necessary arrangements for the future.'

Mitchell gave him a hard look.' If that's how you feel, then maybe the bad news I thought I was bringing you will turn out to contain at least a little comfort.' Briefly he outlined the present state of their enquiries into their son's whereabouts and Justin Chase's death.

Hillard took the news calmly. 'I'm not altogether surprised. I've been thinking a lot these last few days. I never believed his reason for going to the cottage. He's not a temperamental worker. His bedroom's always been good enough, and, anyhow, his thesis was almost finished. He wouldn't have needed all that much peace and quiet to tidy it up. We never disturb him when he's working. I thought he might have met a girl and taken her to the cottage.'

He agreed at once to a search of Lee's room. 'Anything if it'll help find him.' He directed Mitchell up to a tiny cell leading from a tinier landing. It contained a narrow bed, a single wardrobe, a chest of drawers and a dressing-table, obviously used as a desk and holding a Compaq PC. The drawers each side of the kneehole contained cardboard boxes filled with notes, hand-written jottings on scraps of paper. Lower drawers held finished work, neatly printed out with more columns of letters, numbers and symbols than words in sentences.

The walls were bare except for girlish flowered paper and there appeared to be no books until the WPC, who had joined him after making tea for the Hillards, found some in boxes in the wardrobe. There were not many, but Mitchell supposed that wherever Lee had gone he had taken the rest with him. In addition to books, the wardrobe contained only a shabby pair of trousers with a Marks & Spencer label.

The real find was tucked into the back of a file in the bottom drawer of the chest. Several handwritten drafts of a letter of application for a job as a computer analyst were accompanied by a list of companies that included Cantrells. Mitchell tucked the sheets into a plastic bag, together with his other useful discovery, a crumpled yellow envelope, on the back of which was written, 'Charlie's new No.', followed by a row of figures.

Sidney Hillard seemed cheered rather than depressed by the police's new interest in his son. It was evidently easier for him to contemplate physical harm having come to the young man than that he should have decided to reject his parents completely. It was also easier for him to believe. He had persuaded his wife to lie down for a while in order to give Mitchell his full co-operation.

Asked for details of anyone he thought Lee might have contacted since leaving home, he puckered his brow. Then he produced the same list of his elder son's supposed friends and acquaintances as the police had already been given by the younger one, whose opinion he shared. 'This Justin didn't sound like our Lee's sort of friend. Lee was usually on his own, but when he did mix in it was with quiet types. Nathan thinks he was just someone Lee met and he fantasised about being his friend.

'He did get quite pally with the chap called Charlie, though. He didn't seem Lee's type either but he was the one made all the running. One bit, he was here quite often. Mavis couldn't stand him and I wasn't keen but the lad was old enough to choose his own friends. Bit of a smarmy type. Mavis had a bee in her bonnet about him coming just to pinch ideas out of Lee's papers to put into his own, but, as far as I could see, he wasn't writing any. He'd finished with all that university stuff and had a job in Barrow.'

'Do you know where?'

Hillard shook his head. 'Not exactly, but I know it was one of several in a row. He was soon fed up with something when the novelty wore off and the hard work started. He always seemed to have plenty of money though.'

Mitchell remarked mildly, 'I hear the poor chap came to a sticky end.'

'That's right. He was a bit of a slippery customer but he didn't deserve that. Burnt to a cinder whilst he was doing a bit of overtime one evening. I don't think they ever discovered what caused the fire. Ironic, really, to meet his end doing overtime when he was actually a bit of a bum.'

Remember Jennifer's telephone call, Mitchell asked if Charlie had ever talked about his hobbies. Hillard sniffed. 'I don't know about talking but he was definitely keen on gardens. In fact, it's a bit off of me to call him a bum when he turned yon bottom end over for me last year. Before that it was a wilderness and I'm getting beyond doing it. Young Charlie dug out all the couch grass and left it raked and ready to seed.' Mitchell admired the stretch of healthy new grass that now covered the area indicated. Hillard sighed. 'Waste of good growing space, I suppose, but it's easy to manage and it looks neat and tidy.'

The little man looked with interest at the job applications and willingly gave Mitchell permission to borrow them. 'It would have been a good thing for Lee, getting a job and moving away from here – but you don't think he did, do you? You think he's dead.'

Mitchell stopped off at the Millton station to drop off his borrowed WPC, report their findings and use the station's telephone. He read the number on the yellow envelope through the plastic bag, and rang Charlie's new number. When an elderly voice answered, he asked for him. The old lady sounded on the verge of tears as she explained that Charlie had been dead for more than two months. As the manner of his death was described briefly, the voice disintegrated.

Mitchell commiserated and asked the old woman if she were Charlie's mother. He learned that she was his former landlady and that Charlie's mother had given him up for adoption at birth. After a series of foster parents had rejected him he had been brought up in a children's home. If he were a friend of Charlie's, she would be glad to meet him to talk about Charlie. As Mitchell was a man though, and she didn't know him, it would have to be in a public place.

Mitchell commended her caution and willingly agreed to a tea kiosk in Barrow market place as an appropriate spot. When she had been reassured by his warrant card, they could move to somewhere more comfortable and private. The drive took him only a quarter of an hour and, as he approached the designated kiosk, he found it easy to pick out the woman he had come to see.

Miss Pickford was the only patron of the place over thirty. She was proud of her seventy-seven years to which she owned without being asked. Mitchell was genuinely surprised at the revelation and said so. A rapport established, she was eager to answer his questions until the warrant card was produced. Far from reassuring, it seemed to scare her.

She began to talk about herself. Because she could hardly afford to maintain and heat the house she had lived in most of her life, she had begun to take in paying guests. She had seen lodgings offered on a card in a corner shop and been surprised at how much could be asked for a bed and breakfast service.

Anxious to ingratiate himself again, Mitchell praised her initiative and asked about her house. When she seemed at ease again, he asked, 'When did Charlie come to stay with you?'

She bit her lip and her eyes filled again. 'He arrived the same week I put my card in. It was like having a son again.'

Gently, for him, Mitchell asked, 'You've lost a son?'

Miss Pickford twisted her gnarled hands. 'I lost him as soon as I got him. My young man let me down. I was lucky my parents didn't throw me out but they wouldn't let me keep my baby. I never married. I worked as a nanny for a few happy years and then I had to come back home to nurse my parents. All the time I sat and watched them dying I was imagining that my own son would come back to me and, later, when Charlie moved in, I thought my dream was happening.'

'He wasn't...'

'Oh no. He wasn't the right age to be my Leslie, not by a long way. But I thought of Charlie that way. I'd lost my son and he'd lost his mother and we belonged together.'

Their cups were empty and Mitchell signalled for them to be refilled. The coffee was abominable but drinking Ginny's had inured him. He took a courageous swig before asking, 'So, you got on well, you and Charlie?'

Miss Pickford gave Mitchell a rueful smile. 'I loved him, but I knew he wasn't always a good boy. I knew he was in trouble at work. Still, what could you expect with no mother to guide him and teach him what was right? Sometimes he couldn't pay his rent but I let him stay. I cooked meals for the two of us after he was dismissed. In his way, he paid me well because he kept my garden trim all the time he was with me. He was insecure, easily led and he got into bad company.'

Mitchell finished his coffee with a grimace and the old woman scrabbled in her bag for her purse. 'It's my turn to buy. Perhaps you'll have a sandwich with it this time.'

Mitchell had seen the kiosk's curled-up offerings under the glass counter. He shook his head. 'It's a gentleman's privilege to entertain a lady. Perhaps you won't mind if I made a phone call and after that I'd be delighted if you'd let me take you to lunch.'

Miss Pickford blushed an ugly red and Mitchell felt ashamed of patronising her. He took his mobile phone a few yards away from the distraction of waitresses' shrieks of laughter and rang Barrow station. The desk sergeant would be able to direct him to the sort of restaurant where a maiden lady would feel comfortable having lunch.

The café, when they arrived, was all that he had hoped, small, clean and quiet with a homely English menu. He was not surprised when his guest asked to be fed whatever he was ordering for himself. Now he had to whip up as much sympathy for Lee Hillard as she had felt for her former lodger.

Her face lit up when Lee was mentioned. 'Do you know him too? I'm very fond of Lee. I'm sure he kept Charlie out of worse trouble. You aren't a Barrow man, are you? How did you meet them?'

Mitchell said, carefully, 'I've only met one of them.' An idea occurred to him. 'You don't have a picture of Charlie, do you?'

She nodded. 'Yes. I've several at home and I keep one in my handbag.'

'Could I see it?'

She wiped her mouth and fingers with her napkin, reached to the floor for her bag and drew out a postcard-sized picture of a man in a sunny garden, stripped to the waist and leaning on a spade. Mitchell took it and looked into the face of his neighbour.

'Miss Pickford, I have to tell you that the man in this picture is alive and living in Cloughton in Yorkshire. He's a neighbour of mine and he's working for a company called Cantrells.'

She stared at him, her fork half-way to her mouth. 'No, it's Lee who's in Yorkshire...' But he could see that she believed him and he watched her face as she worked out the implications of what she had been told. After a moment she dropped her eyes and said quietly, 'I'm sorry but I don't think I can eat any more.'

Later, as Mitchell, having queued with Bellamy, collected a Chinese meal for two, he regarded the considerable number of polystyrene boxes an enigmatic, doe-eyed girl was packing into their plastic carrier bag and wondered how many Chinese in their own country ate meals with so many courses.

Bellamy's flat was the first floor of a very large house set back on a wide road out of the town. He pointed out proudly that his windows on one side overlooked Furness Abbey. Mitchell was surprised to see rooms that satisfied his own standards of tidiness. Bellamy, correctly interpreting his glance around the place, laughed. 'Don't think I do it. Single DCIs can afford a daily woman.'

Mitchell was not impressed. 'You'd better

not get too used to it if it's only temporary. How did it come about, anyway? You were a big cagey on the phone. What happened to your super?'

But Bellamy continued to be cagey. The great man had left the district for personal reasons. Between mouthfuls of sweet and sour, he described the tribulations of the greatness thrust upon him and Mitchell described his day.

He had taken Miss Pickford home, where, once she had brought herself to accept that there was a serious charge to bring against Charlie Potts, she had told him all she knew. Charlie was in trouble at work because of some trick he had played on his firm's computer. She didn't understand quite what it was. Someone a bit cleverer than he was had got on to it and he had to disappear quickly.

Miss Pickford had suggested he should get some advice from his friend Lee who understood such things. She had hoped it might be possible to put things right and she was convinced that Lee was a good influence on Charlie.

Bellamy scraped the remains from two of the cartons on to his plate. 'So, Charlie set fire to himself whilst he was trying to cover his tracks? Or was it suicide, taking the firm down with him? Or was he just going to set fire to the firm and didn't get away fast enough? I've felt bad about skimping that case but things were at their most chaotic here when it happened. I'd only just taken on this job and, since the insurance company paid up and no one else was harmed and the fire service couldn't prove it was arson...' His voice died away as he saw that Mitchell had more to reveal.

'Charlie's alive and well and living across the road from us in Cloughton.' He watched Bellamy's mouth fall open. 'It really would help if you could look at the file again.'

'You can come and see it for yourself tomorrow. The building caught fire about midnight and one body was found in it. We checked the list of employees. One was missing and he was in bother. We went through the list of possible conclusions I've just mentioned and decided that he'd got a bit more than he deserved.

'I wasn't entirely happy. His GP came up with a tattoo and an appendix scar as distinguishing marks. The arm with the tattoo was particularly badly burned, which seemed a bit iffy, but no one else was missing – well, not till these folk in Millton popped up a couple of weeks ago. When the remains of Charlie Potts's signet ring and neck chain were found we let it go. You think it was this other chap, Hillard?'

Mitchell nodded. 'As I see it, Hillard and the landlady played right into Charlie's hands. Hillard was hard up for friends and desperate to get away from his mother. He confided in Charlie about his various job applications and his forthcoming interview at Cantrells. Until he'd actually got a job, he wouldn't want his mother going into a decline and moaning about his duty to her and how ungrateful he was, so he was keeping it all under his hat.

'Charlie probably appealed to him to tell his folk, instead, that he needed the cottage for peace and quiet to study. Then he'd give the key to Charlie, who'd lie low there until the dust settled.'

Bellamy wiped the grease from his mouth with a paper napkin covered with Chinese symbols. 'And then you think he had the better idea of attending Hillard's interview and taking his job?'

'From what I've heard of them both, Charlie would show up better in an interview than Lee himself, especially when he was armed with Lee's qualifications.'

Together, the two officers gathered cartons, scraped plates into a waste bin and considered Mitchell's theories.

'It hangs together but you've a lot of evidence to collect.'

Mitchell agreed. 'I've started.' He fished in his briefcase and produced a packet containing half a dozen or so picture postcards of Lake District scenes. 'These are all signed "Love, Lee" and say he's making progress with the thesis. Presumably Charlie was supposed to post one every week so the Hillards wouldn't worry. Miss Pickford was loath to show me his room. She got a rotten deal. In exchange for probably the best meal she's had this week I took away all the pleasure she's had in her acquaintance with Charlie. She really thought she'd managed to keep him from a life of serious crime. It wasn't much of a swap and she couldn't even finish her pie.'

Bellamy looked surprised. 'Is this the Benny Mitchell I know and love? You need taking to the pub, mate.'

The remedy was applied without delay. For reasons he could not explain to himself, Mitchell made no mention of Virginia's harassment as they bared their souls over several pints. He was not sure that this was still the old Nigel. There was not time to explain it all properly. He was not in this part of the country to further his own concerns – and, finally, neither of them was sufficiently sober.

Virginia was feeling ill at ease and unsettled. It was not the sort of discomfort she often suffered for very long. When her life failed to satisfy her, she paused to analyse the problem and then dealt with it. She felt hemmed in by her present trouble. The experts were dealing with it and any weighing in with her own solution could wreck her husband's career.

It irked her to have returned to her parents' house. She had been extremely happy with them in the past but now it was no longer her place. Certainly the small house they had bought after she and Alex left home was no place for four lively children. On the other hand, she was glad to be away from her own present home which she now associated with impotent fear. What she resented most of all was not being in control of her own life.

When she saw Superintendent Kleever's car draw up outside she could not decide if she were pleased or sorry. Her mother brought him into the sitting-room, produced a tray with coffee and cups, then disappeared with the twins to the kitchen at the back of the house.

Declan and Caitlin appeared from upstairs to see who the visitor was. 'Say hello to the superintendent,' she chided them.

Declan showed his disapproval of their guest by repeating just the word required. Caitlin was more friendly and graciously accepted a packet of fruit drops. Dispatched back upstairs, they could be heard squabbling. Caitlin's voice predominated. 'I shan't share them because you weren't polite!'

Kleever laughed and settled himself in her father's chair. After a few minutes' small talk he repeated to her his usual reassurances. She had his men watching her. The card that had come with the flowers and the letter were being analysed. Her father's telephone number was ex-directory so there was little danger of any calls here.

'He's found a way round that,' Virginia objected, 'or how could he have called me in the first place?'

Kleever shrugged. 'He might have caught sight of your number in one of your friends' personal phone books – or asked one of the children. There are scores of ways. He could even be one of the people you've given it to.'

'Is that supposed to cheer me up?'

'Unfortunately, Virginia, I haven't come to cheer you up. I'd be silly to try until we've caught him. You wouldn't accept facile reassurances. You're too intelligent a woman. I haven't talked to you since Benny left. I've just called to keep in touch and see if there have been any further developments.'

'I'd have let you know. And, if I hadn't. Dad would have told you. There hasn't been anything since the letter. It's a week now. Do you think he's given up because you've made things too difficult for him, or even because he's had his fun and has got tired of it all?'

Kleever shook his head soberly. Virginia pushed the hair out of her eyes and sighed.

'I don't think so either. The silence is harder to bear than the harassment. It's a different kind of harassment, actually, leaving me to wonder when and what next.'

Kleever got up. 'I have to get back. I just wanted to warn you to stay vigilant, even here. You will stay here as long as your husband's away?' Virginia nodded reluctantly. 'Good. He may be gathering his forces. Next time might be the big one.'

'The big what? What do you mean?'

Kleever went to the door. 'I don't know. I wish I did.'

'Not the children?'

'I don't know that either. All you can do is stay with your family and keep your wits about you.'

14

On Sunday morning, Mitchell nursed a sore head, an unusual experience for him. He had been grateful when Nigel had insisted on his staying the night and christening his new futon. Mitchell had found it not the most comfortable of resting places.

He had spent most of the early hours reviewing the progress of his investigation. His impostor was now identified pretty conclusively and no one who knew all the facts – at present, just himself and Nigel – doubted that Charlie Potts had killed both Lee Hillard and Justin Chase. He'd get back to Cloughton as soon as possible and put more men on to tailing young Charlie. He'd keep his fingers crossed that Cantrell would have respected his instructions and treated his new employee as usual.

Maybe he should have sent someone else over here and gone to the factory himself. On the other hand, he trusted Caroline and, thanks to his mobile, he was in constant touch with all his team. In addition, Nigel was allowing more privileges to an old friend than he would have done to someone he didn't know. It could be that there would be evidence from the Barrow end of the case that would supply grounds for an arrest sooner than his own team could find them.

Eventually, Mitchell had fallen into a heavy sleep from which Nigel had to rouse him. He was aggrieved. Nigel had sunk more beer than he had himself.

His host disappeared to keep a previously arranged golfing appointment and Mitchell continued his appraisal of his first case. Knowing he could trust Nigel to deal with a further examination of the factory fire remains, he made a mental list of the tasks still to be completed before he could return to his family. He owed a good lunch to Nigel in return for supper and a night's lodging. Before that, he ought to see Nathan Hillard and bring him up to date with the search for his brother.

Since Ginny was safe in her parents' household, Mitchell was tempted to take a quick drive along the completely unspoilt coast road this afternoon. He had travelled along a short stretch when taking Miss Pickford home and been enchanted by a quick glimpse of a spot called Bardsea where oaks grew right down to the sea.

Nigel returned, scarlet and sweating, having followed his game by running the six miles home. Carrying a photocopy of Miss Pickford's statement, Mitchell arrived back at the flat whilst he was showering. The old woman had been in tears for most of her visit to the station and he'd been thankful on both their accounts as she finally put her name to a typed version of what she had told him.

Over lunch, Nigel offered, as Mitchell had hoped he would, to return to his office that evening where the two of them could go through the file on the death of Charlie Potts. This justified his afternoon on the beach. There, he battled with a fierce off-shore wind and tried to banish all thoughts of work. He failed to banish his anxiety for his wife and retired to the car to ring his in-laws who confirmed her immediate safety.

Soon afterwards he returned to the flat and prowled the rooms in impatient anticipation of further revelations about the way Lee Hillard had been spirited away. To distract himself he decided to prepare their evening meal. Nigel might be a mini-step higher up the career ladder but Mitchell knew himself to be by far the better cook.

However, he was to be denied his eagerly awaited perusal of the Barrow force's files. His phone rang. After listening to the brief message, Mitchell paused only to scribble a quick note of apology that he propped against the kettle before leaping into his car and making all speed back to Cloughton.

On the same Sunday morning, Declan

Mitchell had remembered that he had left his recorder at home.

'Never mind,' his grandfather comforted. 'You can do some extra practice in the evenings next week.'

'Will I go home tonight or will I go to school from here in the morning?'

'From here,' his grandmother told him. 'You like staying with us, don't you?'

Declan nodded. 'I would if my recorder was here. It's my lesson tomorrow and you have to drop out of the group if you forget it twice. I forgot mine in the first week when we'd just moved.'

'You didn't forget it,' his mother put in. 'We hadn't unpacked it. That didn't count.'

'I expect it did. Miss Gatting says she won't listen to excuses...'

When the child had introduced the topic for the fourth time, his grandfather took his part. 'Why don't we pop over after tea? We can pick up the twins' teddy bears at the same time.'

Remembering the rumpus at the previous day's bedtime as the twins had roared for these items and refused to be consoled by the basket of furry animals generously offered by Caitlin, Virginia was soon persuaded. Besides, by the time they returned from the excursion it would be too late for a session round the Ludo board that, unfortunately, her father had unearthed from the depths of a cupboard.

After much discussion, it was decided by the two older children that Grandad would drive, Mummy would come to look round to see if anything else had been forgotten and they would go along for the ride. Grandma Hannah could bathe the twins and promise them that the teddies were on their way. The party departed in the dusk, leaving Hannah well content with her part in the plan.

Virginia and her father first smelled smoke and noticed the strange orange light in the sky when they were still two streets away from Fulton Road. They glanced at each other, the same thought in both their minds. A left turn two minutes later confirmed their suspicions.

Instinct told Browne to take his family back home. His training as a policeman made him park a little distance away from the inferno in order to check that the fire brigade had been called and the houses either side of his daughter's house had been evacuated. Keeping a sharp eye on his car and its inmates, he helped to control the gathering crowd until, only moments later, firemen and their engines arrived to take over.

Virginia's voice was steady. 'This is arson, Dad.' Browne could see that his daughter had herself well in hand. He fumbled in the car's glove compartment, withdrew a small camera and spoke to her in a low tone. 'We'll have some pictures of this crowd. Arsonists come to watch the fun. Lock the car after me and take the children straight home.'

As he departed, his daughter obeyed his first command and ignored the second. Resigned to her stubbornness, Browne remained close to the car and adjusted the camera's telescopic lens before pointing it at the gathering spectators. Glancing back at his family from time to time he saw his grandchildren's noses flattened against the window as they succumbed to the fascination of the flames.

He knew children were natural pyromaniacs. He could remember himself and his mates starting fires in Ecclesall woods in Sheffield when he was a boy of about ten. He had loved the power and intensity of fire, and its lawlessness, free from anyone's control. It respected no one and nothing and it had become more mysterious and less familiar to children who no longer had coal fires in the grate at home. To Declan and Caitlin this was merely fun.

Caitlin had managed to wind the window down and, before she had obeyed her mother's order to close it immediately, he had heard her exclaim, 'All those sparks are better than fireworks!'

They sobered at Virginia's sharp tone and were silent for a minute, until Declan asked, 'Can we just go in for a minute, quickly, so that we're not burned, to see if we can get my recorder out?'

Virginia softened her tone. 'I'll buy you another one, Declan. I'll get it in the morning and bring it to school in time for your lesson.'

Satisfied that she never broke a promise, the boy turned back to his enjoyment of the spectacle. Virginia watched too and, suddenly, she felt she knew her persecutor. Not his name, of course, but his nature. Now she appreciated what she had learned from Professor Klein. Her stalker had no affection whatsoever for her, not even a perverted one. He wanted to frighten her, feel power over her.

She owed him nothing. She had not led him, however innocently, to believe she was offering him any kind of relationship. By this last act that was supposed to terrorise her, he had freed her. All this time, she had felt half sorry for him. Now, she wanted him behind bars, not just because that would make her feel safe but because it was what he deserved. Virginia was sure the man knew she was not in the house. He didn't want to kill her because then he couldn't go on frightening her.

She could not deny to herself that she had

been afraid, but the part of that fear that had been guilt had gone, allowing her to feel the stirrings of the mental resilience that, before, she had always taken for granted.

This all seemed to have taken a considerable time to work out but her offspring still sat, faces squashed against the windows, mesmerised, whilst her father, a short distance from the car, was still busy with his camera. On-duty officers were keeping spectators well back and she could see the firemen's hoses extended against the wall of flame. She willed the fire to win, to damage the house irreparably so that they could begin again somewhere else.

With every pane of glass that cracked, Virginia felt more liberated as the fury of the flames exorcised her own. By this last destructive act her enemy had given her back most of what he had taken from her. Her life was her own again. Her family was left with just the clothes they were wearing and the few possessions they had taken for their short visit to the Brownes. It was reprehensible in a mother of four that all she could feel was triumph.

Virginia had noticed Kleever's car drawn up beside the marked police cars nearer to their house but she had not seen the superintendent himself among the small group of officers guarding the scene. Now, however, he was coming towards them, his expression grave. She wound the window down to speak to him.

'Virginia, I can't tell you how sorry I am. I should have seen this coming.'

When she told him, 'I'm glad you didn't,' he blinked.

Jennifer hoped she was going to be blessed with Mitchell's luck. Looking back to the time when they were both DCs, she remembered many times when he had talked her into ignoring standard police practice and taking the shortest way to finding out what they needed to know. Almost always, his reprimands had had their stings withdrawn before they were administered because Mitchell had produced a breakthrough, large or small, that had got the current case moving again towards a satisfactory conclusion.

He seldom flagrantly disobeyed an order, merely plunging into a course of action that seemed most likely to give the desired result most quickly. The course usually disregarded completely the whole system of regulations put in place to protect the general public from policemen like himself. Mitchell was of the opinion that the public was best served by the speedy identification and punishment of criminals by the most practical means.

As Jennifer had expected he had given joyful assent to her plan to scare the surgery employees with the threat of an analysis of their voices. She had often been his reluctant tool, but she considered this scheme worth the risk of Kleever's wrath. She had dissuaded him from attending the surgery in person, claiming the right to perform her own experiment without suggesting that she was anxious to protect his promotion.

Instead, she had brought Caroline with her and the two of them had enjoyed a skirmish with the sour-faced receptionist. It seemed to Jennifer that Debbie's indignation was caused less by having to attend the surgery on a Sunday than by being obliged to share the others' ignorance as to the reason for it.

As they waited for Dr Simpson to arrive, she tried to anticipate all his objections to her request. All the other surgeries in the town summoned patients by buzzer. However, all the pregnant girls who had received the calls she was investigating, except for one, were registered here. He would no doubt tell her she had no right to enforce her request, but why should any of them refuse this opportunity to refute suspicion?

The practice nurse's 306 lined itself up neatly beside Jennifer's red Fiesta and he and Dr Simpson both climbed out of it. When she explained the purpose of her visit, the doctor made none of the objections she had rehearsed. He remarked merely, 'I hope and expect the words you ask us to recite will not be a repetition of the nasty suggestions made to some of our patients.'

Reassured on this point, he volunteered to make the first recording, 'partly to set a good example and partly because I have guests to return to.' Jennifer took him into the practice nurse's tiny office and placed a tape recorder on the desk.

Dr Simpson regarded it, unimpressed. 'I expected a bit more sophisticated technology.'

Jennifer tried to sound off-hand. 'All the clever stuff goes into smaller and smaller packages these days.' He read from the card she handed him without further comment, first, as required, in his normal voice, and then in a whisper.

He departed after sending in his cleaner's husband to be the next victim. This man regarded the card with some dismay, then looked at Jennifer in appeal. 'Can't I just say summat?'

They settled for his repeating the written words, phrase by phrase as Jennifer read them out, then he departed thankfully, sending in Damian Johnson. The nurse seemed equally embarrassed. Jennifer sought to put him at ease by thanking him for the use of his office and promising not to disturb any of his papers or equipment. She gave her instructions as before and he read from the card in a wooden tone, but fluently. When he was asked to whisper the words, he was silent.

'Go on,' Jennifer prompted. 'Just the same as before.' When the silence continued, she held her breath. Then Damian Johnson began to whisper.

As Mitchell moved his paperwork around on his desk in an effort to reduce the amount, there was a tap at his door. Before he could reply, Kleever came in, white-faced and obviously furious. He shut the door silently and trod soundlessly, signs Mitchell was beginning to recognise as not auspicious.

His superintendent had obviously discovered where Sergeant Taylor had gone and disapproved to the extent they had anticipated. Here came his demotion unless she rushed in in the next minute or two with a confession.

Kleever's visit, however, had another purpose. He remained standing as he offered Mitchell a stilted apology for not preventing last night's attack on his house.

'Forget it, sir. At least forget trying to take any of the blame.'

'Your wife said something very odd to me last night.' He described Virginia's strange satisfaction at the devastation of her home.

Mitchell nodded, understanding Kleever's bewilderment.

Receiving news of the fire in Barrow the previous night, he had driven like a madman back to Cloughton to console his wife, only to find she was completely back to her normal self and telling him the fire was the reason. This, together with the fact that his family was unharmed, enabled him to be magnanimous. Thanks to his in-laws' generosity, they were not out on the street and, if the cramped conditions became unbearable, a police house was on offer until other arrangements could be made. He forbore to express his opinion of the way the superintendent was handling his case. 'Neither of us blames anyone except the man who lit the fire.'

'You're convinced it's our man?'

Mitchell nodded. 'Sergeant Taylor suggested bored children or even Steve Thacker wanting to work off a grudge but I'm convinced it's part of the harassment of my wife. I had a session with the fire people last night. They were telling me they can work out where a fire has started by looking for where it's burned the longest. This one was started with petrol being poured on our bed. Their chief gave me a lecture for my pains. He said when they tell the police a fire is arson they don't want to know because they have to regard it as a serious crime. There's precious little chance of catching the person responsible so they don't even record it as arson.'

'He's probably right I suppose he pointed out that we're responding quickly enough to this one because it's an attack on one of our own.'

Mitchell nodded. 'No joy from the house to house?'

Kleever shook his head and walked abruptly to the door. Mitchell realised that the superintendent had not relished apologising to a subordinate officer but that didn't seem to explain his pinched features and the carefully controlled movements that betrayed his anger. Since it had not been mentioned, the cause was unlikely to be the unorthodox experiment being carried out at the surgery.

Mitchell did not like mysteries and this one could be easily resolved. 'Have I done something to upset you, sir?'

Kleever paused in the doorway. 'I hope it was not you. Someone has had the temerity to steal my car from outside the main entrance to the station.'

'I'll get on to it right away.'

'Uniforms are "on to it" already. I think we can leave it to them.' On this ungrateful note, Kleever departed, shutting the door behind him without so much as a click.

At the end of Monday, Mitchell took his own debriefing. Jennifer arrived late, having been delayed in the foyer by an irate Kleever. She apologised and explained. 'I know it's annoying but isn't he going a bit OTT? I wonder if he thinks high ranking policemen should be immune to the crimes his underlings are trying to prevent.'

'He is in a paddy.' One of the DCs borrowed from headquarters spoke up to agree. 'Up to now, he's seemed a pretty even-tempered bloke except when there's been good reason to be angry. Not like Petty, flying off the handle if you didn't get your salute quite right.'

Caroline looked at them witheringly. 'The man's car's been taken. Do you know a single male, old enough to drive, who can cope when his car isn't functioning? Second only to his penis, it's his badge of manhood...'

Mitchell called the meeting to order and began a general sharing of information by telling the shift what he had learned in Barrow. 'Nigel sends greetings to everyone who remembers him.'

'He wants you to ring him as soon as possible,' Jennifer interrupted. 'Claxton on the desk said he'd already told you but I was to remind you.'

Mitchell nodded. 'Thanks. He was saying something about coming over to see everyone. I didn't realise he was in a hurry. I won't be able to put him up. We aren't sure where we're going ourselves yet. Let's get on.'

He called on Clement who had been sent to UMIST to find out as much as possible about the student life of the three men concerned in the present case. Justin Chase had been well spoken of by everyone Clement asked. Two of his sporting records still remained unbroken and he had been awarded an Upper Second class degree, together with a testimonial to the effect that he would have been awarded a First if he had not been preoccupied with putting UMIST on the sporting map. Lee Hillard was remembered, if at all, as an industrious nonentity. His post graduate papers contained no new ideas but were valuable to more original thinkers because they contained the results of much painstaking collecting and recording of data that saved everyone else's time.

'What about Charlie Potts and the story that he dropped out?'

Clement shook his head. 'He didn't. He was discreetly sent down for some sort of computer fraud. They tried to explain it to me but, in the end, they made some notes for me to put into the file in case anyone else here might be able to follow it.'

He subsided on this modest note and Mitchell called on Jennifer and Caroline to give their account of the arrest of Damian

Johnson. This too was brief, the two officers referring all who wanted full details to the sheets that would shortly be placed in the file.

Jennifer remained behind when the rest of the shift departed so that they could hear, Mitchell for the first time, the tape that she had recorded at the surgery earlier. Johnson's monologue begun in a whisper, condemned the sluttish girls he had been obliged to attend, who had taken their pleasure in sexual intimacy without the responsibility of commitment to a marriage partner and without thought for the health and well-being of their babies. He spoke in phrases that might have been lifted from an old fashioned textbook but the menace in his tone was more than a pregnant girl, with her hormones and her emotions in disarray, would wish to hear.

The whisper became a voice monotone as Johnson began to talk about his own situation. 'When things are wrong between you like that, you feel sad and helpless, then you get angry, then you go mad. Other couples go to bed for pleasure, to make up quarrels, to enjoy each other. Our bed is where my worst fears come true, where I'm not wanted, where I feel ugly and useless.

'It's not her fault. It isn't because she's having an affair or because she hates me. It's just there and I feel it's my fault. If you're a man, you always feel it's your fault. You must have let yourself go, put on weight, not done well enough at work, lost her respect...'

There was silence and Mitchell reached over to switch off the tape. Jennifer gestured to him to leave it. After a while the voice began again. 'It's all very well being celibate if you're a monk in a cell, with books and prayers and no temptations, but not with her warm body beside you every night in bed. And then to spend all day in here...' The voice had dropped to a whisper again. '...looking after the pregnancies of cheap sluts who love no-one but themselves and are only free from filthy diseases that would ruin the lives of their children because ... because...' The voice disintegrated into sobs and a click on the tape indicated where Jennifer had switched off the machine.

She caught Mitchell's disappointed expression. 'It's all right He's given us something a bit more specific in writing.'

'Poor bugger. He'd have done better to throttle his missus.'

'But he still loves her. By the way, Kleever thinks we've made a clean sweep. He says the only reason Johnson hasn't coughed to calling Ginny is that he'll go down for longer if it's for tangling with one of ours. He says it's easier to believe in one caller making two types of call than for two callers to be at work simultaneously.'

Mitchell considered for some time before asking, 'So, where was Johnson last night?'

Jennifer sighed. 'What time are we talking about? It sounds as though I've talked myself into another job.'

15

As his door closed and Jennifer's footsteps grew fainter, Mitchell remained at his desk feeling a mixture of guilt and weariness. The latter predominated. His eyelids were drooping and his mind was exercised with just-before-sleep fancies when the telephone on his desk startled him awake again.

The voice of Claxton on the desk announced, 'That chap Foggin's here, wanting to speak to Clement. No one else will do. I've told him he's off duty so he's settled himself to wait here all night.'

Mitchell had a soft spot for the genus cantankerous, on most occasions perfectly understanding its point of view. Going down to the foyer, he discovered Foggin, dogless, and enquired after the animal anxiously. After that, Foggin was Mitchell's man.

'I've remembered summat as might sort out yon bonfire business.'

'Really?'

'I wanted to tell the young chap, give 'im first chance with it. After all, 'e were t'one as 'ad the sense to come to me in t'first place.'

'Quite,' Mitchell agreed solemnly. 'I'll

make sure the credit for this goes to DC Clement.' Foggin nodded his satisfaction. 'So, you've remembered something else about the man you met on our field?'

Foggin shook his head vigorously and Mitchell's spirits fell. 'About what, then?'

'About 'is barrer.'

'His wheelbarrow? What about it?'

'It were rusty and split, like, down one side at t'front.'

'I thought you said it was dusk and there wasn't enough light to see his face.'

'Ah, granted. But I nicked me ruddy finger in't crack and bled like a pig for a minute. 'Ad to wrap me 'anky round it and it weren't all that clean. Still, it 'ealed up reight enough. And that guy's coat got tore on it, on the barrer, I mean.'

'The man's coat?'

'You don't listen. I said the guy's. Do I make another o' them statements now?'

Mitchell grinned. 'You know the drill already. I wonder if you'd do something else for us. Could you let our lab have a drop of your blood? We need to compare it so that–'

'You don't 'ave to spell it out. I'm not stupid. 'E could say it were somebody else's bloodstains if you 'adn't tested mine. I'll 'ave to do me duty then, won't I?'

Mr Foggin was enjoying himself enormously. Mitchell left Claxton to make the arrangements whilst he grabbed the nearest telephone. He identified himself and cut into the technician's refusal to be hurried. 'It's not that. I'm apologising. I said that the scraps of the guy's clothing wouldn't be much use to us.' He explained his new interest in the despised shreds. 'You didn't take any notice, did you? You've still got them? I'll never try to teach you your job again.'

There was a short silence before the technician remarked, 'I'll be back before your scraps arrive. I'm just taking the pigs to have their wings trimmed.'

On Tuesday morning the uniformed constables making house-to-house enquiries following the firing of Mitchell's house were working with scant enthusiasm. If Mitchell's immediate neighbours had had their curtains drawn against the dusk and had seen nothing, it was unlikely they would learn much from the inhabitants of the rather superior blocks of flats around the corner.

The flats were in three blocks or 'houses' and PCs Dexter and Thompson had been allocated to St Oswald's House. Thompson wondered who the blessed Oswald had been and what possible connection he might have had with Cloughton. Dexter told Thompson to keep his mind on the job and expressed the opinion that the fire was just an excuse to sniff round the place quite literally.

'Drugs, you mean?'

Dexter nodded. 'Young Shaun Grant lives in this block.'

'They get shirty here if you call it a block, remind you it's not a thirteen-storey monstrosity thrown up by the council.'

'...and his mate, Jonathan Stepney,' Dexter went on, ignoring the interruption, 'lives in St Hilda's down the road. Claxton was telling me...'

Thompson looked back to where Dexter stood on a small square landing, made to allow stone steps to turn back on themselves. 'Go on.'

Dexter continued to stare out of the window. Thompson came back down half a flight to join him. 'What is it?'

'Only the super's car, and it looks as if it's had a little accident.' Both officers paused to take pleasure in the large dent in the back offside wing of Kleever's car.

'Sure it's his?' Thompson envied the younger officer his keen sight.

Dexter squinted. 'The bit of the registration plate they haven't muddied up matches his. Yes, I'm sure.' They ran down the steps they had just climbed, reached the street and continued towards the damaged vehicle. Soon left behind, Thompson contributed towards his colleague's efforts with a yell.

Dexter ran faster but, even so, the two

youths had time not only to get out of the car but to attempt to open the boot before making off. They entered the third apartment block before he could reach them. He stood and panted, using breath he could ill afford to curse his colleague.

As Thompson stood, scarlet with shame, the two officers who had been canvassing St Hilda's came towards them. One had seen a youth, standing on the pavement, talking to the driver. 'I'm pretty sure it was Shaun Grant. He didn't go home, went off in the other direction towards the park.'

The frustrated Dexter was dismissive. 'So, is it a crime to go for a walk?'

'We'll pick him up to help with our enquiries.'

'I'm sure he'll tell us the names of his new friends when he finds out they were naughty enough to smash up the super's car.'

'The super's?' The St Hilda's men blinked. 'We'd better get it in and give it the works. Good job it's not Petty's. He'd hold us personally responsible for every scratch on the bloody paint work.'

At almost lunchtime, Mitchell was back at the telephone. He had had strict instructions that Kleever should be notified immediately his vehicle was sighted. Since the superintendent was presently giving a lecture to the cadets at the police college in

Wakefield, transported there with sad loss of dignity in a car from the pool, the best Mitchell could do was leave a message. He spoke to an assistant of an assistant asking that Kleever should be told that the BMW had been found and that the prospects of tracing the thieves by a forensic examination of it were good. He decided to withhold news of the damage. Shaun Grant could be frightened into naming his friends and, since the youth who had ridden in the passenger seat had wrenched at the misshapen boot with his bare hands, his prints would satisfy the magistrates. With luck, they would find drugs in the boot and Kleever might even feel, in the end, that things had worked out for the best.

Mitchell dialled again. He introduced himself and agreed that he supposed he was that cute girl Carrie's boss. As economically as possible he explained the reason for the small favour he was asking and was assured of Cantrells' willingness to co-operate with any police operation whatsoever.

However, in such a small firm, small, only in number of employees, it would be difficult to be discreet about intercepting personal telephone calls to an individual. 'Tell you what, though, Inspector. Cantrells can do you better than that. The company's been working on a real neat little scheme for...'

Mitchell suspended his attention until the string of technicalities came to an end. Hillard was to be sent personally to hand over the finished job to the customer. It would be good practice for his PR skills, and it would mean he wouldn't be there to take his calls. Mitchell thanked him and rang off.

'What was all that about?' Jennifer had opened the door and been beckoned in.

'You first.'

'OK. Johnson has a cast iron alibi for the whole of Sunday. I've checked it out and it's all there.' She handed over a couple of typed sheets.'

Mitchell nodded and described his visit from Mr Foggin. 'I'm off to impound Charlie's wheelbarrow. I shall make sure they drop everything to deal with it. I've just been making sure that, if his woman's in, she won't ring him at work to warn him about it. We don't want him doing a runner at this stage.'

'Who's tailing him this morning?'

'Clement. Who's tailing Ginny right now?'

Jennifer sighed. 'Benny, I honestly have no idea.'

By lunchtime Mitchell considered he had spent his morning sufficiently virtuously to indulge himself by returning Nigel's call. When acting DCI Bellamy had completed his message Mitchell replaced the receiver carefully and sat for a full minute, his body still, his mind whirling.

Then, with his plan of action made, he reached again for the telephone, inordinately thankful that he had secured the name of the assistant of the assistant in Wakefield to whom he had spoken earlier. She had not yet gone to eat her lunch. 'Have you had a chance yet,' he asked her, 'to deliver my message to Superintendent Kleever?'

She apologised profusely. 'They had an early coffee break. It was over before I went up at eleven, expecting them to be free, as planned. It was because the superintendent wanted a longer session for his talk and questions. I'll make quite sure he–'

'*No!* Sorry, but could you please forget the whole matter. Don't tell him anything, that I rang even.'

She was understanding. 'A hoax call, was it?'

Mitchell considered. 'I suppose you might say that it was.'

Clement's spell of keeping watch on Charlie Potts had been enlivened only by driving his car, in pursuit of his quarry's, the mile and a half across town from Cantrells to Sedley brothers plc. Some time later, PC Dexter came to relieve him and it was only on his way back to headquarters that he saw anything interesting enough to report to his DI.

314

It was a brilliant winter day of hard, clear colours and stark lines. He had a perfect right to half an hour for his lunch, he told himself. He rejected the stuffy canteen in favour of a polystyrene cup of coffee and a hot bacon sandwich from the kiosk by the entrance to the park. He ate and drank hastily, then entered the green haven to stroll in what would probably be the only sunshine between now and Christmas.

He allowed himself twenty minutes for his walk and found he could smile tolerantly as he passed the town's young people, coiled, snake-like, round one another, gathering strength to spend the three or four hours of the working afternoon apart. For the first time, he could look back to the days when he and Joanne had behaved similarly and feel thankful for what they had had, rather than bitter for what was lost.

He glanced at his watch and saw that he would have to hurry to be in time for the afternoon briefing. Taking a last look round, he observed that one couple on a nearby bench were well past their teens. Perhaps aware of his scrutiny, they drew apart and he recognised Clare Chase and Warren. He would not, he decided, report his observation to his colleagues.

When Jennifer tapped on the door and came into Mitchell's office he was standing, his back towards her, staring out of the window. When he did not turn round she apologised for disturbing him. 'It's just that I've had another session with Damian Johnson. I'm convinced he's had nothing to do with Ginny. When he'd got a diatribe on sluttish parents out of his system, he told me he was no more than distantly acquainted with her. He said he'd never do anything to upset a good marriage with nice kids. He said...' She paused to recollect how Johnson had expressed the idea. 'He said, "It was a sort of madness that came over me. Yes, I'm jealous, but even in madness I'm not the sort to destroy what's good just because I can't have it." Something very like that. He convinced me.'

She was still addressing Mitchell's back. 'Benny?' He turned and she took in his white face. 'Whatever's up?' He was still silent. 'You need some lunch.'

Mitchell found his tongue. 'I haven't time. I've got something to deal with.'

'Is it private?'

He considered. 'Not from you.'

'Then come and eat. It's obviously my turn to be Dutch uncle.' She went out, leaving him to follow, remembering all the times they had taken each other to task during their professional acquaintance and their personal friendship. She saw that his mind was on something far different and, beyond asking, 'Not the canteen, I take it?' left him to his troubled thoughts.

Fifteen minutes later, looking at him over two halves of bitter and two plates of goulash on the table between them, she instructed, 'Start at the beginning and finish at the end.'

He nodded, consumed most of his beer and reverted to something approaching his normal manner. 'Kleever's car went missing and he made a hell of a fuss.' Jennifer nodded. 'He even considered cancelling his college lecture over it.'

'Really? Why?'

'Good question. He had to go, of course. He came to my office before he left to tell me to include Ginny when we charged Johnson and to let him know as soon as there was a whisper about his car.' Jennifer nodded. 'When there was a quiet moment, I gave Nigel a ring. Apparently he'd tried to get me again this morning, twice in fact.'

'And?'

'I'd left him a note when I left, to explain why I'd run off in a hurry. Told him very briefly about Ginny and about the fire. When I got hold of him this morning he told me Kleever was their super in Cumbria, the one who left in a hurry and gave him his taste of glory.'

'Why didn't he tell you that while you were up there?'

'Because we were still feeling a bit strange with each other? After all, I didn't feel comfortable enough to confide in him about Ginny until there was a reason to. Besides, they'd all been told not to talk about it. Apparently he took a shine to one of their uniformed PCs and she wasn't interested in him. He seemed to give up but then she began to be harassed in much the same way as Ginny has been. There was a hell of a stink about it. The PC was accusing him but it was his word against hers about everything. The last development was a fire in her flat.'

Jennifer was silent now and after a minute Mitchell resumed his account. 'Nothing could be proved. Kleever was moved here in his own interests. He had friends in the hierarchy who made sure the story didn't come with him.' There was another pause, then Mitchell spoke with a measure of his usual animation. 'And now he's in a hell of a tizz about his car going missing.' He stood up suddenly, overturning his chair and drawing the attention of all the other diners to them. 'I'm going to watch them take it apart, every nut and bolt. And I'll get someone in Wakefield to lock Kleever up till I get there…'

Jennifer remained seated and held him with her eye. 'You're going to stop making an exhibition of yourself. You're going to eat your perfectly good lunch because it could be a while before you can stop to eat again. Then we're going to make succinct notes on what you've just told me so that you can give a coherent account of it to Superintendent Jameson, who'll probably involve the ACC. Then you're going to leave it to him and you and I are not going to let Ginny out of our sight until this situation resolves itself. Does Kleever know we have his car?'

Mitchell shrugged and explained between mouthfuls about the message he had left and then withdrawn.

Jennifer considered. 'He'd find it difficult to get out of having lunch there and it's a three-quarter-hour drive from Wakefield.'

'He could invent an emergency.'

'Possibly. He could also countermand your instructions to the lab.'

Mitchell had himself in hand again. Pushing away his empty plate, he winked at Jennifer. 'Permission to leave the table, Miss? I'll ring Jameson first and let him speak to the lab. Then I'd better do whatever he says. Could you....?'

'I'll pick Ginny up now. Where will she be?'

'If she isn't with Tom and Hannah, they'll tell you.' He scribbled his in-laws' number on a page of his pocketbook and handed it to her. 'Wherever you take her, let them know.'

The two officers left the restaurant together, ignoring the curious glances from all sides.

At his shift's debriefing that evening, Mitchell stayed alert only by a tremendous exercise of will-power. He gave the latest details of the charges against Damian Johnson and Charles Potts. His team, however, was agog with the novelty of having hunted down a superior officer who was guilty, almost certainly, of a particularly despicable offence. For some of the more discerning, already their enjoyment of the joke was giving way to concern, not only about public confidence in the police force but about how far it was safe to trust brother officers if a 'bad apple' could reach such a level of seniority.

Mitchell knew they had a right to have their questions answered and remained as patient as possible. Kleever, he told them, was denying all charges against him as he had done in Cumbria. This time, though, there was rather more evidence against him. He repeated what most of them had already heard. 'All that is perhaps mostly circumstantial, but the lab's examination of the car was helpful. The boot contained a briefcase, covered in the superintendent's prints and only his, and containing items of my wife's underwear stolen from her washing line and the mobile phone belonging to Justin Chase. This has been removed from the station's lost property collection after it was brought in by a member of the public.' He explained the significance of this particular phone.

'No wonder your nose was kept well out of it.' This was from Caroline. 'Where is he now?'

'In the charge of the ACC. Geographically where, I neither know nor care, so long as he remains in custody.'

'Where's DS Taylor?'

Mitchell looked at Clement. 'I'm not sure. You'd need to apply to my in-laws for that information. Wherever she is, Virginia's with her.'

Clement added defiantly, 'I don't think she likes me. I think she even thought I was behind all this business with your wife.' For once, Mitchell could think of no reply.

A DC slipped into the room. Mitchell waved him to a chair as he prepared to dismiss his shift. 'Better late than never, I suppose. No, don't tell me where you've been. I think we've cleared the decks for the immediate present. We're all entitled to an evening off.'

'Some of us aren't going to get it,' the tardy DC volunteered from his seat at the back. 'Sergeant Claxton's had a call from the Catholic High School. Between the end of school and the staff coming back to get things organised for an open evening, our old friends have knocked off all their computers.'

Postscript

Thursday, December 16th was a significant day in the lives of a number of persons whose fortunes had been linked with those of DI Benedict Mitchell during these first weeks in his new post.

Steve Thacker heard that Gemma had been taken into the maternity hospital late on the previous night. He had rewarded his informant with, 'So what?' But then he had drifted away from his drinking companions to give himself space to consider this new aspect of himself. Steve Thacker, the father.

It was no big deal. Anyone could do it. Well, almost anyone. He was going to keep well away. Show a bit of interest now and he'd be involved. Up to his neck before he knew where he was. Nevertheless, his feet drew him to the hospital gates. He wasn't going in, of course. Just to the telephone kiosk. He's look up the number. He wouldn't give his name, just ask what was happening.

It was hardly surprising that his temper flared when some high and mighty, jumped-up nurse asked, 'Are you a relative, sir?'

'Only the kid's bloody father, that's all!'

That soon changed her tune. Gemma was fine, they told him, but they were just a bit worried about the baby. It was possible they would have to do a section...

They'd better be careful with his bloody baby. He dropped the receiver and hot-footed it up the drive. Helpful staff directed him to the delivery room and he submitted with ill grace to hand washing and gown. Thus attired, he met Gemma's expression of astonishment with a sheepish grin. The two midwives demanded one last push. He watched her screw up her face and heard a sound, half grunt, half groan, that seemed to project a yelling, bloody bundle of baby into a midwife's hands.

She wrapped the child in a cotton sheet and turned to him. 'Want to hold your son?' She placed him in Steve's arms and he looked down. The baby reminded him of a little, featherless bird he had found on a path as a child and had tried for some time to revive.

Gemma listened to his apologies, his stammered regrets, his promises to go straight for the sake of this little creature. The midwives had tactfully retreated. Gemma was quite moved. She could see that Steve meant every word – for now. With luck, he'd stay in this frame of mind for as long as a week. That would be nice. She'd learned to be grateful for small mercies.

At eight o'clock Mr Charles Potts picked at his first breakfast on remand.

Rather later the same morning, a letter addressed to Dr Simpson was delivered, together with many others to the surgery. It concerned Megan Scott, the only mother-to-be in any real danger from Damian Johnson's threat. The hospital reported a negative result to its tests. For once the doctor would have some good news to deliver.

By the time Dr Simpson's morning surgery began, Nigel Bellamy was parking his car in the station yard in Barrow in Furness and preparing himself to resume duty in his former position of detective inspector. The new superintendent took over his duties this morning. Nigel had enjoyed his taste of power and had renewed his determination to earn himself a permanent position as a chief inspector. With luck, something might turn up on his old patch.

At twenty minutes to eleven the bell rang for morning break at South Cloughton High School. Form 4B, august members of Upper School as from September, watched their juniors race out into the playground. The fourth-form boys followed at a sedate pace and, seemingly casually, repaired to the bicycle sheds where some of them managed to puff at quite half a cigarette before the master on duty was seen to be moving in their direction. The law-abiding girls were standing, goose-pimpled and teeth chattering, exchanging gossip. Melanie Patchett and company sidled into the forbidden cloakrooms where a wall of coats hid them sufficiently for the female teacher patrolling inside the building to pretend she had not seen them. On her way, Melanie had grabbed the recently emancipated Harriet by the elbow. 'Come an' get a load of this!'

Harriet glowed. She had got her best present before Christmas even began. She was in the gang!

Mr and Mrs Hillard too were in for a pleasant surprise. At ten-fifty, having had coffee as usual twenty minutes earlier, Mavis Hillard was gathering cups and telling her husband, coherently for her, that she would wash them up with the lunch dishes just this once.

The telephone rang as she departed for the kitchen. Sidney Hillard picked up the receiver and heard his daughter-in-law. Now that the truth about Lee's death had been established and it was not possible to have a proper funeral, she and Nathan thought a memorial service would be nice. What did he think? Would it upset Mavis?

'To hell with Mavis for once. Lee deserves at least that. I'm very glad you thought of it.'

This independence surprised and delighted Mrs Hillard junior. So much so that she added, 'By the way, we're hoping that you'll come and spend Christmas Day with us.'

At two thirty in the afternoon, Mitchell and Virginia sat on red plastic chairs, their knees – Mitchell's anyway – squashed by the backs of identical chairs in the row in front. The Vernon Road Junior and Infants School's Christmas concert was proceeding before them. Caitlin, her face looking sallower than ever against the sparkling white robe she wore, had been the only unbeautiful angel in the nursery class's Nativity Tableau. She had also, Mitchell had been pleased to note, been the only one to heed her teacher's embargo on waving to parents.

Now Declan, clutching the new recorder, promised and delivered by Virginia on the day after the fire, joined his fellow members of the recorder club. He was to play a solo verse of a carol and his mother prayed as he approached the top E flat in the last line that he found so difficult. 'You have to cover up only half of the hole with your thumb, and it's underneath, so you can't see how much half is.'

The recorder produced an agonised squeak, several tones above the required note. Declan kept his composure and finished his piece before leaving the stage with tears rolling down his cheeks.

Mitchell's children had been in bed three hours when Warren and Clare Chase left the restaurant in which they had enjoyed – in some ways at least – what they had agreed should be their last occasion alone together. He was tall and authoritative in his manner. A taxi whose driver had been approaching another couple veered towards them when Warren raised his hand.

He gave Clare the lingering kiss of a lover, then took a step away from her. 'Let's leave it there. Don't let's spoil it. I can't give you what Justin did. You can't share my burden for the church. We comforted each other in a time of need and I feel no guilt for that. Write to me from Scotland if you ever need anything, and be sure I'll never forget you.'

His final kisses were those of a brother, one on each of her cheeks. He did not stop to wave or watch as her taxi drove away.

At the police Christmas ball, it was almost midnight when Adrian Clement and Caroline Webster grew so physically tired from dancing that they were obliged to retire to the bar. Neither expected the evening to result in a serious relationship between them. Both recognised it as a sign of Clement's regeneration as a whole member of society. His sadness for the loss of his wife and child would never leave him, but it would not, in future, isolate him.

Caroline had felt touched and privileged when he had offered his diffident invitation. The two of them had enjoyed each other's company, affection, sexuality, and they intended to enjoy them for at least several hours longer.

The Mitchells too had enjoyed the police ball, though they had left slightly before Mitchell's younger colleagues. Earlier in the week they had moved their possessions into a police house from where, after Christmas, they would make more permanent arrangements. Both sets of parents were willing baby-sitters, but the children might be restless and unsettled in the strange house.

When Virginia and Mitchell tiptoed upstairs, however, the three youngest children were sound asleep. Declan, thumb in mouth, looked up as his bedroom door creaked. 'Why might Daddy have to go to work on Christmas Day?'

'Because Superintendent Kleever had to go away and it makes extra work for the rest of us.'

'Where's he gone?'

Virginia was the quicker thinker. 'He left some unfinished business in Barrow, where Uncle Nigel works. He's got to see about it.'

Declan nodded, satisfied. They tucked him in and had reached the door when he spoke again. 'I could have played that top E flat on my old recorder.'

Mitchell kept the chuckle out of his voice. 'I know what you mean, son. I could still hit sixes if I hadn't got rid of that old cricket bat I had when I was at school. You can spend the holidays getting used to the new one.'

Declan sat up again. 'You're saying I'm making excuses, aren't you? Wasn't Kat a lovely angel?'

Mitchell nodded. 'Caitlin was the best angel of them all. And you were the bravest boy.'

The publishers hope that this book has given you enjoyable reading. Large Print books are especially designed to be as easy to see and hold as possible. If you wish a complete list of our books please ask at your local library or write directly to:

Magna Large Print Books
Magna House, Long Preston,
Skipton, North Yorkshire.
BD23 4ND

This Large Print Book for the partially sighted, who cannot read normal print, is published under the auspices of

THE ULVERSCROFT FOUNDATION

Other MAGNA Titles
In Large Print

LYN ANDREWS
Angels Of Mercy

HELEN CANNAM
Spy For Cromwell

EMMA DARCY
The Velvet Tiger

SUE DYSON
Fairfield Rose

J. M. GREGSON
To Kill A Wife

MEG HUTCHINSON
A Promise Given

TIM WILSON
A Singing Grave

RICHARD WOODMAN
The Cruise Of The Commissioner